"What about you ~~...~~ nothing for yourse~~lf...~~

Her gaze brushed his, and for a moment Levi thought she'd confess some dream of her own. Then she shrugged as if dismissing it. "You do right by my kin, preacher, and I'll be satisfied."

So brave. He might have given another woman a brotherly hug to encourage her, but something told him Callie wouldn't take kindly to the gesture.

Lord, I thought You sent me here. I thought You were offering me a chance to be the man You want me to be. Give me the words. Help me win her over, for her sake and mine.

"You don't believe I'll take care of you all," he said aloud.

She shrugged as if she didn't believe much of anything.

He released her shoulders. "I want to help you, Miss Murphy. I want to honor your brother's wishes."

She scrubbed at her cheek, but not before he saw the tears that had dampened them. "Adam's gone. Besides, it wasn't as if you two were partners."

Partners. The most sacred of ideals where she came from. And that gave him an inkling of how to proceed.

"We weren't partners," he acknowledged. "But you and I might be."

Regina Scott has always wanted to be a writer. Since her first book was published in 1998, her stories have traveled the globe, with translations in many languages. Fascinated by history, she learned to fence and sail a tall ship. She and her husband reside in Washington State with an overactive Irish terrier. You can find her online, blogging at nineteenteen.com. Learn more about her at reginascott.com or connect with her on Facebook at Facebook.com/authorreginascott.

Visit the Author Profile page at Harlequin.com.

REGINA SCOTT

His Frontier
Christmas Family

◈ **HARLEQUIN**® LOVE INSPIRED® HISTORICAL

Recycling programs for this product may not exist in your area.

LOVE INSPIRED BOOKS

ISBN-13: 978-0-373-42550-1

His Frontier Christmas Family

www.Harlequin.com

Printed in U.S.A.

Therefore, if anyone is in Christ, the new creation has come. The old has gone, the new is here!
—*2 Corinthians* 5:17

To Kristy J. Manhattan, my fool dream,
and to the Lord, for encouraging us
to dream beyond ourselves.

Chapter One

Near Seattle, Washington Territory
December 1874

Someone was watching her.

Callie Murphy kept her fingers moving as she pinned another diaper to the clothesline stretching from the cabin to the closest fir tree. She felt as if a gaze was fixed on her back, pressing against the buckskin coat that covered her cotton shirt and trousers. She had to be mistaken.

Her brother Adam had filed for a homestead a good five miles south of Seattle. He'd wanted space and quiet, claiming he was tired of the crowded gold rush camps in which they'd been raised. Mr. Kingerly and his wife lived a mile away, and the kindly older man would walk up to Callie if he wanted her help with something. The last stranger had passed this way months ago.

Still, she couldn't help glancing around. The one-room cabin stood in the center of the clearing her brother had widened in the forest, but the forest was trying to reclaim it. Already ferns poked up heads along the edges, and blackberry vines, withering with the coming winter, snaked across the dirt. As for the forest beyond, the most movement was a bird flitting from branch to branch.

In the wash basket at her feet, Adam's daughter blew bubbles, her round face a wreath of smiles. With shiny black curls and big blue eyes, six-month-old Mica reminded Callie of the porcelain-headed baby dolls on display in a Seattle mercantile window, especially around Christmas. The little girl looked far more like her late mother, Anna, than anyone on her father's side of the family. Every Murphy, including Callie and her little brothers Frisco and Sutter, had hair the color of amber and eyes like slate.

"Hush, little baby, don't say a word," Callie sang softly, feeling that itch between her shoulder blades that said her watcher was still there. "Mama's gonna buy you a mockingbird."

Mica gurgled her delight, rocking from side to side to the tune.

"And if that mockingbird don't sing," Callie continued. "Mama's gonna buy you a diamond ring."

Mica laughed.

Callie shook her head. Who was she to promise diamond rings? That was almost as bad as Pa's promises, saying he'd strike it rich. Always one more hill to climb, one more creek to pan. Always little to show for months of labor. That was the way of the men she'd met. They either dreamed dreams too big to realize or thought only of themselves.

"If you're looking to rob us," she called into the forest, "it's only fair to tell you we got nothing of worth."

The forest was still, as if everything was waiting. In defiance, she bent and picked up another diaper, hanging it alongside the others. It didn't matter who was watching or why. She had one goal: to keep her, Frisco, Sutter and Mica safe until Adam returned. She'd protected her family most of her life, starting with her younger twin brothers after her mother had died of influenza, now with them and Mica. She knew what she was doing.

Still, this feeling was too much like the last time she'd lived on the gold fields, five years ago at the Vital Creek strike in the British Territories. At fifteen then, she'd just started getting her womanly curves. Most of the miners had noticed.

"You don't strike it rich, Murphy," one had told her father, "you let me know. I'll buy your daughter off you."

Pa had thrown himself at the fellow, and Adam had jumped in right after. That was when she'd started wearing loose clothing, washing and combing her hair less often, keeping her head down and her rifle close.

She almost shuddered at the memory, but she refused to give her watcher the satisfaction of knowing she was nervous, and for good reason. She'd grown complacent in their little hideaway. Her rifle was hanging on its hook over the hearth.

As if she felt the same concern, Mica frowned.

Callie made herself brighten at the baby braced in the wash basket as she retrieved one of the boys' shirts. "Isn't it a nice day to hang the clothes, Mica?"

A twig snapped in the woods. Ice raced up her spine. Callie stepped closer to Mica, bent as if to choose another piece of clothing and closed her hand on the stick she used to stir the wash.

"Excuse me."

Callie whirled, stick raised like a club with Mica behind her. The fellow standing there held up his hands as if in surrender.

"Sorry I startled you. I'm looking for the Murphy family."

Callie eyed him. He looked about Adam's age, with curly hair a shade darker than hers and eyes so deep a blue they were nearly black. Something about those eyes seemed sad, weary, as if he'd come a long distance and still had a ways to go. He didn't look particularly dangerous.

She held the stick high anyway.

"What do you want with the Murphys?" she asked.

"I have news about their brother Adam," he explained. "Are you California?"

This time she did shudder. Why had Pa picked such silly names for his children? Adam had the only name that sounded normal, and only because Pa had thought the first boy in the family should be called after the first man in the Bible. When Callie had asked her mother, God rest her soul, about why she hadn't protested, Ma had smiled.

"You know your pa," she'd said. "When he gets an idea in his head, there's no arguing with him."

That was why they'd followed him from San Francisco in the south to the British Territories in the north.

Still, only family knew Callie's real name, which meant this man must have talked to Adam. She lowered the stick but kept it at the ready.

"I'm Adam Murphy's sister," she acknowledged. "What do you know about my brother?"

He dropped his hands and took a step closer. Her fingers tightened on the stick. He must have noticed, for he paused.

"I mean you no harm. My name is Levi Wallin. I'm a minister."

A minister? Now, that made no sense. Why would a minister bring her news from Adam?

"I don't know your game, mister," she told him, "but I think you better leave. I have two other brothers, and they don't take kindly to strangers."

He frowned. If he really was a minister, he'd probably lecture her on being kind to strangers, respecting her elders, even though he could only be five or six years her senior. That was what ministers did, she'd learned from the few she'd met—criticize her, show her exactly how different she was, why she would never fit in with good society. She figured the best thing to do was let them go their own way while she went hers.

But this fellow didn't show any sign of leaving. "I knew your brother well," he said, voice soft. "Adam had honey-colored hair, just like you, and his eyes were lighter. He was a little shorter than me, but that didn't stop him from fighting for his place or protecting his family. When Gap-Tooth Harding offered to buy you, every man in camp weighed in on one side or the other."

Now Callie frowned. "You were at Vital Creek?"

"To my sorrow," he admitted. "Scout Rankin and I had a claim at the opposite end of town from yours. I met Adam in a card game at Gillis's. He cleaned me out."

Just when she wanted to trust him! "Now I know you're lying. Preachers don't gamble."

He smiled, and something inside her bubbled up as warm as a hot spring. "I wasn't a preacher then."

He wasn't one now that she could see. Those rough wool trousers and caped duster looked warm, but they weren't nearly nice enough to belong to a fancy minister. Ministers liked to show how important they were, how much better, smarter. If that was what it took to win God's favor, she never would.

"Well, whatever you are," Callie told him, "I'm not sure what to do with you."

"I'd like to talk to you and your brothers." He nodded toward Mica in the basket. "And your husband, of course."

He wasn't the first to assume Mica was her daughter instead of her niece, for all the differences in their coloring. She told him what she told the others. "I don't have a husband."

Again, she waited for the expected response—the gasp, the finger shaking, the prediction she would suffer for her sins.

Instead, his eyes widened. "Adam has a daughter? Where's his wife?"

She could lie, claim Adam's wife was in the house with a gun at the ready, but suddenly Callie felt as weary as this fellow looked. She jerked her head over her shoulder. "Buried over there. I'm in charge until Adam gets back."

He moved closer yet, carefully, as if unsure whether she'd hit him or snatch up the baby and run. She considered doing both, but he was close enough that she could see the lines fanning out from the corners of his eyes. Worry lines, Ma had called them, and she'd had her share. What worried this man?

"That's a heavy burden," he murmured. "I can see why Adam wanted me to help."

"Adam asked you to help?"

He nodded. She studied his face, but he didn't avoid

her gaze or blink rapidly like she'd known some men to do when lying.

She drew in a breath. "I wish he'd thought of us before hightailing it back to the gold fields the minute his wife Anna died of a fever. But you needn't worry, mister. My brothers and I are handling things just fine. We'll make it through until Adam gets back for the winter. If you see him before we do, just remind him that if he doesn't live on his claim in the next two months, we could lose it."

His face sagged, and he put a hand on her arm. "I'm sorry, Miss Murphy. Adam won't make it back in time. He died three months ago. I only received word yesterday."

There was no good way to say it. Even if he'd been a minister eight years instead of eight months, Levi thought he'd have stumbled telling Callie Murphy what had happened to her brother. Adam had been so alive, so feisty, so determined to strike it rich. It was hard for Levi to believe all that energy had been snuffed out.

"Are you sure?" he'd asked the two grizzled miners who'd stopped by Wallin Landing with the news and to bring him Adam's belongings and the note to the Murphys.

They'd hung their heads, avoided his gaze.

"Surer than we wish we was," one of the old timers gritted out. "He caught pneumonia and couldn't fight it off. All that's left of Adam Murphy now is a pile of regrets."

Levi knew something about regrets.

He kept his hand on Callie's arm now, ready to catch her if she fainted. She didn't so much as sway. Her eyes, a mixture of blue and gray that reminded him of the swirling waters of Puget Sound, narrowed on him.

"Prove it."

She spat out the words, as if he'd lie about anything so important. How ironic. He'd lied enough over the years, to escape punishment, to win something he'd wanted, to make himself appear more important. Now he was telling the truth, and she didn't believe him.

"My horse is tied out front," he said. "I have Adam's letter in my saddlebag. Come with me, and I'll give it to you."

Her jaw worked as if she fought hard words. "I'm not going anywhere with you. And I don't trust you out of my sight."

She was either the most suspicious woman he'd ever met, or the wisest. She was also plenty brave, ready to lay into him with that stick. Having been raised in the gold camps and now living so far out, she probably had to take precautions. He hadn't intended to look dangerous, but then, he'd used his boyish charm too many times in the past to think that danger couldn't look pleasing.

"Then maybe I can help you until your brothers get back." He bent to reach for the clothes, and she stepped in front of him.

"You want to help?" she challenged. "The pump's been stuck for weeks. We have to lug all the water through the woods from the creek. Fix the pump, and we'll talk."

Levi straightened. "Fair enough." He located the pump near the back of the cabin and went over to it. Easy enough to spot the problem. The device was orange with rust. He glanced up to ask her whether she had any oil, and words left him with his breath.

She'd picked up the baby and stood there, swaying from side to side, singing softly. The buckskin coat and trousers, so common on the gold fields, still hinted of a figure. The sunlight shafting through the forest sparked around her, sending gold skipping along her hair.

Levi turned his back on her. *Oh, no. You have no business admiring Adam Murphy's little sister. You have a lot of work to do before you're fit to be a husband to any woman.*

A movement in the bushes caught his eye, and a moment later two boys about eight years of age scampered into the clearing, dragging a burlap sack between them. The pair was identical, down to the dirt on their round cheeks and the mud on their worn boots. Sutter's Mill Murphy and San Francisco Murphy. Back at Vital Creek, the miners used to make a game of guessing which boy was which.

"Look what we got, Callie," one crowed.

"Old man Kingerly didn't even try to stop us," the other bragged.

Callie shot Levi a look before hurrying to meet them. "He agreed to give you that, didn't he?" She tipped her head toward the house.

The closest boy glanced Levi's way and stiffened, then elbowed his brother. The other looked toward Levi and dropped his corner of the sack.

"Sure," he said. "Of course."

"Who's that?" his brother demanded.

"That's Preacher Wallin," Callie answered them. "He came to tell us something important. I think we should go inside to hear it."

Her brothers exchanged glances, then the one retrieved his corner of the sack, and they dragged it toward the house. The shapes bumping against the material told him they had at least one pumpkin in the batch.

Callie followed them, baby up in one arm. The little one seemed to like him. She blinked big blue eyes surrounded by long black lashes and offered him a wide smile that revealed a set of four teeth. He remembered his oldest nieces being that age before he and Scout had set out to seek their fortune.

Regret stabbed him. He'd missed more than six years with his family chasing after something he had never needed. He'd thought striking it rich would give him standing, make him a man. He'd become a man all right, and not one his father would ever have wanted him to be. He would spend the rest of his life atoning for what he'd done on the gold fields. The Murphy family was only one step along the way.

Callie paused beside him as if she wanted to ask him something. She barely came to his shoulder, so he bent his head to give her his full attention. The blue-gray of her eyes was cool, assessing, as if she could see his darkest secret. He willed himself not to flinch.

She reached down, grasped the handle of the pump with her free hand and tried to yank it up. It didn't move.

"Pump's still broke," she pronounced, straightening. She passed him for the door.

Levi was the last one inside. "The pump is rusted solid. Unless you have some oil and a wrench, it's likely going to stay that way."

She shrugged as if she didn't care or doubted he would be of much use regardless. He suspected her nonchalance had more to do with the fact that she had no way to procure oil or a wrench.

In fact, she had no way to procure much of anything

if the state of the cabin was any indication. It held a single room, though a ladder against one wall told of a loft overhead. Unlike his brothers' sturdy cabins, this one was more crudely made. The logs hadn't been seasoned properly, and the chinking was falling out in places, letting the sunlight spear through. The windows at the front and back held no glass; only shutters kept out the wind. The stone fireplace was barely big enough to keep the place warm. The shelves next to it listed, even though they held no more than a sagging sack of flour and some tough-looking carrots.

How could Adam have left his family in such dire straits?

A bedstead piled with quilts lay against one wall, with a plank table and benches near the fire. The boys dropped their sack by the table and climbed up on a bench. Callie, still holding the baby, went to stand at the head of the table. She frowned at Levi, before turning to her brothers. Her face softened.

"The preacher brought us news about Adam," she said. "I warn you—it ain't good."

Her brothers' eyes widened, and they looked to Levi.

He stepped forward until he stood at the end of the table. "I'm very sorry, boys. Your brother has passed on."

They frowned in unison, mirror images of each other.

"Passed on to where?" one demanded.

"Were there better pickings there?" the other asked.

Levi's heart tightened. "Much better pickings. Adam is in heaven."

The first boy turned to his sister. "Where's the Heaven strike? In Washington Territory?"

"Nah," his brother scoffed. "It's in Idaho, you dolt."

The first boy scowled. Callie was regarding Levi, challenge in her eyes.

He squared his shoulders. "What I'm trying to say is that your brother Adam has died, boys. But he didn't want you to worry. He asked me to take care of you, and I will. I want you all to come live with me."

Chapter Two

Callie was so shocked that she clutched Mica close to keep from dropping her. Live with him? Was he touched in the head?

Her brothers looked just as surprised, mouths hanging open, their normally busy bodies stilled. As usual, Frisco recovered first.

"Why'd we want to come live with you?" he demanded, hands braced on the table. "Callie takes care of us real good."

"Always has," Sutter agreed.

"Always will," Callie promised them.

As if she thought so, too, Mica rested her head against Callie's shoulder. Frisco and Sutter climbed off the bench and pressed against Callie's side.

The preacher didn't look dismayed to find them all ranged against him. He merely inclined his head.

"Your sister has done a good job," he said, gaze moving from face to face. "But even Callie has to get tired once in a while."

How did he know? She'd been so careful not to let her brothers see it. Neither of them knew the nights she broke down and cried, trying to think of a way to change their circumstances. She was up before they were, in bed long after they climbed to the loft. There weren't enough hours in the day for tending to the claim let alone all the washing and cooking and cleaning.

Adam and Pa had both promised better things.

"Just you wait, Callie," Pa would say, eyes bright and cheeks flushed like he was feverish. "One day you'll dress in fine silks and live in a big house with servants to do all the work."

He'd had a fever all right. Gold fever. This preacher seemed no different.

"We get by," she told him, warmed by her brothers on either side. "What are you offering that's any better?"

He took a step closer and spread his hands, as if intent on making his case. He had nice hands, strong-looking and not too soft, like he could wield a pick or shovel if he needed to. He was slender for a man, but those broad shoulders and long legs seemed made to crouch beside a stream for hours panning.

And when had she started judging men by their ability to hunt for gold!

"I have a solid house," he said, "with a good roof and a big hearth."

That would be nice. Frisco and Sutter kept having to reposition the tick they slept on to stay out of the drips from the roof when it rained.

"Our house is solid," Frisco blustered.

The preacher had to know that was a lie, but he inclined his head again. "I also have a kitchen stove, plenty of food set aside for winter, a separate bedroom and a sleeping loft overhead."

Her brothers brightened, but Callie had spotted the

fly in the ointment. "Who do you figure's sleeping in the bed?" she asked.

His brows shot up. Preachers—they never liked to talk about practical things, like sleeping arrangements or taking turns in the privy.

"You and the baby would have the bedroom," he assured her. "I'll bunk in the loft with the boys."

Sutter and Frisco looked around her at each other, and she was fairly sure they didn't like the idea of having the preacher so close at night. She'd heard them open the shutters in the loft after they were supposed to be asleep, the thud of their feet against the logs as they climbed down. And she'd stayed awake until she'd heard them climb back up again.

Still, she couldn't believe the preacher would be so generous. "You'd take us into your own home," she challenged. "People you barely know?"

He smiled. "I knew Adam. He saved my life once, gave me food when I was starving. I was his friend. That makes us friends, too."

Friends, he said. She had had few over the years, young men her age mostly, and they'd quickly lost each other as families traveled to different strikes. She couldn't believe this man was her friend. She couldn't make herself believe any of it—Adam's death, this stranger's kindness. Either Levi Wallin was one of those do-gooders who donated to the poor only to brag about it, or he was after something.

"We don't need your pity, preacher," she said.

He smiled. Such a nice smile, lifting his lips, brightening his eyes. She could imagine people doing anything he wanted when he smiled at them that way.

"I'm not offering to help you from pity," he promised

her. "Adam asked me to look out for you. Some people might say he gave me guardianship of you all."

Her brothers stiffened. So did Callie.

"Don't much care what others say," she told him. "I don't need a guardian. I've been taking care of my family since I was twelve. And I'll reach my majority in six months."

He didn't argue the fact. If he really did remember Vital Creek, he'd know about the parties Pa threw on any of his children's birthdays, with music and treats. Anyone who recalled those would know she would turn one-and-twenty in the spring.

"Still, Adam asked me to take care of you," he pointed out. "Perhaps you'd like to read his letter now." He turned for the front door before she could respond. "I'll be right back." He strode out of the house.

Frisco and Sutter ran after him to peer out the cracks in the shutter.

"He has a horse," Frisco reported.

"A nice one," Sutter agreed.

They would know. They'd seen their share of sway-back nags over the years.

"He talks nice, too," Frisco acknowledged. He turned from the shutter. "Do you think he's telling the truth, Callie?"

She shrugged. "Even if he was, would you want to live with a preacher?"

Sutter stepped closer to Frisco, nudged his shoulder. Most folks thought her brothers were identical, but she could tell the difference. Frisco was a little bigger, a little heavier, and Sutter's eyes had more gray in them. Frisco was the leader, Sutter the follower. And both looked to Callie to make the hard decisions.

Like now, when this stranger wanted them to leave the only home they'd ever known.

The preacher returned, crossed to her side and handed her a piece of paper, even as her brothers came to join them. He'd left the door open as if to give her more light to read by, but the little black lines and dots still swam before her eyes.

Were these really Adam's last words?

She handed the letter to Frisco. "Here. Read it aloud."

Her brother swallowed, then looked down at the paper.

"Callie, Frisco, Sutter and Mica," he started, each word slow as he sounded them out. He glanced up at Callie with a grin. "See there, Callie? That's my name next to yours."

The preacher smiled as if he appreciated her brother's excitement. Between their moves and the remote location of the claim, Frisco and Sutter had never been in school, but Callie took pride that they had learned their letters from Anna.

"I see it," she told Frisco. "Read the rest."

He bent over the paper. "I promised you all to come back before winter, but I think I'm done for."

Sutter sucked in a breath, and Frisco looked up again, face paling.

"Go on," Callie said, throat tight.

"Real cold up here. You remember. But don't worry. Levi Wallin will take care of you. He knows about living like we did. He understands."

Callie looked up to find Levi watching her. No one who hadn't lived in the camps could appreciate the life they'd led. Even the townsfolk in Seattle called her and her brothers wild, uncouth, like they were animals instead of people. Levi Wallin might have visited the gold fields, befriended Adam, but he was still a preacher.

"Tell Mica about me when she asks," Frisco continued, voice wavering more from emotion than reading skills now, Callie thought. "Tell her I loved her and her ma. Tell her I only wanted to dress her in fine silks and give her a big house with servants."

Callie dashed a tear from her cheek. She'd tell Mica about Adam, but never that he'd wasted his life, like his father before him, chasing after a fool dream.

"Think of me kindly," Frisco finished with a sniff. "Your loving brother Adam."

Sutter's face was puckered. "Why'd he have to go and die?"

"Everyone dies," Frisco said, crumpling the note in his fist. "Ma, Pa, Adam, Anna. Callie will die one day. So will you."

"I won't!" Sutter shouted, giving him a shove.

"Boys!" Callie blinked back tears. "That's enough. Frisco's right—everyone dies someday. It might be sooner or it might be later. None of us knows."

As Frisco rubbed at his eyes with his free hand, she gathered him closer. Sutter crowded on her other side. Adam was really dead. He and Pa had fought with the fellow who'd tried to buy her. Now it looked as if her brother had simply given her away. Didn't he think she could raise the boys and Mica alone? Hadn't he trusted her? What was she supposed to do now?

"I remember how it felt to lose my pa," the preacher said, in a quiet, thoughtful voice that was respectful of what they were feeling. "I was eight when he was killed in a logging accident."

So maybe he knew a little about loss. Frisco didn't respond, but Sutter raised his head. "What did you do?"

"I relied on my family and friends," he said.

Now Frisco looked up at Callie. "You're family, Callie. What do you think we should do?"

At least her little brothers trusted her. Even Mica was regarding her with hope shining in her blue eyes.

Still, what choice did she have? She'd been counting on Adam returning before the freeze set in. She needed another pair of hands to get everything ready for winter. Her brothers were too young yet for some of the tasks, and they weren't very good about taking care of Mica so she could work elsewhere on the claim. They kept finding more interesting things to do, leaving the baby unattended. But she couldn't hunt or chop wood carrying a baby.

Besides, with Adam gone, how could they keep the claim? She couldn't file for her own for another six months.

She met the preacher's gaze. Once more that deep blue pulled her in, whispered of something more, something better. If only she could make herself believe.

"I think," she told her brothers, "that we should get to know Adam's friend a little better."

Levi smiled. Though he liked to think he'd outgrown the grin Ma had always called mischievous, he knew a smile could go a long way toward calming concerns, soothing troubled hearts. The Murphys had no reason to trust him other than a recommendation from their dead brother. A brother who might still be alive if he hadn't yielded to the siren's call of gold.

"You live around here, preacher?" Callie asked him.

They were all watching him. Even the baby blinked her eyes before fixing them on his face as if fascinated.

"I'm the pastor of the church at Wallin Landing, up north on Lake Union," he told them. He still couldn't quite believe it. He'd tutored under a missionary on the gold fields, traveled to San Francisco to be trained and ordained. He'd intended to return north to the men who needed hope in the gold rush camps, to help Thaddeus Bilgin, his mentor. Then he'd discovered that his family had built a church and was ready to request a pastor. They couldn't know how they'd honored him by offering him the role. His first duty had been to perform the marriage ceremony for his closest brother, John, and his bride, Dottie.

But Callie didn't look impressed that he was the pastor of a church at such a young age. Her eyes were narrowed again. "Levi Wallin, Wallin Landing. Must be nice to have a family who owns a whole town."

He'd never considered his family wealthy, until he'd left them. Now he knew they had riches beyond anything he would have found panning—love, friendship, encouragement, faith. Still, he didn't want to give Callie the wrong impression and have her be disappointed when she saw Wallin Landing.

"Not much of a town," he explained. "Yet. It was our pa's dream to build a community. We have a church, a store and post office, a dispensary and a school." He nodded to her brothers. "My brother James's wife is the teacher. You could learn all kinds of things there, boys."

First Frisco and then Sutter nodded. At least, he thought he had the names pinned to the right person.

Frisco stuck out his chin. "I reckon we know enough without going to some stupid school."

"And I reckon there's always more to know," Callie countered. She held out the baby to him. "Here. Take Mica for a ride in her wagon. Leave the door open so I can see you. No running off this time. Me and the preacher need to talk."

Frisco accepted the baby, who babbled her delight at his company. With looks that held a world of doubt, the twins headed for the door.

Callie took a step closer to Levi. Her hair was parted down the middle and plaited to hang on either side of her face, making her look sad and worn. But even if it had been pinned up like most ladies wore it these days, he thought she'd still look sad. She certainly had reason.

"Did they give him a good burial?" she asked.

If someone from Seattle had asked him that question, he would have extolled the wisdom of the minister who delivered the eulogy, numbered the attendees who had honored the deceased with their presence and described the casket and the flowers. After watching men die in the northern wilderness, he was fairly sure what Callie was really asking.

"A team of six men buried him good and deep. Nothing will disturb Adam's rest."

She nodded, shifting back and forth on her feet as she gazed out the open door. With a rattle, the boys passed, dragging a rickety wagon with Mica bundled in the bed. He heard Callie's sigh, felt it inside.

"I'm sorry," Levi said. "He was too young to die."

"So was Anna," she murmured, rubbing at her arm. "That's Mica's mother. Our ma and pa died too young, for that matter. Pa stayed in the stream so long he contracted pneumonia. I wouldn't be surprised if Adam went the same way."

She and her little brothers had seen too much death. She was younger than his sister Beth. She ought to be giggling over fashion plates, planning for a bright future. What sort of future had her father and brother bequeathed her? She was all the family the boys and the baby had left. The need to help her was so strong that he wondered she couldn't see it hanging between them.

"A man I knew at Vital Creek was fond of saying that life is for the living," he murmured. "What do you want to do with your life, Miss Murphy?"

She made a face. "Not so much a matter of wanting as what must be done. Frisco and Sutter need to go to school, learn a trade. I won't have them dying with a pan in their hands, too. And someone has to raise Mica."

Levi closed the distance between them, put both hands on her shoulders. Though they seemed far too narrow, there was a strength in them. "What about Callie? Do you want nothing for yourself?"

Her gaze brushed his, and for a moment he thought she'd confess some dream of her own. Then she shrugged as if dismissing it. "You do right by my kin, preacher, and I'll be satisfied. I can always find my own way later."

So brave. He might have given another woman a brotherly hug to encourage her, but something told him Callie wouldn't take kindly to the gesture. She was all prickles and thorns, a hedge thrown up in defense of the heart within, he suspected. He wasn't sure how to convince her he only meant the best for all of them.

Lord, I thought You sent me here. I thought You were offering me a chance to be the man You want me to be. Give me the words. Help me win her over, for her sake and mine.

"You don't believe I'll take care of you all," he said aloud.

She shrugged as if she didn't believe much of anything.

He released her shoulders. "I want to help you, Miss Murphy. Adam supported me when no one else would. I want to honor his wishes."

She scrubbed at her cheek, but not before he saw the tears that had dampened them. "Adam's gone. Besides, it wasn't as if you two were partners."

Partners. The most sacred of ideals where she came from. And that gave him an inkling of how to proceed.

"We weren't partners," he acknowledged. "But you and I might be."

She turned her gaze his way again. "How do you figure?"

"We both want the best for your brothers and little Mica. We should work together."

She cocked her head. "I'm listening."

"You, your brothers and Mica can come to live at Wallin Landing as my wards. I'll see your brothers and Mica clothed, fed, housed and educated. I'll help you find a future for yourself."

Still she regarded him. "How do I know I can trust you?"

"When two people decide to partner on a mining claim, how do they know they can trust each other?"

"They give their word and shake hands," she allowed.

"I give you my word that you and your family will be safe at Wallin Landing." He stuck out his hand.

She eyed his hand, and for a moment he thought she'd refuse. Then she slipped her fingers into his, sending a tingle up his arm. "And I give you my word to help you raise Frisco, Sutter and Mica," she said.

He shook her hand. "Partners?"

"Partners for now," she agreed. "But don't expect anything more."

Releasing her, Levi frowned. "What more would I want?"

She shook her head. "Sometimes you ask the silliest questions for a man who claims to have been on the gold fields. You just hold up your end of the bargain, preacher, or this will be the shortest partnership you ever heard of. Wallin Landing may be north of Seattle, but I can still walk away."

Chapter Three

Levi Wallin came back the next day with a wagon. By that time, Callie had talked herself into going with him.

She had a number of concerns. For one thing, she still wasn't sure she'd made the right decision by agreeing to partner him. It was fine and good to say he wanted to help, but once he was back at his church, everything neat and tidy and clean, surely he'd start to regret his promise to her. What sort of fellow willingly took on four more mouths to feed, the raising of two boys and a baby? She'd accepted that responsibility out of love; she was kin, after all. What was Levi Wallin's reason?

He said he had been Adam's friend, and it seemed he owed Adam a favor for helping him. This was a mighty big favor. The preacher might recall some of the same events she did at Vital Creek, but she didn't remember meeting him there, couldn't see his face along the crowded stream of her memories. Charity only went so far, and this partnership was a fair piece further. She simply couldn't figure him out.

And their visitors didn't make matters easier.

Carrying Mica in her arms, she'd walked the mile to

the Kingerly claim to confirm the elderly farmer had indeed given her brothers the pumpkin and turnips they'd dragged home. She'd returned to find two men with her brothers at the back of the cabin. Their rough, heavy clothing and the pans affixed to their horses' trap told her what they were before they introduced themselves. Zachariah Turnpeth and Willard Young claimed to be prospectors heading home for the winter. They begged a room for the night. It was one of the unwritten rules of the gold fields. You shared bedding, food, drink, clothing, equipment. About the only thing you didn't share was your claim. Only the worst of the worst came between a man and his claim.

But she wasn't about to let strangers stay in the cabin.

"You can pitch your tent out back," Callie told the older men. "We've no grain for the horses, but you're welcome to share our dinner."

Her brothers scowled at her as if they thought she should be more generous. As little food was left, she knew she was being generous indeed.

The twins were quick to quiz the prospectors on where they'd panned, what they'd done as she'd fed them all roast pumpkin and turnips.

"Alike as two peas in a pod," Zachariah said with a smile to Callie.

"Puts me in mind of Fred Murphy's young'uns at Vital Creek," Willard agreed. "They'd be around seven now."

Callie looked at them askance, but Frisco puffed out his chest. "Eight," he declared.

"You knew Pa?" Sutter asked.

Callie waited to hear their answer.

"If your pa was Fred Murphy, we did," Zachariah admitted.

"And that means your brother was Adam Murphy," Willard said. "We was real sorry to hear about his passing." He scratched gray hair well receded from his narrow face and glanced around. "A shame he couldn't make it back before Christmas."

"Yes, it is," Callie murmured, eyes feeling hot.

Zachariah reached out a hand and ruffled Frisco's hair, earning him no better than a frown. "I don't suppose he sent anything home for his brothers."

"Not a thing," Sutter said with a sigh. "And now we have to leave."

"Leave?" Zachariah turned to Callie. Both of the miners watched her as if she was about to confess she'd been voted president. "Where are you going? North to pan?"

In winter? Oh, but they had the fever bad. "No. We're going to live with a friend at Wallin Landing. It will be better than this."

Sutter smashed the pumpkin on his tin plate with a wooden spoon. "Most anything would be better than this."

Callie couldn't argue. Adam had been a terrible homesteader. He'd bought them a goat for milk, but the ornery thing had run off weeks ago. Foxes had carried off the chickens. He'd never managed enough money for a horse and plow, so the most they'd been able to grow came from Anna's vegetable patch behind the house. Callie was just thankful the woods teemed with game and wild fruits and vegetables. But even that bounty was growing scarce as winter approached.

Frisco scooted closer to the table, glanced between

the two men. "Sutter and me could come north with you, when you head back."

Sutter nodded. "We got pans."

Heat rushed up her. Callie slammed her hands down on the table. "No! No panning, no sluicing. Finish up and head for bed. We have a long way to go in the morning."

The prospectors had shoveled in the food as if they suspected she was going to snatch it away, then slipped out the back door. And Callie had spent the next hour or so packing up her family's things, such as they were.

She'd hardly slept that night, but more to make sure her brothers didn't run off with Zachariah and Willard than with concern over the change she was making. She was glad to see the men gone in the morning, the only sign the holes in the ground where they'd driven their tent pegs. Wearing her brother's old flannel shirt and trousers, belted around her waist to keep them close, suspenders over her shoulder to keep them up, she'd barely finished feeding Mica mashed pumpkin when Sutter dashed in the door.

"He's coming!"

Callie's stomach dipped and rose back up again. So much for not being nervous. Gathering Mica close as she shoved her father's hat on top of her hair, she followed her brother out onto the slab of rock that served as a front step.

Though he was still dressed in those rough clothes she found hard to credit to a preacher, Levi Wallin had brought two horses with him this time. They were both big and strong, coats a shiny black in the pale sunlight. They were hitched to a long farm wagon with an open bed, the kind Adam had always wanted to buy. Frisco was trotting alongside as if to guide them.

It only took two trips to load their things. Adam had left with his pack, most of the panning supplies and some of the dishes, but she still had her father's pack and the one Ma had used plus Mica's wagon. Their belongings fit inside Levi's wagon with room to spare. She had Sutter bring the quilts their mother had sewn and pile them in a corner of the wagon next to the bench. Pulling on her coat, she glanced around one more time.

This was supposed to be home. Maybe one day she could come back. Maybe no one would want a claim so far out. Maybe she could file for it herself in six months.

Maybe she better leave before tears fell.

Her brothers were already snuggled in the quilts when she came out with Mica in one arm and her rifle in the other. The preacher approached her, and she offered him the baby so she could climb up.

He hesitated, then took the little girl from Callie's grip. He held her out, feet dangling, as if concerned she might spit on his clothes. Mica bubbled a giggle and wiggled happily.

Callie sighed. "Here, like this." She lay the rifle on the bench, then repositioned Levi's arms to better support the baby. Some muscles there—hard and firm. Touching them made her fingers warm. She took a step away from him.

As Mica gazed up at him, the preacher reared back his head, neck stretching, as if distancing himself from the smiling baby in his arms.

"She won't bite," Callie told him.

"Yet," Frisco predicted.

The preacher's usually charming smile was strained. "It's been a long time since I held a baby. I was the youngest in my family, and I moved away when my brothers' oldest children were about this age."

So that was the problem. Callie patted his arm and offered him a smile. "You'll do fine. Just hang on to her until I climb up and stow the rifle, then hand her to me."

That went smoothly enough, until Levi climbed up onto the bench, reins in one fist. His trousers brushed hers as he settled on the narrow seat, and his sleeve rubbed along her arm as he shook the reins and called to the horses. The wagon turned with the team, bringing her and Levi shoulder to shoulder. Each touch sent a tremor through her.

No, no, no. She'd spent the last five years avoiding such contact with men. She'd all but decided she would never marry. She certainly didn't want to get all fluttery over a minister of all people, someone who would only judge her and find her wanting. And how did she know he wouldn't go tearing off to the gold fields one day like every other man she'd ever known? She'd had quite enough of that for one lifetime.

Not even Levi Wallin's charming smile could convince her otherwise.

What was wrong with him? Every flick of the reins, every bump of the wagon made him more aware of Callie Murphy sitting beside him. He'd thought his change of heart and his religious studies had helped him become a new man. But had he just traded gold fever for petticoat fever?

He remembered what it had been like when Asa Mercer had brought women from the East Coast to the lonely bachelors in Seattle. His brothers Drew, Simon and James owed their wives to Mercer's efforts. Even now, seven years later, men still far outnumbered the women in Seattle. That was one of the reasons his sister Beth had written for a mail-order bride for their brother John.

But Levi had no intention of taking a bride. Not for a long while, if ever. His time on the gold fields had shown him the kind of man he was deep down. No wife deserved a husband like that. He had started to rebuild his life, but he had a long way to go.

His brothers didn't understand. They had all been so pleased, and not a little surprised, to find that their little brother had become a minister. They remembered the scrapes he'd gotten into as a youth—stealing Ma's blackberry pie off the window ledge where it had been set to cool and claiming a bear had lumbered by. Trying to show his oldest brother Drew he was strong enough to master an ax and bringing down a tree so close to the house it shaved off a corner of the back porch. Attempting to prove himself a man by gambling himself into a debt so deep his entire family had had to chip in to raise him out of it.

The last thoughtless act still made him shudder. He'd worked on Drew's logging crew for months to pay everyone back. And then he and Scout had heard about the gold strike in the British Territories and run off to make their fortunes.

"You'll see," Levi had promised his friend. "We'll come home rich. They'll *have* to respect us."

Respect had seemed all important then. He was the youngest of his family, Scout the only son of a father who couldn't have cared less. They had wanted something to call their own, a way to make people look at them with pride. Filling their pockets with gold had sounded easy.

Their adventures had not only failed to find them

gold but lost Levi his respect for himself. And no one
except Scout, Thaddeus and God knew how far Levi
had fallen. It would be a long time before he felt himself worthy of respect again.

The best he could do now was help the Murphy family. He glanced at Callie sitting beside him. She wore a
slouch hat that hid her hair and shadowed her face as she
gazed down at the baby in her arms. The movement of
the wagon must have lulled little Mica to sleep, for thick
black lashes swept across her pearly cheeks.

He couldn't forget the feel of the child in his arms—
so tiny, so fragile. Her big blue eyes had gazed at him
so trustingly. She was too young to know the things he'd
seen, the things he'd done.

*Thank You, Lord, for this opportunity to make amends
and help a friend.*

Peace brushed him like the wings of a dove, reminding him of why he had started down this path. God had
never abandoned him, no matter how far Levi had run.
He'd been waiting with open arms for Levi to come
home. It was a blessing to return the favor with the Murphys.

"How far do we got to go?" one of her brothers asked
behind him. The belligerent tone likely belonged to
Frisco.

"Will it take much longer?" Sutter whined.

Levi smiled. He'd been the same way once, eager for
things to start now. "Have you ridden to Seattle before?"

"'Course we have," Frisco said, tone now aggrieved.

"Well, it's that much again to Wallin Landing," Levi
told him.

He glanced back in time to see Frisco slide deeper
into the pile of quilts. "That could be hours."

"Days," Sutter moaned.

"Maybe we could stop in Seattle," Callie suggested. "Stretch our legs."

"Get a sarsaparilla," Levi offered.

Sutter perked up. Frisco pushed himself closer to the bench. "You got money, preacher?"

Callie scowled at her brother. "I got money, the last of what Adam sent us a few months ago. There's no call to bother the preacher."

"It's no problem," Levi assured her. "I said I'd provide for you all."

Frisco leaned up between them, arms braced on the back of the bench. "That's real nice of you, preacher. And maybe we could get something to eat at one of them fancy hotels."

"San Francisco Murphy," Callie said, her voice a low rumble, like a thunderstorm heading their way.

Her brother's eyes widened, and he ducked back into the wagon bed. "It was just an idea. A fellow can't live on pumpkin and pinecones."

"I never fed you pinecones," Callie complained. "But maybe I should." She shot Levi a glance. Behind that stern look, he thought he saw a twinkle in her blue-gray eyes. "You got pinecones up your way, preacher?"

"Plenty of them," Levi assured her. "My brother chops down a lot of trees. I'm sure he could find a few cones, maybe some sawdust."

"There you go," Callie said, facing front. "Everything a growing boy needs."

"You're no fun," Frisco grumbled.

"I'd eat pinecones," Sutter told him. "If I had to."

"Would not!"

"Would, too!"

Before Levi could move, the two were rolling around in the bed of the wagon, pushing and pummeling each other. With a jolt, he realized their movements were shoving the packs toward the rear of the open wagon.

Callie must have seen the problem as well. "That's enough!" she cried. "You'll cost us our things."

Neither brother paid her the least heed. Face turning red, she reached back a hand, but, holding the baby, she couldn't seem to catch hold of either boy.

"Hang on," Levi told her.

She cast him a glance, then resolutely grabbed the side of the bench.

Levi slapped down on the reins, and the horses lunged forward. The movement sent both boys flying into the quilts. Levi reined in, allowing the horses to draw the wagon to the side of the road and stop. Then he turned and gazed down at two scowling faces. Somehow, he thought he'd looked at Drew with just that amount of defiance when his older brother had taken over leadership of the family after Pa had died.

"You wanted to get to Seattle as fast as possible," he reminded them. "Every time you act up, I'm stopping this wagon. I've slept out under the stars before, in colder weather than this. If you want to take a week to go five miles, I'm your man."

They didn't so much as exchange glances this time.

"No," they chorused.

"Good," Levi said. "Then pull those packs up closer to the bench and get comfortable."

The two scurried to comply.

"By the way," Levi continued with a wink to Callie, "I hear there are bandits in these parts. Keep your eyes peeled, and sing out if you spot one."

The twins' heads jerked up, and they nodded eagerly.

As soon as they'd settled themselves back among the quilts, Levi faced front and called to the horses.

"Bandits," Callie said, skepticism in her voice. Even Mica, who must have been awakened by the sudden movements, was frowning at him.

Levi shrugged. "My brother and his wife were set upon out this way."

Callie's eyes widened.

He felt a tug of guilt and leaned closer, speaking low for her ears alone. "Eight years ago. I haven't heard of any trouble recently."

"Are those bandits?" Sutter called.

A chill ran up him. They were rolling around a bend, so Levi could easily spare a look back. Callie turned as well, shoulder brushing his. Two riders were coming along the road. The pair was far enough behind that Levi couldn't make out their faces under their broad-brimmed hats. He forced himself to focus on guiding the horses around the curve.

"Do you know them?" Callie murmured beside him.

"I don't think so," Levi told her. "You?"

Her cheeks were pale. "We had visitors last night. Might be them. Horses look right."

"There's another bend coming up," Levi said. "We'll check then."

As the horses trotted around the curve, Levi and Callie turned once more. She was so close he could feel the warmth of her.

The way behind lay empty.

Callie met his gaze. "Where did they go? I didn't see any tracks leading off this one."

Neither had he. Were they waiting around the last

bend, making sure he didn't get another look at them? Why the secrecy? What were they trying to hide?

And what had drawn them out this way?

Chapter Four

Callie kept her head high as they rolled into Seattle. She'd been a little concerned about the men Sutter had spotted on the road, but the pair had never caught up with them. Obviously bored, Frisco and Sutter had curled themselves in Ma's quilts.

They perked up as Levi guided the horses down Second Avenue. Callie wished she could be as excited. New buildings crowded either side of the wide, muddy street, signs overhead showing pictures of boots, hats and a mortar and pestle. Men in a variety of garb, from fine wool coats and high-crowned hats to rough trousers and tweed caps, moved among the shops, boots clomping on the boardwalk. The few ladies among them walked with bonnets covering their hair and cloaks covering their swaying skirts. Callie's hand went to finger her lank locks spilling out below her hat. It had been too cold the last few weeks to take a bath and wash her hair, even if she'd felt it fair to ask her brothers to lug enough water from the creek.

Many of the people were glancing their way with curious looks. She could almost hear their whispers.

There go those wild Murphy brats.
Someone ought to teach them better.
They shouldn't be allowed near civilized folk.

"We gonna get that sarsaparilla, preacher?" Frisco asked, leaning over the edge of the wagon as if ready to dive into the mud of the street to escape.

"You sit back down," Callie ordered before Levi could answer. "I won't have you causing trouble."

Frisco heaved another sigh and threw himself once more among the quilts.

"We should rest the horses," Levi told her. He nodded ahead to one of the few brick buildings she'd seen. "Why don't we stop at the Pastry Emporium?"

Immediately her brothers chorused their support, rousing Mica, who beamed at them all as if delighted to wake in such company.

Callie eyed the building with its green-and-white-striped awning over the wide front window, the bright painted sign overhead. A lady in a bow-spangled dress was just entering.

"Looks mighty fancy to me," Callie told him. "I doubt they'd want our business."

Levi raised his brows. "I assure you, Miss Murphy, the owner Maddie Haggerty has seen far worse than two eager boys. She's an old friend of the family."

Oh, but he moved in fine circles. First a whole town, now a prosperous Seattle business owner. Callie hefted Mica close as Levi drew the horses to the hitching post and jumped down to tie them. As Frisco and Sutter ran to press their noses to the sparkling glass of the front window, Levi held out his arms to Callie. "Coming, Miss Murphy?"

Callie faced front. "I'll wait here. Someone should watch the wagon."

Out of the corners of her eyes she saw his arms fall. "That shouldn't be necessary. We'll only be inside a short while, and we can see the wagon from the window."

Callie hunched her shoulders. "We're carrying all our worldly goods, preacher. I ain't taking chances."

"On anything, it seems," he said.

Callie shot him a look. The sun glinted on the golden curls against his forehead, made the blue of his eyes sparkle nearly as much as the clear glass window. Still, she couldn't let his sweet looks sway her. "I came this far, didn't I?"

He took a step back, holding up his hands as if in surrender. "As you like, Miss Murphy. The boys and I will only be a moment." Turning, he strode for the door, her brothers on either side.

Callie sighed. She shouldn't have been so hard on him. He was only being kind. He wasn't used to having people judge him. In her experience, ministers were the ones who generally led the judging.

As if to comfort her, Mica cuddled closer. Callie rested her cheek against the baby's silky hair. At least Mica didn't complain. She'd made do with goat's milk after her mother had died, opened her mouth eagerly for whatever mashed fruit, vegetable or grain Callie could manage after the goat escaped. She laughed and wiggled through every rough diaper, every tepid bath.

"And if that diamond ring turns to brass," Callie sang, rocking her gently, "Mama's gonna buy you a looking glass."

Mica sighed happily.

"Pardon me, ma'am."

Callie looked up to find a fellow on horseback next to the wagon. His hat was as black as the horse, his eyes only a shade or two brighter. The planes of his face were hard. A shiver went through her, and Callie swallowed.

Seeing he had her attention, he nodded. "I know those horses, but I don't know you."

She was not about to be accused of horse thievery. Callie narrowed her eyes at him before turning to stare straight ahead. "Don't much care what you know, mister. I advise you to ride on."

He didn't even shift in the saddle, and his voice came out cold. "I'm afraid I can't do that until you tell me how you came by James Wallin's horses."

Callie glanced his way. One hand had strayed closer to the gun at his hip. She stiffened, arms tightening around Mica. She'd never reach the rifle under the bench in time.

Her brothers' laughter echoed behind her as they came out onto the boardwalk to the tinkle of the shop bell.

"Hey, Callie," Frisco called, "look what we got—a whole roll, all for you. With frosting!"

"Who's that?" Sutter asked.

Figure on Sutter to notice the man on horseback. Callie refused to take her eyes off the fellow until she knew he wasn't going to shoot one of them.

"Deputy McCormick," Levi said. "How can we help you?"

Deputy? So this fellow was the law in Seattle.

He nodded past Callie as if acknowledging Levi. "No help necessary. You answered my question." His hand moved away from the gun to finger the brim of his hat. "Good day, ma'am."

"A moment," Levi called, just when she thought she might relax. As Sutter scrambled up into the bed of the wagon and Frisco handed Callie the roll wrapped in paper, Levi came around to face the lawman.

"These are the Murphys from out around Columbia," he told the deputy. "I'm taking them to Wallin Landing to live. We were followed part of the way by a pair of riders. I didn't like the looks of them."

The lawman nodded. "I'll head that direction when I can. Thanks for letting me know." With a flick of the reins, he rode on.

Callie drew in a breath at last. Sutter leaned out of the wagon bed, as if watching the deputy until he turned the corner. Frisco pressed against the side of the wagon next to Callie.

"Go on and eat it," Frisco said, slate-colored eyes bright as silver in the sunlight. "It's cinnamon."

She could see some of the red-brown spice clinging to the corner of his mouth, and her own mouth turned up in a smile. "Was it good?"

"Oh, yes." He glanced at Levi, who had also been watching the lawman. "Thanks, preacher."

Levi collected himself and smiled at her brother. "You're welcome, Frisco. Climb aboard, now. We still have a ways to go."

With a sigh that sounded far less happy, her brother trudged toward the back of the wagon.

Levi turned his smile on Callie. "I'm glad to see Deputy McCormick checking on you, making sure you were safe out here."

Callie snorted. "Wasn't me he was worried about. It was the horses. He thought I'd stolen them."

She expected Levi to argue, but he chuckled. "Wouldn't be the first time someone made off with Lance and Percy." He patted the closest horse before going to untie them. "You remember those bandits I mentioned? They took these beauties, left my brother and his betrothed alone in the wilderness."

Sutter popped up behind her. "How'd they get home?"

Callie was fairly sure he was asking about the horses, not Levi's family, but Levi nodded to him as he climbed into his seat and took up the reins. "James and his sweetheart navigated the forest alone for three days before our brother Simon tracked them and brought them home. The deputy and James both searched for the horses, but Rina was the one who rescued the pair."

"Rina?" Callie asked with a frown.

Levi called to the horses, who pulled the wagon down the street toward where trees dotted the horizon at the north. "His betrothed, now his wife. She can be impressive."

Frisco popped up as well. "Wait, ain't she the lady you said taught school?"

"That's right."

Her brothers exchanged glances. Callie knew what they must be thinking. A schoolteacher who could fight off horse thieves?

Maybe going to Wallin Landing would turn out better than she'd thought, for all of them.

Levi smiled at how quickly Callie consumed the treat from Maddie. The Irishwoman was a good cook, but the way Callie inhaled the aroma, dug her fingers into the soft dough, that was about the best cinnamon roll ever baked. She caught him watching her as she finished and ducked her head, right hand rubbing at her left shoulder.

"When are we gonna get there?" Frisco whined.

"Another hour," Levi promised him.

The answering sigh could have toppled a cedar.

"We can sing to pass the time," Callie said, shifting Mica on her lap.

Frisco humphed. "You always want to sing."

She ignored him, looking thoughtful. "Something spritely like we did around the fire at night."

Sutter popped up. "How about 'Sweet Betsy from Pike'?"

Levi wasn't sure what his congregation would think if he drove in to Wallin Landing belting a bawdy song from the gold fields. "What about 'Get on Board'?"

Callie brightened. "We know that. Adam brought it back from his last trip." She started singing the first verse.

"The gospel train is coming.
I hear it just at hand.
I hear the car wheels moving.
And rumbling through the land."

She had a clear, sweet voice, both the sound and the glow on her face drawing him in. The feeling reminded him of summer outings on the lake with his family, friends gathered around a hearth. He and her brothers joined her on the chorus and other verses, while Mica swayed in time.

"Well done," he complimented her when they finished and her brothers plopped back down among the quilts.

She blushed a soft pink. "I always liked music, sung or played. Something about it touches me inside." She pressed a hand to her heart, and Mica grabbed her fingers. With a smile, she lowered her hand. "That probably sounds odd to you."

"Not at all," Levi told her, ducking under a low-hanging branch. "I feel that way about the Bible. Thaddeus Bilgin, the minister who took me under his wing at Vital Creek, encouraged me to start reading it again. Every time I open it, the words are new."

She smoothed the buckskin of her coat. "Never have read the Bible."

Levi grinned at her. "Now, that's something I can help you change."

Her hand stilled. "I expect I'll be too busy."

Not if he could help it.

Just the memory of his old friend made his spirits lift. Thaddeus had taught him a lot of things, both spiritual and practical. The two of them still corresponded now that Thaddeus was settled in Vancouver.

His spirits lifted even higher as the first farms at the edge of Wallin Landing came into view. Their neighbor Mr. Paul raised his hand as they passed. Mrs. Ruflagger called a greeting as she walked her ducks down to the lake. Funny how they both treated him kindly now that he was the minister. The elderly farmer had spent half of Levi's life chasing him out of the crops, and the wise farmwife had spent an equal amount of time dragging him out of the lake. A good thing they didn't know what he'd done on the gold fields. They might not be so forgiving.

The steeple rising through the trees in the distance reminded him of the One who had forgiven all.

"Almost there," he called to the boys.

Frisco and Sutter bobbed up, looking around eagerly.

Callie raised her head, and Mica reached out as if she could make the wagon go faster.

He called to Lance and Percy, and the horses leaned into the harness, carrying the wagon up the rise onto the promontory that held the church buildings.

His brothers had built the chapel to inspire. The steeple loomed higher than the ancient fir and cedar surrounding it. The clean white paint gleamed in the sunlight and cheered on a rainy day. The windows on the north looked out onto Lake Union. Beth had wanted stained glass but Levi had convinced her to use clear panes. The vista reminded worshippers that they served a mighty God, capable of creating such a wonder. He couldn't come near the place without feeling a sense of pride.

To one side lay a long, steep-roofed log hall, ready to serve as a place for local gatherings. Rina was planning to use it for the school's Christmas theatrical in a few weeks. On the other side of the church, completing the triangle of buildings, stood the parsonage.

Frisco and Sutter leaped from the wagon before Levi had even brought it to a complete stop. Whooping and hollering, they ran toward the door of the two-story log house.

"Stop!" Callie ordered them, sitting taller on the seat and earning her a surprised look from Mica. Her brothers skidded on the path. "You come back and help the preacher and me unload."

Their shoulders slumped, but they returned to the wagon.

"Plenty of time to explore," Levi promised them, climbing down. "In fact, after we get everything settled, I'd be happy to show you around."

Frisco tugged up on his worn trousers. "No need, preacher. We're pretty good at finding our own way." Sutter nodded.

Still defiant. Levi went around to the rear of the wagon and pulled out a pack like the one he'd used on the gold fields. Memories threatened, but he put them aside.

"Just as well," he said. "My brothers would probably skin me alive if I showed you our secret fishing hole."

Sutter grinned, but Frisco scowled.

"Here." Levi shoved the pack at him. "Take this inside. Sutter, go see if Callie needs help with Mica."

Muttering under his breath, Frisco took the pack and headed for the house. Levi shouldered the other pack and pulled out Mica's little wagon. As he came around from the back, Callie was standing on the ground and handing the baby to Sutter.

"And mind you no fighting while she's in your arms," she admonished him.

"I know that," Sutter said, making a face. "I'm not stupid, contrary to what *some* folks think."

"None of you is stupid," Levi assured him, putting a hand on his shoulder.

Callie seemed to be avoiding his gaze. "Some folks may not think you're so smart, preacher, bringing us to live with you like this."

Levi bent to put his eyes on a level with hers. "As I heard from someone I know, *don't much care what others say.*"

He thought he saw a smile tugging at her lips. She had a pretty mouth—pink-lipped, warm, soft-looking.

"You're here!"

His sister's cry forced his gaze away from Callie. Levi drew in a breath. He had to get control of these wayward thoughts. He and Scout had bragged about the number of hearts they'd break once they were rich. Well, he'd bragged. Scout had merely smiled dreamily. That had been years ago. Surely Levi was a gentleman now. He'd become a minister. He wasn't supposed to notice that his new ward's lips looked as sweet as strawberries.

But he couldn't help noticing how her eyes widened as Beth approached.

His sister was an acknowledged force of nature in Wallin Landing. Anyone looking at her artfully piled blond hair and frilly pink dress topped by a fur-trimmed short cape would think she had nothing to do all day but pamper herself. The truth was that Beth generally had a hand in anything good that happened at Wallin Landing. Though she was only a couple years older than Callie, she managed the food and lodging for the logging crew, took care of her cabin, helped teach at the school and care for the youngest ones with his sister-in-law Nora and had staked her own claim at the north of Wallin Landing.

Now she advanced on them, hands outstretched as if she meant to gather them all close. Sutter must have seen the gesture, for he beat a hasty retreat to the parsonage with Mica. Callie took a step back as well, as if she would follow.

Beth didn't give her a chance. She enfolded Callie in a hug. "Welcome, welcome! I'm so glad you're here! You can't imagine how long I've wished for someone closer to my own age. Dottie's not too far, of course, but she's a wife and mother. You and I can't be more than a year or two apart, so that's neither here nor there. You must tell me everything about you. I can already see you're wonderfully practical—trousers must be so much easier to work in." Beth drew back, beaming as widely as the baby.

Callie stared at her a moment, then looked to Levi.

"This is my sister Beth," Levi explained. "She lives near the parsonage."

"Not far away at all," Beth agreed. "It's an easy walk. I'm sure we'll find all kinds of reasons to visit—to share recipes, compare sewing patterns, prepare for Christmas. Oh! Have you read the latest issue of *Godey's Lady's Book*? That pink-striped walking dress would be perfect on you."

Callie took another step back. "Thank you, but I have a baby and two boys to care for. Excuse me." She turned and ran for the house.

Beth's face fell. "Oh, Levi, I'm so sorry. I didn't mean to scare her."

Levi shook his head. "It's not your fault. She's skittish as a fawn, Beth. You can't understand what it's like to live in the gold camps, the only girl surrounded by rough men."

Beth put her hands on her hips. "No, with five older brothers and a logging crew for company, I couldn't possibly imagine."

"Five older brothers and a logging crew who adore you," Levi corrected her. "I get the impression Callie Murphy has had to kick and fight for everything she has, and she's taken her share of punches."

Beth dropped her hands with a sigh. "Then how can we make her feel at home?"

"I'm not sure," Levi admitted, eyeing the parsonage. "But I promise you I won't stop trying."

Chapter Five

$\sim$

Callie shut the door and leaned against it, heart pounding faster than it should. She ought to have known the preacher's sister would be a perfect young miss. Their family owned a whole town! Was it possible someone like that, all bows and smiles, could be friends with her? She may have kept her family together, but she wasn't a perfect young miss. She didn't have recipes. She just threw what she had in a pot. And as for reading a book…

Noise and movement suddenly pierced her panicked mind. Frisco and Sutter were down on the floor, rolling and punching, while Mica sat on the rug to one side, clapping her hands as if encouraging them.

Callie shoved off the door and waded into the fight. "Enough! Both of you!" She grabbed Frisco by the collar and heaved. He broke away from Sutter, kicking. Sutter rolled out of reach.

She released Frisco and pointed to the farthest corner. "Go on, git! You stand there a moment and think."

Sutter stuck out his tongue at Frisco as his twin slunk away.

Callie pointed to the opposite corner. "And Sutter, you get over there. You have some thinking to do, too."

Sutter's jaw tightened, but he loped to the corner and set his back to her.

Callie went to pick up Mica. The baby gurgled a welcome, seemingly as content to be in Callie's arms as watching the wrestling match before her. Callie shook her head.

"What am I going to do with you?" she asked her brothers. "It was bad enough you fighting at the claim. Wasn't much there you could hurt except each other. The preacher and his family are used to nicer things. They won't appreciate you behaving like a pair of bear cubs in the spring."

Frisco sniffed, gaze on the log wall. "Never said I wanted to come."

"Me, neither," Sutter reminded her.

"Well, we're here," Callie informed them. "And it's up to us to make the best of it."

Her brothers' silence said otherwise.

Cuddling Mica, she glanced around the room for the first time. This was the cabin Adam should have built. The log walls were planed to fit tightly together; the chinking, where it was needed, was firm and clean. She couldn't feel any breeze coming through the plank floor, couldn't see an ounce of sunlight peering in except through the windows. And there wasn't a trace of smoke staining the stone fireplace at one end.

Sutter stood near the hearth, nose to the wall. Behind him was a plank table flanked by benches, and beyond him, marvel of marvels, sat a stove. She'd only seen one before, in a high-price cookhouse in Vancouver. She caught Sutter glancing at the black-and-silver beast as if just as awed by it.

At the opposite end of the room, Frisco stood stiff-backed near open stairs leading up to the loft. Several wood chairs and a carved bench were clustered close by on a colorful rag rug. Quilted cushions covered the seats. Behind them, three windows looked out onto the lake. They had shutters that could be closed against the night, but they were surrounded by red and white curtains, tied back with bows.

Of course.

Behind her, the door opened, and Callie stiffened. Turning, she was more than a little relieved to find Levi alone. He brought in the last pack and her rifle, moving slowly as if he thought she might bolt otherwise. He wasn't far off.

His smile faded as he glanced from Frisco to Sutter. "Everything all right?"

"Just fine," Callie told him. "Frisco, Sutter, help the preacher bring in the quilts."

Her brothers ran for the door, no doubt eager to escape.

"Don't let them out of your sight," she warned Levi.

Brows up, he left the pack and gun and hurried after her brothers.

They returned immediately with the quilts, dropping them at Callie's feet. Then Frisco grabbed the pack with his and Sutter's belongings. "Where are we bunking?"

Levi nodded to the stairs. "In the loft. Why don't you go look around while I show Callie the rest of the house? Leave space for me to sleep."

The last was said to air, for her brothers were already halfway across the room, Sutter's arms filled with quilts.

"They're high-spirited," Callie told him, hearing a defiant note in her voice.

"So was I." Levi turned his look to her with a smile. "Welcome to your new home. This is the main living area." He nodded toward the stove. "The door by the hearth leads to a covered walkway to the church."

Apparently the people of Wallin Landing didn't want their pastor to get wet. Mica nodded as if she approved.

He turned toward the stairs again, taking Callie under them to where a door opened to another room. "This is where you and Mica will be sleeping."

Callie ventured inside. The space was easily three times the size of the tent Ma and Pa had shared and nearly as big as Adam's entire cabin. An iron bedstead rested against one wall, with a wooden chest at its foot. There was even a little table beside the bed with a glass lantern on it. The quilt was purple, blue and white, like waves on a wind-tossed sea, and purple curtains hung at the window. It was fancier than the best hotel room Pa had ever rented for them.

Callie's throat felt tight. "You sure you want to give this up, preacher?"

His smile was prettier than the first show of color in the creek. "For you and Mica, of course."

Now her eyes felt hot. Callie blinked against the tears building.

"Will it do?" he asked, head cocked.

Callie could only nod, afraid her voice would betray her.

His smile deepened.

"You'll probably want your own quilt on the bed," he said, moving forward to tug at the covering. "Ma sewed this one for me. I can't believe it made the journey to Vital Creek and back."

"I can't believe someone didn't steal it from you," Callie said, fighting a pang at the sight of the quilt being bundled up in his arms. "Vital Creek was mighty cold, even in the summer."

He chuckled. "It was at that. I didn't bathe for months." He seemed to recollect himself, for pink tinged his high cheekbones. "If you'll tell me what you want in here, I'll leave you to settle in."

Callie pointed through the door to the pack, rifle and quilts, and he carried them into the room and bowed out. She shut the door behind him. Swallowing, she glanced around again, then her eyes lit on the door latch. She raised a brow.

"No lock," she told Mica. "Guess we'll have to shove the chest over the door every night."

Mica nodded.

Callie ventured to the bed and lay the baby down on it. Mica immediately righted herself, wiggling on the surface as if she loved the feel of her new bed. Was it really as soft as it looked? Callie bent, braced her hands on either side of Mica and pushed down. Mica positively bounced. Something squeaked.

Callie frowned at the noise, but Mica grunted, eyes on Callie and chin tipped as if asking to bounce again. Callie obliged her. Mica collapsed in a fit of giggles.

Callie was more interested in what had caused that squeak. She'd done her best not to share her bed with mice over the years, and she wasn't about to start now. She bent and peered under the bed. Not even dust marred the plank surface. In the shadowed light, however, she could see what appeared to be a net of metal under the mattress, holding the bed in place.

She straightened. "Well! What do you know about that?"

Mica wiggled, asking to be bounced again.

Callie gave her one more, then set about unpacking. Ma's quilt, worn as it was, didn't look nearly so pretty on the iron bedstead, but at least it made the place feel a bit more like home. And who was she to complain? A real cookstove, a room all to herself and Mica and a bed with springs. It was more than she'd ever dreamed of.

There has to be a price.

She shook the thought away. Just because everything good had cost too much on the gold fields didn't mean she had to pay here. So far, Levi had been good to his word. This was a great deal better than their claim.

Perhaps that was why, when her fingers brushed the smooth shell of her mother's comb and the fabric of her dress at the bottom of the pack, she hesitated. It was the last dress Ma had owned, other than the one they'd buried her in. Callie had been saving it to cut up for Mica. Maybe there was a better use for it, for the time being.

Maybe it was time she thought about trying to fit in again.

As soon as Callie shut the bedroom door, Levi drew in a breath. She'd liked the room. He wasn't sure why that pleased him so much. But he'd seen the tears come to her eyes, the way she'd gazed about as if awed by her surroundings. It seemed all she needed was a little peace and quiet. Surely he could give her that. He'd already convinced Beth to come back tomorrow. He could handle this.

Something thumped outside, followed by a knock at the door. Levi hurried to answer.

His brother John stood there, tall infant chair beside him. John was his closest brother in age, though he'd flourished under Drew's leadership where Levi had challenged their older brother at every turn. Slightly shorter and stockier than Levi, with mahogany-colored hair and their mother's green eyes, he had never looked happier since marrying a few months ago.

"Dottie thought you might need this," he said, giving the chair a push. It rolled forward and bumped against the threshold.

"Is that Drew's high chair?" Levi asked, eyeing it.

"It was," John acknowledged. "He loaned it to Dottie for Peter, and I made a few improvements. But Peter's big enough that he prefers to sit at the table with us now."

The pride in his voice was unmistakable. Though the little boy was Dottie's son, John had fully entered into the role of father, even before their marriage.

"I'm sure Callie will appreciate it," Levi said, lifting the wheeled contraption into the house. He leaned closer to his brother. "Listen, John, would you tell the others to wait a few days before welcoming Callie and her family? They're still accustoming themselves to the changes."

John, always the peacemaker, nodded sagely. "Of course. If a book would help, I'd be happy to bring some from the library. *Culpeper's Complete Herbal* and *Robinson Crusoe* for the boys, perhaps. *The Courtship of Miles Standish* for Miss Murphy. That was always Beth's favorite."

Courtship? "I'll pass along your offer."

With a nod, John strode off, whistling.

Levi shut the door. John was a hopeless romantic, devouring the adventure novels their father had left them. He'd recently finished building and equipping the community library he hoped to open after Christmas. But somehow, Levi didn't think Callie would be interested in reading about someone else's courtship. He could only hope it was his brother's kind nature that had prompted him to suggest it, and not an attempt at matchmaking.

He stepped back into the room and wheeled the little chair over to the table. He could imagine Mica smiling from it. She smiled at everything.

Unlike Callie. Her smiles were so rare that they were like the sun coming out after the rain. What would it take to make her smile more often?

There was a perfunctory tap on the door before his brother James strolled in.

"I saw Lance and Percy from the store, so I thought I'd fetch them," he announced, glancing around. "Where's your new family?"

Levi hurried to intercept him before James could wander any farther into the house. "Getting settled and needing a little time to get used to things," Levi told him.

"Ah." James wiggled his brows. Though James was older, he resembled Levi the most, from his dark blond hair and deep blue eyes to his slender build and tall height. The main difference lay in their hair. Where James's was straight and short, Levi's was longer and curlier. That had always seemed odd to Levi. James was the tease, the jokester in the family. Somehow it seemed as if he should be the one with curly hair.

"Perhaps I should warn you," he said now. "Rina would like to evaluate the boys so she knows where to place them in school."

Levi glanced at the empty stairs, already concerned about the silence from the loft. "Give them a day or two."

"I'd be happy to give them all the time in the world," James assured him, "but I bow to my wife, who knows far more about educating young minds than I ever will."

"I'll speak to her," Levi promised, taking his arm and attempting to escort him to the door.

"Do you have everything you need?" James asked, resisting and glancing about as if hoping to catch a glimpse of Callie and the boys. "What about a cradle for the baby? Dottie gave us ours back recently."

"Tomorrow," Levi said, pulling a little harder.

He thought he heard the squeak of James's boots against the plank floor. "I could bring you something from the store—an extra set of dishes? More flour? A bear trap?"

"We're fine," Levi assured him, straining to wrestle his brother over the threshold.

James planted his hands on either side of the open door, eyes widening as he looked past Levi. "Yes, I can see that you are. Quite fine indeed."

What was he talking about? He was fairly sure his brother was just teasing him, but Levi couldn't stop himself from glancing over his shoulder just in case.

Callie had come out of the bedroom. Gone were the slouch hat and the rough buckskin coat. Her honey-colored hair was held up behind her by an abalone comb and flowing about her shoulders in waves. The blue printed calico dress was likely too cold for a winter's day, but it outlined her form and brought color to her cheeks. Or perhaps it was Levi's and James's approving looks that made her blush.

She raised her chin and marched toward the stove, Mica waving a greeting from her arms.

"Isn't it time to get supper started?" she asked with a look to James.

Levi's brother cleared his throat. "Not until I properly welcome you, dear lady." He removed his hands from the doorjamb and sketched an elegant bow. "I'm Levi's brother, James. And you must be the lovely Miss Murphy."

Though his brother was devoted to his schoolteacher wife, he still went out of his way to be gallant to the ladies, young and old. Another woman would have simpered and blushed.

With one hand, Callie pulled a pan from the rack above the stove. "Nice to meet you, Mr. Wallin. If you'll excuse me, I should earn my keep." She brought the pan down on the stove with a clatter.

"I thought you brought a ward, not a housekeeper," James murmured to Levi, brow up.

"We have a few things to work out," Levi said, and he managed to push his brother out at last.

He closed the door and turned to Callie. For all her bravado, she was shifting from foot to foot as if unsure what to do next. Mica peeped over her shoulder and wrinkled her nose at Levi.

"I thought I'd cook for you," he said, moving closer. As he passed the infant chair, he gave it a push that set it rolling toward Callie.

She turned as if noticing the rumble of the wheels against the planks. "What's that?"

"A present from my brothers," Levi told her. "For Mica."

The little girl was already reaching out a hand and

wiggling her fingers as if wanting to draw the chair closer. Callie tilted her head to study the contraption. "Why? What's it for?"

"If I may?" Levi held out his arms.

Callie hesitated a moment, then handed him the baby.

He was more sure of how to hold the little girl this time. But it probably wouldn't have mattered if he hadn't been. Mica smiled up at him, cheeks pink and eyes sparkling. Levi gave in to the thought of rocking her a moment, her weight soft in his arms, before sliding her into the seat.

Mica blinked, then shifted as if getting comfortable. Her smile spread, and she set up a delighted chatter.

Callie looked less impressed, eyes narrowing.

"It rolls," Levi explained, demonstrating. Mica slapped her hands down on the tray in front of her and crowed her approval. "You can take her to wherever you're working without having to carry her." He gave the chair a little push, and Mica squealed, bright and pure.

Callie's hand came down over Levi's on the back on the chair. "Do *not* show the twins."

He had a sudden image of Frisco and Sutter, batting the baby and chair between them. He cast a glance toward the stairs. "I won't."

Mica scooted as if hoping to get the chair moving again. He held it steady, trying not to relish the feeling of Callie's hand warm against his.

"How were they doing when you checked on them?" she asked.

He rubbed behind his ear with his free hand, then stopped when he noticed the nervous gesture. "I haven't had a chance."

Callie's eyes widened, and she released him to back away. "You watch Mica. If I haven't returned in a quarter hour, send for that deputy. I may need rescue."

Chapter Six

Levi Wallin had filed a claim he couldn't pan.

That's all Callie could think as she lifted her mother's skirts and climbed the stairs to the loft. He wasn't sure how to deal with a baby, couldn't keep his family from overrunning his house.

And he had no idea how to handle her brothers.

Callie shook her head at the sight that met her at the top of the stairs. The loft was one long room, peeled logs bracing a roof that no doubt kept out the rain, with a stone hearth at one end and a window with a shutter at the other. Three pallets and two trunks lay waiting. Perhaps it was the dim light that had inspired her brothers to try to start a fire in the grate.

With what looked like one of Levi's shirts as tinder.

"Here," Callie barked. "Now."

She must have sounded sufficiently commanding, for both her brothers obeyed.

"What do you think you're doing?" she demanded, hands on her hips.

Frisco raised his chin. "Setting up the room, like you asked."

"It's kind of cold up here," Sutter agreed.

It was warmer than the house they'd left. "Where'd you get that shirt?"

Sutter nodded to one of the trunks. "In there." He leaned closer and lowered his voice. "He has near a dozen!"

Another mark of a preacher, not that she'd mention it. "And what did you do with *your* clothes?"

Sutter cast a quick glance at the pack, which they'd left along one wall, the quilts piled up around it.

"They're fine where they are," Frisco blustered. "We ain't staying long."

Sutter nodded. "We was figuring to head north as soon as the thaw sets in."

Callie bent to put her face on a level with theirs. "You are not heading north. This is our home now. You want to live out of a pack? Fine. But you take Ma's quilts, and you lay them on the beds. She didn't work that hard to have them dumped on the floor."

He and Sutter both looked to the pallets along the far wall as if noticing them for the first time.

Sutter glanced back at her. "We get our own beds?"

"Looks that way," Callie said, straightening.

"I get the quilt with the velvet patch," Sutter yelled, diving for the pile.

Frisco wrinkled his nose. "You can have it. Someone spilled tea on it."

Callie felt a pang of guilt. They had so few things left from her mother—the dress Callie was wearing, the quilts pieced together from cast-off clothing, the gold ring Pa had given Ma—in promise, he'd said, not only for the many years they'd spend together but the gold he would heap at her feet. Adam had given the ring to

Anna, and now Callie kept it for Mica. After all, Callie wasn't planning to marry.

"I'll wash it when I can," Callie said, moving forward to take the quilt from Sutter. "Use another one for now."

While her brothers prepared their beds, Callie retrieved Levi's shirt. Fine material, soft under her hands. Did it feel good against those broad shoulders?

What was she thinking?

She wadded it up with the quilt for washing, then escorted her brothers downstairs for supper. The preacher had said he was well stocked for food, though she hadn't noticed any, come to think of it. She blew out a breath. Another area where he was lacking. Maybe she should go hunting.

She had barely reached the ground floor when the scents assailed her—warm bread and the tang of onion.

"What are you cooking, preacher?" Frisco called, hurrying closer to where Levi stood by the stove, Sutter right behind.

Callie deposited the quilt and shirt in the bedroom before going to the table. Mica had been pushed up to the edge of it in the funny little chair and was waving around a wooden spoon. Every few swipes she brought it to her mouth to gnaw on. Time to feed that baby. But with what? If Levi didn't know how to hold her, he likely didn't know what kind of food she needed, either.

"My mother called it rag-oo," he was telling her brothers now, lifting the lid on a copper pan to give whatever was inside a stir. Callie's mouth started watering.

She made herself slide in next to Levi instead. He'd wrapped a cloth around his waist; already it was splattered with red and brown dots. She wasn't sure why seeing him mussed pleased her. "I need to feed Mica," she explained. "You got anything I can mash?"

"There's a cupboard built into that wall," he answered, pulling back the metal spoon. "Help yourself."

She went to check. Sure enough, two little handles opened to a cupboard so stocked, Callie could only stare. Jar upon jar crammed on the shelves—red tomatoes, purple plums, golden applesauce, blackberry preserves, pearly onions swimming around blood-red beets, dusky green asparagus and brighter green beans. Oh, what she could do with all this!

She grabbed a jar of applesauce and carried it back to the table.

Frisco was already sitting on the bench. "When do we eat?" he asked Levi.

Levi covered his hand with a corner of the cloth at his waist and eased open the oven. "I'd say a quarter hour, by the look of the biscuits."

"Biscuits?" Sutter hurried to the table and slid in beside Frisco. Mica called her welcome to them both.

Callie's feet carried her to Levi's side, her gaze latched on the browning morsels in the oven. "You know how to bake biscuits?"

He nodded, and she almost cried out in loss as he closed the oven door and shut out the sight of the food she hadn't eaten since Anna had died. "Ma insisted we all learn to fend for ourselves," he explained. "Cooking, cleaning, sewing."

"See there, Callie?" Frisco called. "You won't have to do anything anymore. The preacher's gonna take care of us all."

She didn't believe that for a moment. Lots of prospectors learned how to pry open a tin and heat it over the fire. That didn't make them good cooks. Besides, it wasn't fair to expect Levi to do all the work.

"We ain't greenhorns," she told her brothers. "We don't need to be coddled. I expect you can help with chores."

Frisco pouted.

Letting her brothers think on the matter, Callie turned to the sideboard beyond Levi. She was thankful to see porcelain-covered cast-iron plates and cups instead of fine china. She wouldn't have trusted the boys with anything breakable. A drawer in the sideboard provided access to forks and such. She carried them all to the table.

"Make yourself useful while you wait," she told Frisco.

He crossed his arms over his chest. "Why should I?"

"We might eat faster," Callie pointed out as Levi looked up with a frown.

Frisco began setting the table. Sutter pitched in.

As Callie passed Levi again, she nudged him with her shoulder to get his attention. "This rag-oo—can a baby eat it?"

He lifted the lid, and she thought her nose might fly off her face she inhaled the scent so hard. "Maybe the gravy and some of the softer vegetables."

"Good enough," Callie said and went to fill a bowl with applesauce, as well.

Frisco and Sutter had the places set. Anna had taught them how. On the trail, everyone had just grabbed what they could and sat around the fire to pull out what was in the pot or on the spit. She hadn't had a table until Adam had built one for his bride.

Her eyes were feeling warm again. She was not going to let Levi see her cry. Besides, her brothers might think she was unhappy with the accommodations, and the truth was she was beginning to think partnering with the preacher just might work out.

"I can cook, you know," she told him as she opened the jar and doled out a portion of the applesauce for the rest of them. "If you kill it, I can skin it."

"Impressive," he said with a smile, opening the door to check on the biscuits again. She purposely did not look in that direction. "Beth still prefers that we dress the meat before giving it to her."

Callie nearly dropped the jar. "She puts dresses on the food?"

She thought she heard him choke. Had he taken a bite of the rag-oo? Maybe it wasn't as good as it smelled.

Frisco must have heard the sound as well, because he frowned. "You all right, preacher?"

Levi gasped in a breath. "Fine. There's cider under the sideboard. Pour it around, will you?"

By the time Callie had finished, he was bringing the food to the table. Frisco reached for the pot as Levi sat down.

"Grace first," he warned her brother.

Sutter frowned. "Who's Grace?"

The preacher's color deepened. "Grace is what we call the prayer we say before eating, to thank God for the food and His other blessings."

Now Frisco frowned. "Why? God didn't cook this. You did."

Callie had nearly forgotten the custom, and she felt that twinge of guilt again. "Anna said a prayer before we ate," she reminded her brothers. "So did Ma. Fold your hands like this." She clasped her hands together and watched as her brothers followed suit. "Now bow your heads and close your eyes."

"All right," Sutter said with a sidelong glance at his brother. "But nobody better touch the food."

"I promise," Levi said. He was all seriousness, except for the gleam in those deep blue eyes. She made sure her brothers had bowed their heads before doing so herself.

"Dear Lord," Levi said, voice soft and warm, "thank You for the land to grow these vegetables, the woods to hunt this meat. Thank You for bringing us together at this table. May the food and fellowship bless us, and may we always bless You. Amen."

"Amen," Callie echoed, lifting her head. What a nice thought, to thank God for things. Why didn't more preachers talk about things like that?

"Is 'Amen' like 'the end'?" Sutter asked as Frisco reached once more for the pot.

"It actually means 'so be it'," Levi said, intercepting the food. "It's a way of saying you agree with the prayer. Pass me your plates, and I'll serve."

"Don't be stingy," Frisco urged him.

He wasn't. Levi piled the rag-oo on their plates, then popped on several biscuits. Callie alternated between taking a bite and giving a spoonful to Mica. The meat was tender, the gravy thick and spicy, and the biscuits? They melted in her mouth, light as a cloud. She nearly sighed aloud.

"I was thinking," Frisco said, digging into his third helping. "Callie really should help Mica more. It's hard for her to cook and such when she's minding the baby."

That was true, but her brothers hadn't seemed to notice or care before now.

"It would be a real blessing, preacher," Frisco continued, his smile making him look appropriately innocent, "if you was to cook for us every night. For Callie's sake."

"And Mica's," Sutter added.

Callie met Levi's gaze and saw a smile. He knew what her brothers were up to. Something warm rose inside her. She wasn't alone anymore.

"I agree with your sister that everyone in the house should help with the chores," he said. "Even Mica when she gets a little older."

Mica blew applesauce bubbles at him.

"I can chop wood," Sutter ventured.

Frisco elbowed him. "Cannot. Callie won't let us near the hatchet."

"Not after you tried to chop down the apple tree Anna planted," Callie reminded them.

"I can teach you to use a hand ax properly," Levi said, mopping up the last of the gravy on his plate with a biscuit. "But that's just part of the task. Once the wood is chopped, you have to stack it near the door, out of the rain where it will dry. And you have to carry the dry wood to bins, one here by the stove and one in the loft."

"I'll fill the one downstairs, you do the one up," Frisco told Sutter.

"You can take turns filling the upper and lower bins," Callie said. "And you can set and clear the table and learn to wash the dishes."

Frisco pushed back from the table. "And what are you going to be doing?"

"Oh, all the washing and cleaning," Callie said. "Mending your clothes. And, I expect, when spring comes around again, there will still be some planting and tending to be done."

Sutter made a face. "You didn't do all that at the claim. Why do you have to do it here?"

Callie's face heated, but Levi stepped in smoothly.

"It had to be hard for Callie to do that all alone," he pointed out. "When we pull together, the sled goes farther, faster."

Sutter grinned. "You got a sled?"

"What he means," Callie put in, "is that when we all work together, it's easier on everyone."

Levi nodded. "I've lived in a house where everyone pitched in so that it was well tended. And I've roughed it in a quilt and tarp by a stream alone. There's nothing to beat clean clothes, a roof over your head and family around you."

"And good food," Frisco agreed with a satisfied sigh.

Callie felt the draw of Levi's words, as well. To live in a house with a roof that didn't leak, where a fire warmed her, where good food filled her. Where she had help with all the many things that must be done.

Where Levi Wallin smiled at her across the table like he was her husband and she was his wife.

She sucked in a breath and dropped her gaze. That was just a fool dream, no different from Pa's stories of big houses and servants. She was grateful for the opportunity to have her family cared for. She wasn't ready to think about more, because she'd learned long ago that more never came.

Levi caught himself smiling as he headed for bed that night, then schooled his face before the twins caught sight of it. It didn't do any good to dwell on Callie Murphy—her bright eyes, her soft sighs, her sweet voice. He had pledged himself to be her partner, to help her raise her brothers and niece. It was as simple as that.

And she didn't trust him in any regard. After sending her brothers upstairs to bed, she had bid him good-night and carried Mica into the bedroom. A moment later, he had heard the scrape of wood against wood, and something had darkened the light coming under the door.

"Everything all right in there?" he'd called.

"Fine," she'd called back. "Just moving furniture."

That's when he'd realized she'd shoved the chest Drew had carved for him across the door. She was protecting herself and Mica. From him.

He supposed he ought to be insulted, but all he could think was that Callie Murphy was once again being wise. She didn't know him well enough yet to realize he would never have demanded her attentions.

As he came up into the loft, moonlight trickling down the center of the space, he could just make out Callie's brothers, snuggled under the quilts they had brought from their brother's cabin. He and John had carried the extra pallets over from John's house and Simon's. The beds had served for company there. Now they were serving his new family.

The boys had left the one closest to the hearth for Levi. Another time he might have been touched they'd given him the warmest spot, but he suspected the reason had nothing to do with his comfort. Positioning him near the hearth left the stairs clear for them to escape as soon as he was asleep.

He had to duck his head under the pitched roof, but he went to the pallet, hefted it and carried it over to the other side of the loft, near the window.

"What are you doing?" Sutter asked, proving that at least one of them was awake.

"A wise guide once told me it was best to keep your feet warm and your head cool," Levi told him, repositioning the tick near the stairs. "Good night, Sutter."

"Good night, preacher."

Frisco's fake snore let Levi know what the boy thought of the conversation.

Whatever their plans had been, Callie's brothers were still in their beds when Levi woke the next morning. His conscience was heavy enough with thoughts of the past that he was a light sleeper, so he felt fairly confident the boys hadn't sneaked past him in the night. After taking them to see the church, however, he wasn't so sure.

He had made Callie and her family porridge and bacon for breakfast. Once more the boys had wolfed the food down while Callie ate more daintily as she fed Mica. The baby didn't seem to care what she ate. Everything, like everyone, was met with a smile.

The boys seemed to have slept in their clothes by the number of new wrinkles, but Callie had changed back into her trousers and shirt, suspenders up over her shoulders. She seemed determined to help, stirring the porridge, turning the bacon in the pan.

"I thought I'd show you all around this morning," Levi told them. "You didn't get to see much of Wallin Landing yesterday."

Callie glanced up from feeding Mica a spoonful of porridge. Those blue-gray eyes were thoughtful, but she didn't question his suggestion.

"And there's that fishing hole," Sutter reminded him.

Levi smiled. "Right you are. Let's get everything cleaned up, and we'll start out."

Sutter tipped up his porridge bowl and licked out the last. "There you go. All clean."

"He means washed," Callie said, cheeks turning pink. "And it wouldn't hurt if you two washed yourself, as well."

"I ain't lugging water from the lake," Frisco said, crossing his arms over his chest.

"You don't have to," Levi told him. "There's a pump just outside in the breezeway."

"Does it work?" Frisco asked suspiciously.

"Let's find out," Levi said.

He showed them how to raise the handle on the pump, filled up a pot and brought it in to heat on the stove. The color in Callie's cheeks stayed high as she used the cloth Levi gave her to wash the baby's and her brother's faces, necks and ears. When she started rubbing the cloth over her own neck, Levi had to turn away again.

Partner. Ward. Adam's little sister.

He had to remember that. But he thought he might be walking just a bit fast as he started out of the parsonage at last.

Fog shrouded the area, masking the top of the steeple and clinging to the trees.

"That's my parents' original claim," Levi explained, voice coming out hushed. He pointed down the hill. "The cabin on the right was where my brothers and sister and I were raised. The three men on my older brother's logging crew live in it now. And at the back of the clearing, that long building is the school."

"I thought you were gonna show us where to fish," Frisco said with a frown.

"I will," Levi promised. "But the church is right here. Might as well look in it first."

The boys shrugged, but Callie followed him willingly enough along the breezeway. In her arms, Mica sang to herself, voice high and piping, as if ready to join the church choir.

"The whole community pitched in to erect these buildings," Levi explained. "The parsonage, the church and the hall next door. It took months of work, squeezed in around planting, farming and harvest."

"Nice when folks work together like that," Callie murmured as if impressed.

"Your brothers must know something about building," Sutter allowed.

"My brothers know something about a lot of things," Levi agreed. "Maybe someday I will, too. Now, a word of warning. I didn't have a chance to come in and clean since Sunday, so it might be a little dusty."

Callie cast him a glance as if she didn't understand the humility as he opened the door.

The chapel was a simple construction, one long room with a door at the back and another at the side near the altar, an aisle along each wall and down the middle flanked by white-washed pews. Usually, his gaze was drawn to the cross over the altar. It was made of wood found on the shores and polished until every grain gleamed. Now he jerked to a stop, staring at the toppled benches, the velvet bags they used for offering strewn here and there, the communion plates scattered across the altar.

Callie whirled. "San Francisco Murphy, what have you done!"

Levi turned as well, but the boys had disappeared from the doorway, and he wouldn't have been surprised to see them pelting for the woods.

Chapter Seven

What was she to say? How could her brothers have been so mean-spirited as to wreck a church the whole community had pitched in to build? True, nothing appeared to be broken, but it just seemed disrespectful. The people of Wallin Landing must have wanted a church real bad to work so hard to make this one. Which was kind of odd. Most prospectors lamented when the first preacher showed up in camp. And if he had wanted a building, he'd have had to erect one himself.

"I told you, you have to watch them every minute," she said to Levi. She took Mica from him and went to gather up the little velvet bags that had been tossed about. What did a church need with red purses, anyway? Mica reached for one, but Callie took it away from her, eliciting one of Mica's rare frowns.

He righted a bench with a thud. "Likely they didn't mean any harm."

"But they caused it nonetheless." She moved to the table at the top of the room and stacked the tin plates. Did they eat here, too? Mica smacked her lips as if she thought so.

"I should have expected something like this," he said, banging another bench into place. "I uprooted them. They just returned the favor."

Callie whirled, earning her a giggle from Mica. "Don't you dare condone such behavior! You can't coddle them, or they won't ever learn how to get on in the world. Did your ma coddle you?"

He turned away, but not before she saw red streaking his cheeks. "A little understanding can't hurt."

Callie couldn't argue that, but she was no longer sure if they were talking about her brothers or him.

It took them a little longer to set the room to rights, then they ventured back outside. Callie was afraid to learn where her brothers had gone. They didn't know the area yet, and they'd talked yesterday about heading north. Of course, she didn't know Wallin Landing, either. How could she find them if they got lost?

Levi must have been looking for them as well, for he caught her arm and pointed down the hill with his free hand.

The horses that had brought them to Wallin Landing were out in the pasture along with Levi's mare, plucking at the brown winter grass. Frisco and Sutter had climbed the rail fence and were waving at the trio, feet swinging.

Callie shook her head. "See? Not an ounce of remorse for what they done."

"They may not realize the potential harm," Levi said, releasing her arm and starting down the hill.

Callie walked beside him, scurrying to keep up with those long legs. Mica giggled each time she bounced. "Then we should make sure they understand."

Sutter had pulled up a clump of grass and was holding it out, as if trying to entice the horses closer. Callie shuddered to think what would happen if her brother actually mounted one of the powerful beasts. As it was, the three horses kept their distance, heads down. Only the flick of their ears told her they heard her brothers' eager calls.

Levi leaned his arms on the fence next to Frisco. "That was some mess in the church."

Frisco nodded, gaze on the horses. "Someone must not like you."

Callie planted her feet between the pair. "San Francisco Murphy, you apologize."

Frisco glanced at her with a frown. "Why?"

Callie threw up one hand, earning her a squeak of surprise from Mica. "*Why*? You just told the preacher you didn't like him and you nearly destroyed his church."

Frisco's frown deepened. "Did not."

"Me, neither," Sutter insisted.

Now Callie frowned. Her brothers could tell some tall tales when they wanted, and they'd fibbed a time or two to escape punishment, but she'd always caught them. Something said they were telling the truth now.

So who had damaged the church?

"I'm glad to hear that, boys," Levi said, voice deepening. "I'd hate to think that you'd try to destroy a place devoted to God, a place meant to provide peace, sanctuary."

Now, that was more like it. Callie nodded her agreement.

"It's a nice church, preacher," Frisco said, turning for the pasture once more. "But I like horses better."

"So did I at your age," Levi assured him. He pushed off the rail. "But there's lots more to see. We can start with the barn over there." He headed in that direction.

Her brothers hopped down and ran ahead toward the large log building.

Callie sighed as she and Mica caught up to him. "Is that all you're going to say about the matter?"

"For now," Levi said, gaze on her brothers. "But I'll take your advice and keep an eye on them." He lengthened his stride to reach her brothers.

He kept them busy the next little while, showing them the barn with the goats, chickens and pair of oxen his oldest brother used in his logging. He let them climb up to the hay loft and roll around in the piles. He pointed out the stack of logs as high as his head that would serve for fuel for the winter.

Sutter's eyes widened.

"I could chop that much wood in a day," Frisco bragged.

Sutter elbowed him. "Could not."

"Could, too!"

Callie was ready to wade in, but Levi stepped between them. "Want to see the school?"

"No," her brothers chorused, and they scampered toward the lake.

Levi loped after them.

"You are going to make them go to school, aren't you?" Callie asked him when she joined them near the biggest cabin.

"Of course," he assured her.

She wished she could believe that, but she couldn't help feeling that Levi Wallin wasn't used to being the authority, despite his calling as a preacher. He acted more like Adam, an indulgent older brother.

Frisco and Sutter needed more. They needed someone who would forge their characters, help them find the strength to refuse the easy path that had ruined their father and brother. She'd done what she could. She needed a real partner.

As the boys headed down a path toward the water, she caught Levi's arm. "Promise me you won't keep giving in to them."

"Promise me you'll let them have a little fun," he countered.

"Fun?" Callie stared at him. "It isn't fun eking out a living, but it has to be done. Most things in life are that way."

He reached out and tucked a hair behind her ear, the touch soft. "Not everything has to be a struggle, Callie. Let me show you."

She took a step back, shifting Mica between them. "I don't need you to show me anything. I raised my brothers alone. I thought you were going to help."

He dropped his hand. "I am helping."

"Not if you let them do as they please, you aren't."

He frowned. "They're just children."

"Children who will grow into men."

His frown only grew. He didn't understand any more than Adam and Pa had. Callie tightened her grip on Mica. "Fine. I'll take the chore back. I don't need your help. We did all right without you."

"No," Levi said, crossing his arms over his chest. "You didn't. And it's about time you faced that fact and stopped lashing out at people who only want to help."

Levi had never seen Callie so fiery. Her eyes flashed like gemstones, two spots of color stood out on her cheeks and her breath came fast.

"If you wanted someone who would do your bidding," she said, "you should never have offered to partner me."

Levi dropped his arms. "I never asked for someone to do my bidding. But no one here is trying to harm you, Callie."

"Tell that to the people who messed up your church," she said, pushing past him. "I'm going to find my brothers."

Levi ran a hand back through his hair.

Father, what am I doing wrong? I only want to help.

And why beholdest thou the mote that is in thy brother's eye, but consider not the beam in thine own eye?

He wasn't surprised that that verse came to mind. He knew he had a lot to make up for. Sometimes, lying in bed at night, he felt the rope rough against his neck, heard the jeers of the miners surrounding him.

You know what we do to claim jumpers, don't you?

Thief!

Liar!

Scoundrel!

A shudder shook him. He wasn't that boy anymore. Thaddeus had convinced the miners involved to keep quiet, giving Levi a chance to atone. He wasn't going to waste it.

He found Callie and her brothers down by the lake. Though the mist was rising, it still hid Mount Rainier from view. With the forest all around, the lake was cupped by green and topped by silver.

Seemingly oblivious to the grandeur, the boys were throwing stones into the water, the plunks echoing even as the ripples widened. As many times as he and his brothers had stood along the shore throwing rocks, Levi was surprised there were any left.

"Lots of fish in that lake," he ventured, joining them. "Some as long as my arm."

Sutter paused in midthrow. "Really?"

Levi held up a hand. "Word of honor."

"I'll catch 'em," Frisco said, hurling a rock out as if planning to knock a fish on the head. "You can cook 'em, preacher."

"With pleasure," Levi assured him. "For now, see that plant growing at the water's edge? That's watercress, and it tastes fine. Pick us some for dinner."

Frisco and Sutter dropped their rocks and moved down the shore.

Levi stepped closer to Callie. "Forgive me. I wasn't trying to tell you how to raise your brothers. You are Mica and the twins' family."

Her gaze had followed her brothers. "And I'm sorry for getting riled. I suppose you're trying, preacher."

"Very trying," Levi agreed with a smile.

She smiled back, brightening the day. "There's hope for you. And for me. But I've been both mother and father these last few months. I suppose I'm not used to sharing the responsibility."

"Neither am I," he confessed. "I was the youngest boy. My brothers claim Ma had a sweet spot for me, not that I noticed with the number of punishments she had to mete out, well deserved."

She cast him a glance, gaze shuttered. "Hard on you, was she?"

His mother's face came to mind, strong, determined, but with love shining from her green eyes. How she'd smiled when he'd excelled, cried when he'd misbehaved. She'd had more cause for concern than most mothers.

"Never," he said. "And I always knew she loved me."

She nodded, gaze returning to her brothers, who were working together to pull up the watercress. "My ma, too. Pa, for that matter, though he had odd notions about how to show it. He thought the next big strike would set us up for life. I tried to tell him the money didn't matter to me, but he kept saying I deserved better."

"I suppose all parents want the best for their children," Levi allowed.

"I suppose," she said, but she didn't sound convinced.

The rest of the day went fairly well. They brought the watercress back, and Levi showed the boys how to set it to stewing. Callie put Mica down for a nap, then swept out the house from top to bottom. As if to make amends, she swept out the church, too. Nice to have a partner again, even if the feeling brought a pang for his last partner, Scout. Would he ever see his friend again? He couldn't blame Scout for avoiding him after what Levi had done.

For his part, he did as she'd suggested and kept an eye on her brothers. He showed Frisco and Sutter how to chop wood, setting up two stumps as their bases so no one would need to take turns. He gave them each a hatchet, as well. If there was one thing his family had in abundance, it was implements to chop down trees. The boys did so well that he sent them to James's store along the lake for a treat, telling them to put it on his bill.

As he watched Callie play with Mica on the rug, warmth wrapped around him. It seemed he had a family of his own.

Thank You, Lord.

He had dinner going on the stove—venison steak John had brought over along with stewed watercress and biscuits with blackberry preserves, when the boys returned. Callie looked up as they entered.

"Mighty fine store you got here, preacher," Frisco announced.

Sutter sucked on his candy stick and nodded.

"We brought you something back." Frisco pulled a tin of beans from his pocket and set it on the table. "Thought it might go with the watercress."

"The man never even noticed it was gone," Sutter bragged.

Callie rose even as Levi sighed.

"Take it back," she ordered her brothers. "Now."

Frisco snatched it off the table. "Why? He has lots of stuff in that old store. He won't miss it."

Levi set down the fork he'd been using to turn the venison and came around the table. "It doesn't matter how much someone has. Chances are, they worked hard for it. If you want something, you need to work for it, too."

Frisco was coloring, and Sutter shuffled his feet.

"We was just trying to put food on the table," Frisco muttered.

Levi's heart went out to the boy, and he squatted to put his face on a level with the twins.

"There's plenty of food here," he told them. "My brothers grow it and share it with us. We can hunt and fish and gather like we did with the watercress. But we aren't going to steal. That's wrong."

Frisco sniffed. "You don't know what it's like to be hungry, preacher."

Levi grimaced, rising. "Oh, but I do. When I was nineteen, my friend Scout and I decided to seek our fortunes on the gold fields."

"Like Pa," Sutter said, wide-eyed.

"And Adam," Frisco reminded him.

"And half the fools in North America," Callie put in.

Levi nodded. "And fools we were. Here, we'd been raised in the wilderness, and we still had no idea how to handle ourselves. We ran out of tinned food in a week, had no money to buy more. We ran out of shot and powder in a month, so we couldn't hunt. Scout tried to make a bow and arrows, but he rarely hit anything. The panning scared away any fish. It got to the point where we were living on mushrooms."

Both the boys were staring at him. So was Callie.

"What did you do?" Sutter asked.

"I snuck into your camp and stole food."

They all started.

"Adam caught me," he admitted. "He saved our lives that day. He gave me and Scout enough sourdough and flour to last a week and made me promise I would come back for help before I tried to steal anything else. So, you see, your brother didn't hold with stealing, either."

"Neither did Ma and Pa," Callie said quietly.

Frisco shuffled his feet. "I'll take it back, say I'm sorry."

"Maybe we could chop wood for his store to make it up to him," Sutter suggested, glancing between Levi and Callie.

Though Levi was certain James had enough wood, he nodded, rising. "Good idea. Now, why don't you wash up? Supper's almost ready."

They ran for the pump.

Callie took a step closer, lowered her voice. "Was that true? Did you try to steal from us?"

Levi couldn't meet her gaze. "I did, to my sorrow."

He felt her sigh, but her voice came out sounding relieved instead of disappointed. "I'm glad Adam offered you food. He was always ready to help a friend. Just like you're helping us now."

Levi turned for the stove before he could speak the words pushing against his lips. If Callie knew why he felt compelled to help her and her family, he very much feared she'd want nothing further to do with him.

Chapter Eight

Callie couldn't help thinking about Levi's story as she settled for the night with Mica in the soft bed. It seemed he did understand a little of what she and her family had endured. Too bad she hadn't seen him when he'd come for food. Maybe she'd find it easier to deal with him now. Then again, if she'd known he'd once tried to steal from them, she might never have agreed to come to Wallin Landing. As it was, she had still pushed the chest over the door that night.

Like the house and church, the chest was built solid. The carved top showed a salmon leaping out of a stream as if it would fly over the trees on either side. Levi must have used it to store his clothing, for she'd found a button at the bottom when she'd opened it to put in her and Mica's things and the items Adam had left.

"It's not much to show for the person he was," Levi had said that evening when he'd given her the bundle the other miners had brought with Adam's letter.

Callie's throat had felt tight. "Not much at all. He deserved better."

Levi had rested his hand on her shoulder, the touch

kind. Warmth penetrated her shirt. He'd left before she could thank him again for his kindness.

The next morning, she pulled on her shirt, trousers and coat and went with Frisco and Sutter down to the store to return the tin of beans. On Levi's suggestion, she left Mica with him. The baby was by far the easiest member of the Murphy family to get along with. Still, Callie felt almost bare without Mica in her arms.

She walked into the store out of the misty morning, and memories wrapped around her. The clutter of fish hooks standing next to cornmeal, bolts of fabric beside bear traps—it was like every gold rush mercantile she'd ever visited. Levi's brother, standing behind the counter at the back of the disordered space, suspenders up over a plaid flannel shirt, looked perfectly comfortable among the crowded surroundings. He listened, face impassive, as Frisco and Sutter stammered out their apology for taking the food and offered to chop wood.

"I have plenty of wood," he told them, glancing from one to the other. "And Pa always said the punishment should fit the crime."

"Crime?" Sutter squealed with a look to Frisco.

"Honest, mister," Frisco said, "it was just a tin of beans."

"A tin of beans?" James Wallin drew himself up, pointing a finger to the ceiling. "Might as well say the sweat off my brow, the very sustenance on which my wife and children depend."

Frisco and Sutter squirmed, and Callie hid a smile. This was better than going to a play at the opera house. And she had a feeling he wasn't going to just pass off her brothers' misdeeds, unlike a certain preacher.

He leaned closer to her brothers and lowered his voice

as if taking them into his confidence. "I am partial to trout. You catch me one big enough to eat, and I'll count our dealings square."

"Yes, sir," Frisco said, backing from the counter.

"As soon as we can," Sutter promised beside him.

James nodded to them, then turned to Callie and offered her a wink. "It seems Levi isn't the only one to wear the trousers in your family. I appreciate a lady of daring."

Callie shrugged. "Not so much daring as necessity. You ever tried panning in a dress?"

James's face turned solemn, but she could see the light in his eyes. "I have never had the pleasure."

She grinned before turning to walk her brothers back up to the main clearing.

As they came past the big cabin, her brothers arguing about which of them would catch James Wallin's big fish, Levi's sister was out on the porch, leaning on a broom. She quickly started sweeping as Callie and the twins approached, but she didn't fool Callie. The porch was clean enough to eat off.

"Oh, good morning, Miss Murphy, boys," she called as if surprised to see them. "How are you enjoying Wallin Landing?"

Frisco paused and scratched behind his ear. "It's passable."

"You have horses," Sutter told her.

She smiled, a dimple popping into view beside her mouth. "Yes, we do. And you must go up to see Simon and Nora's farm. They have a three-legged cow."

Frisco planted his hands on his hips. "You're joshing."

"I promise," Beth told him. "They have a dog, too. He looks a bit like a wolf, but he's very friendly. His name is Fleet, and if it snows you will see him pulling his own sled."

Her brothers exchanged delighted glances.

"Can we go up and see, Callie?" Frisco begged.

"I'm sure it would be fine for the boys to go by themselves," Beth put in. "Nora watches the little ones while the others are in school, so she's sure to be there." She pointed to an opening in the trees at the edge of the clearing. "Just follow that path up the hill."

"It's all right," Callie told her brothers. "I'll come fetch you for chores."

Her brothers ran off.

Beth sighed. "I remember when I was that age. You couldn't keep me in the house."

Seeing her now, her purple-striped gown dotted with bows, lace draping her neck, Callie had a hard time believing she'd been anything like Frisco and Sutter.

Beth rolled the handle of her broom between her hands. "Would you like to come in? I can put the kettle on for tea."

Callie would have preferred to escape to Levi's house, but there was something wistful about Beth's voice. What would it hurt? She could always leave if she felt uncomfortable.

"All right," she agreed.

Beth shoved the broom into a corner of the porch and ran for the door, looking every inch as excited as Frisco and Sutter.

Callie ventured inside. Like Levi's house, the door opened into one large room, with stairs leading up to the second story. Arches on either side of the hearth spoke of a second room beyond, and Callie caught sight of a washtub leaning against a wall. A long plank table near the window could easily seat twenty, and the chairs and benches scattered around the room would have accommodated another dozen or so.

"All your houses are so big," she said.

Beth, who had gone through the closest arch, poked her head back out. "You haven't met Drew yet, have you? Once you see him, you'll know why Pa designed the rooms with space to spare. He expected us all to grow. Do you like honey with your tea?"

Honey. Callie could only nod, afraid she might squeal like Mica if she opened her mouth. As Beth disappeared again, she made herself go to the table and take a seat, folding her hands on the planks. There was dirt under her ragged nails. She tucked her hands under the table.

Beth returned with a plate of tiny white cookies. "Tea will be ready shortly," she promised, taking a seat near Callie. "Are you all settled at the parsonage?"

Levi had used the word, too. That must be what they called a preacher's house. "More or less," Callie acknowledged, wondering whether it would be rude to snatch up one of those cookies.

Beth clasped her hands together as if trying to contain her delight. "And how do you like my brother?"

Callie blinked. "Which one?"

Beth giggled. There was something happy, something engaging about the sound. It reminded Callie of Mica. She couldn't help smiling.

"I do have a lot of brothers," Beth admitted. "This time I was talking about Levi." She reached for a cookie at last. "How are the two of you getting along?"

Callie took a cookie, finding it still warm from the oven. Were those walnuts speckling the white? She tried not to gulp it in one bite, savoring the sweetness. Not for the first time she wished she'd paid more attention to what Anna had done at the hearth.

She caught Beth watching her and swallowed hastily. What could she say to Beth about Levi? In truth, there were moments she liked him quite a lot. Other times she wanted to shout at him, tell him to leave her alone. She certainly didn't want to admit that to his sister.

"He's tolerable," she said.

"My, what…praise." Beth rose. "Let me check the tea."

Callie leaned back as Beth hurried from the table. Those cookies were watching her. But Beth had only taken one. Would she think Callie a lout for taking a second?

Before she could decide, Beth bustled back, two steaming pink and white cups in hand. She set down one in front of Callie. "Best blow on it first. It's hot."

Callie joined her in puffing at the brew before taking a cautious sip. Frowning, she looked down into the amber-colored liquid. "This is tea?"

"Rose hip and chamomile," Beth said, pausing to take a sip.

Pa's tea had been black, oily stuff. He always joked it would put hair on Adam's chest. Even the tea was fancy at Wallin Landing.

"What are your plans for Christmas?" Beth asked, before taking another sip.

Callie drank a little more. It was rather nice, fruity almost, delicate, not unlike Beth Wallin. "Hadn't thought that much about it. A few weeks away yet, isn't it?"

Beth inched forward in her seat. "Yes, but there's so much to do—the decorations, the baking, the geese to pluck. And we'll be having a community dance in the hall on the evening of Christmas Day. I'm trying to find musicians so Simon doesn't always have to play."

Callie nodded, though in truth she wasn't sure what she could do to help. The last few years before moving to Seattle, they'd usually been huddled in some hotel room on Christmas, waiting for the ground to thaw enough to go back to panning. Even Christmas in Adam's cabin had been a simple affair, with oranges as a treat. But a dance, with a real musician? Oh, what she'd give to go to that!

"You're about five and a half feet tall, aren't you?" Beth asked.

Callie frowned at the change of subject. "Near as I can tell."

Beth cocked her head. "Our figures are fairly similar."

Perhaps, but Beth had more curves than Callie ever would. "I suppose."

Beth snapped a nod. "Good. Nora wants to make you a dress, you see. You really can't keep wearing trousers. We can use my measurements and just tuck things up and in a little."

Levi's sister didn't understand. Callie set down her cup. "My trousers work for what I have to do. And I don't have money for a dress."

Beth waved her free hand. "That's all right. It was intended as a gift."

A gift. Charity more like. In the kindest way possible, Beth was telling Callie her clothes weren't good enough.

She wasn't good enough. She didn't fit in.

Callie stared at the cookies, sad she hadn't grabbed a second one while she could, then pushed back her chair. "Thank you, but I make do. I should be going."

Beth's round face puckered as she rose as well. "But we were just starting to get acquainted."

Callie drew in a breath. "I can see you want to be friends, but I should warn you. You probably don't want to get acquainted with me, even if we're panning the same stream here at Wallin Landing. You won't like what you find. Good day."

She hurried for the door before Beth could call her back.

As Callie trudged up the slope toward the parsonage, tears stung her eyes. Levi's sister was only trying to be kind. She truly thought a cup of tea, a present was all it took to be friends. True friends knew all about each other. True friends lifted you up when you were down and cheered you as you rose. Callie might not have ever had a true friend like that, except for Anna, but she'd seen it a rare time or two on the gold fields.

Beth might want to be that kind of friend, but she and Callie were too different. The more Beth learned about Callie, the less she'd want to be friends. Callie couldn't bear losing someone else dear. Maybe when the twins and Mica were grown, she could learn to be a grand lady worthy of associating with Beth Wallin. She'd wear pretty dresses with bows and lace and not care what slopped on them. She'd have dainty cups, drink rarified tea and eat all the cookies she wanted with friends while they chatted about the latest fashions and newest literature.

Well, maybe not the literature.

Partway up the slope, she stopped and stamped her foot. There! She was acting no better than Pa, spinning tales that would never come true. And why was she wishing for the moon, anyway? Her life wasn't nearly so bad. Spending time with these Wallin folk was just giving her notions. She had to remember who she was, where she came from.

She took a deep breath, forcing herself to calm. On either side, the forest lay quiet. Perhaps that was why she heard the snap of something close at hand.

Callie stilled, glancing from side to side. There it came again, that feeling of being watched. Someone was out there. Was that a shape moving through the trees? A bear?

A man?

"Everything all right?"

She whirled at the deep voice behind her, and her gaze landed in the middle of a plaid-flannel-clad chest. Swallowing, she tilted her head back to see a giant of a man, who seemed to be frowning.

"Can I help you?" he asked.

Callie stumbled back. "No! I don't need help. I don't need any of you. Go away, and leave me alone!"

Levi had rocked Mica to sleep. The fact stunned him. Ma had said he'd never stood still long enough to catch a breath, but he'd sat at the table holding the baby and swaying back and forth until jet black lashes drifted over those blue eyes and her little mouth relaxed. Now she was resting on the bed, pillows piled around her so she wouldn't roll off. He'd have to remind James to bring over the cradle. It couldn't be easy for Callie to sleep with the baby. She was probably awakened every time the little girl moved.

The door slammed open, and Callie dashed into the room, face white and hands trembling. Levi strode to meet her. "What's wrong?"

Her breath was coming fast again, but not from anger, he thought. Something had frightened her. "There was a man by the woods. He was huge!"

Levi moved to the door and yanked it open. His brother Drew paused with fist raised to knock.

"I think I frightened your guest," he said, face heavy with regret. "Please let her know I meant no harm."

"I will," Levi promised. "I'll come to see you later. Ask James to bring over that cradle."

Drew nodded, and Levi closed the door. Turning, he saw Callie standing with her hand on her shoulder again, as if trying to hide herself.

"Is he gone?" she asked, voice shaking.

"Yes." Levi crossed to her side. She'd probably push him away, but he thought she needed comforting. He put his arms around her, felt her head rest against his shoulder. The honor of it nearly shook him off his feet.

"It's all right, Callie," he told her. "You'll be fine."

"No, I won't." Her voice wavered in a sob. "I should know how to take care of myself. I've been doing it for years. But everything is different here. I don't know how to talk, how to dress. I don't even know how to drink tea!"

He wasn't sure what she was talking about, but he rubbed a hand along her back, the hide of her coat rough against his fingers. "It is different here from the gold fields," he acknowledged. "But different doesn't have to be bad. You said you liked my cooking."

She sniffed. "You put too much salt in the rag-oo."

He nearly smiled at the petulant tone. "Duly noted. I'll put the salt cellar on the table, and we can each decide how much to add to the plate."

She was silent a moment. "You don't fight enough with me."

Levi paused. "You want me to fight with you?"

He felt her sigh. "I don't know. See? I don't even know that!"

Levi held her out so he could see her face. Tears left a muddy trail in their wake. Her eyes pleaded with him for understanding, for encouragement.

"You know plenty of things," he told her. "I've heard all of my sisters-in-law struggled with how to do much with a baby in their arms. You figured out how to cook and wash with water far away. You took care of Mica when her mother died."

She hung her head. "Doesn't seem like that counts for much in the scheme of things."

"It counts for a lot with me," Levi assured her. "It counts for a lot with Mica, Frisco and Sutter, too. You don't have to change a thing about yourself, Callie, if you don't want to."

"And if I want to change?" She glanced up, lower lip trembling.

He pulled her close. "I'm here to help, whatever you need."

He felt her sigh again as she rested against him, but the tension in her had lessened, leaving her soft in his arms. He ought to be satisfied with the good he'd done, bask in the contentment of knowing he'd brought her a little peace. But something urged him to hold her a little closer, press a kiss against her hair, promise her he'd stay by her side forever, protecting, cherishing.

They were partners. Nothing more. He might understand her, but she would never understand what he'd done.

He drew back. "You don't need to be afraid here. Everywhere you look you'll likely find a Wallin involved. The man who startled you was my brother Drew."

She stuck out her lower lip. "Was he? No wonder everything has to be so big."

Levi chuckled. "Simon's just as tall, but not so muscular. But neither of them would harm a hair on your head."

"I know." She looked away, teeth worrying her lower lip a moment. "Do you think I'm pretty?"

He blinked, as much at the *non sequitur* as the fact that it touched on his thoughts. "Certainly."

Her look swung back to him, eyes narrowing. "But I'd be prettier with a fancy dress, my hair all piled up like a frosted cake."

Levi met her gaze. "You'd be pretty wearing Gap-Tooth Harding's whale skin coat."

She wrinkled her nose, clearly having no idea how adorable she looked while doing so. "That old thing? It was torn, dirty and smelly and...oh."

"Oh," Levi agreed.

Pink suffused her cheeks. "Well, thank you." She stepped back from him. "I appreciate the help, preacher. I feel better now."

Levi inclined his head. "Good enough to stop calling me preacher?"

She frowned. "That's what you are."

"Then I suppose I should call you mother-father-sister-head-of-her-house every time I speak to you."

Her mouth quirked. "Point taken. What do you want me to call you?"

"How about Levi? And I'll call you Callie."

The pink deepened. "All right." She glanced around. "Where's Mica?"

"Napping," Levi reported with some pride. "Where are Frisco and Sutter?"

She gasped, returning to clutch his arm. "Oh, Levi! I let them go up to see your sister-in-law Nora without me. If we hurry, we might be able to save the farm before it's too late."

Chapter Nine

Callie could scarcely catch her breath as she followed Levi up the hill behind the main clearing. First she'd been scared that she'd begun to feel a kinship with Beth, then Levi's brother had startled her, and finally Levi had gathered her close and told her she was pretty. Even if she was dressed in an old rag like Gap-Tooth Harding's nasty coat. Now would be a good time to set a spell and think, but she couldn't leave Levi's sister-in-law besieged by the twins.

Looking over Levi's shoulder, safe in his strong arms, Mica waved at Callie. Callie couldn't help a stab of envy. She'd recently become aware of how nice it was to be held in Levi's arms.

Her cheeks were heating as he led her out onto a plateau. Very likely her face was red. She hoped he'd put it down to the exertion of the climb, though in truth she'd hiked far higher hills following her father and brother.

Now fields, fallow in winter, lay waiting in every direction. Far on the other side, firs rose as if guarding the area. Closer at hand, a long, low house stood surrounded by the remains of a garden. The sprawling building was made of planed lumber painted white with green trim. Flower boxes sat under each window, curlicues edged the roof and a bench swing waited on the deep porch that wrapped around the house. It was the prettiest house Callie had ever seen. The person who owned it must be fairly fancy.

No one answered Levi's knock at the green-lacquered door, but voices sounded nearby.

"That's Frisco," she told Levi.

A sharp yip split the air, and Callie tensed.

Levi smiled. "And that's Fleet. Come on."

He led her around the side of the house to the back door, where a yard opened between the porch and a large vegetable patch. A woman about Callie's height, with flyaway black hair and a matronly figure, was standing on the shaded porch, toddler up in her arms and another clinging to the skirts of her purple plaid gown. The apron around her waist had bows and scallops a plenty, but it was also speckled with every color imaginable, as if she'd collected bits of everything she'd passed.

Out in the yard, Frisco and Sutter were running back and forth, two boys about half their age and size trailing behind like the tail on a kite. And darting among and between them was a sled dog. She'd seen his like in the British Territories, broad chest and bright eyes. This one had black markings over his head and shoulders, as if he were wearing a hooded cape.

"That's some dog," she said as she and Levi stopped to watch the fun.

"His name is Fleet," the woman said, venturing down the stairs and over to Callie and Levi. "I hope you don't mind me letting him play with Frisco and Sutter. He loves the exercise."

He loved the exercise? Her brothers were the ones doing most of the running, cheeks red and mouths open.

Levi nodded to the lady. "Good morning, Nora. I see you've met Callie's brothers." He lifted Mica, whose head was turning back and forth as she followed the commotion across the yard. "This is Mica, and this is Callie Murphy."

Nora bobbed a curtsey as if she'd met someone important. "Very pleased to meet you." She nodded in turn to the children around her. "I'm Nora, in my arms is my Hannah and this is Rina's Charlotte."

The little girl beside her hid her face in the purple plaid.

"Out there you have Rina's Seth and my Lars. They certainly like your brothers. I hope Frisco and Sutter can visit often."

That was the first time anyone had ever said that about her brothers. She was so surprised that Levi had an opportunity to speak first.

"I expect they'll be starting school soon," he said as Mica reached for Hannah. The two little girls clasped hands and smiled at each other. Hannah had her mother's gray eyes and black hair, making her and Mica nearly twins.

"How do you manage them all?" Callie couldn't help asking.

Nora laughed, a warm, happy sound. "Most days it's more like they manage me. We do the chores together, read, cook, eat and take naps when I can convince them. Catherine's Bartholomew is resting inside right now. It all works out."

Callie had an urge to wrap her arms around this

woman and hold her tight. "That's what I did with Frisco and Sutter. And now with Mica."

Nora's broad face saddened. "But I get to send most of them home for supper. You had to do it all. But no more. Now you have us to help."

Were those tears shimmering in the gray gaze? It was as if Nora Wallin had peeled back the curtain, peered into Callie's life and understood how hard she'd worked, how joy and sorrow could mix inside her, how she longed for someplace she would be safe, accepted.

"Thank you," Callie said, feeling her own tears starting again.

Nora's smile brightened her face. "You're welcome. Anything I can do, let me know. I'm already planning a dress, and now that I've seen Frisco and Sutter, I think long trousers will be needed for winter." She blushed, dropping her gaze. "I'm a seamstress, you see. That's what I do, sew for people I love."

If anyone else had told her she was loved on first meeting, Callie would have called them a liar. But there was something so warm, so open about Nora that Callie couldn't doubt her. Emotions clogged her throat, and she looked hurriedly out at her brothers.

"We should probably take them back to the parsonage," she murmured. "They have chores, too."

"You hear that, Fleet?" Nora called. "Frisco and Sutter have to go home."

The two younger boys skidded to a stop, faces hanging.

"Why?" one asked.

Frisco threw out his chest. "We got to help the preacher."

"And we're fishing for the store," Sutter added.

Their two devotees looked impressed.

As Levi went with Mica to round up the younger boys, her brothers sauntered over to Callie's side, the dog pacing them.

Sutter put a hand in the thick fur. "Could we bring Fleet with us, Callie, please?"

"Fleet belongs to Nora and her family," Callie told him.

"Though he goes where he wants," Nora added with a smile.

"We'll come visit again," Callie promised. She glanced at Nora. "And you could come down to the parsonage any time you want."

Despite her best efforts, the suggestion came out hesitant. And why not? It wasn't as if she knew how to phrase an invitation. She'd never had a home she felt comfortable inviting a lady to visit.

"I'd like that," Nora said. "Thank you. Say goodbye to the boys now, Fleet." She reached out her free hand toward the dog.

Fleet backed away. "Noooo!"

Callie gaped.

"He talks!" Sutter rounded on her. "Callie, we got to get a dog like Fleet."

Frisco bent to put his face on a level with the dog's. "What else does he say?"

Nora eyed her dog with evident pride. "Sometimes he says Nora."

Frisco's brows shot up. "Say Frisco," he commanded the dog.

Fleet brought his leg up to scratch behind his shoulder.

"That might be a little hard," Levi commiserated,

joining them as the two younger boys ran up the steps and into the house. "Let's leave him to practice. Good day, Nora."

"A very good day to you all, too." Her smile and the little girls' waves saw them out of the yard.

"I like her," Sutter said as they started down the path for the main clearing. "She's nice."

"You like her dog," Frisco corrected him.

"He's nice, too," Sutter allowed.

"They're all nice," Callie said, hearing the note of longing in her voice. Everyone of Levi's family was going out of their way to make her feel welcome. She needed to find a way to return the favor, especially with Levi.

Levi was smiling as he led Callie and her family back to the parsonage. It looked as if they'd discovered a way to harness the boys' energy. He'd speak to John and Simon about getting Frisco and Sutter involved with the animals. And Callie and Nora seemed to get on; perhaps his kindest sister-in-law could help Callie feel more at home. He was still congratulating himself on how well things were going when Rina arrived that afternoon to evaluate the twins, bringing Mica's cradle with her.

It was a question as to whether Drew's wife, Catherine, or James's wife, Rina, was the most formidable of his sisters-in-law. The regal brunette swept into the parsonage with a pleasant smile, but he was certain entire nations rose and fell behind those changeable hazel eyes.

"Forgive me for not coming to welcome you sooner," she told Callie and the boys, who were clustered around the table looking at books that John had brought over.

Mica banged on her chair with a spoon as if to get their attention.

Rina twitched her lavender wool skirts aside as she joined them. "I'm trying to end lessons at a good place before Christmas, and there's the theatrical to consider."

"The Lake Union School puts on a Christmas play each year," Levi explained.

"This time in the hall," Rina said with a fond look his way.

"But not the church?" Callie put in with her own look to Levi. "We found things moved around yesterday."

Rina frowned. "We won't decorate until a few days before the event, and we aren't going to use the church. Perhaps Beth and Nora were cleaning."

He was fairly sure his sister and Nora hadn't over-turned the benches in the process. By the way Frisco and Sutter were squirming, they were still the most likely culprits. As if she thought so, too, Mica blew bubbles at them.

Rina laid the book and slate she'd been carrying on the table. "Boys, I'd like you to show me how well you read, write and cipher so I know what kind of work to give you in school."

Frisco pushed the slate away. "I'd probably be at the head of the class."

Sutter pulled the book closer. "I like reading."

"Do not!" Frisco declared with a scowl.

Sutter scowled back. "Do, too!"

Levi was ready to intervene, but Callie rose and came around beside him. "That's enough. You ought to thank Mrs. Wallin for visiting us. How'd you like to test in front of the whole school?"

Sutter closed his eyes as if it were a fate too awful

to contemplate. Frisco crossed his arms over his chest. "Don't need to be tested. Ain't going to school."

"That's a shame," Rina said, rearranging the slate closer to him and setting a piece of chalk from her pocket beside it. "We could have used a bright young man such as yourself for the theatrical. Standing up in front of the whole community. Leading the school."

Levi wasn't sure how the lad would take the challenge. Neither was Callie—he could feel her tensing beside him. Mica reached for the chalk.

Frisco grabbed it first. "I suppose I could help. But only until Christmas."

Rina inclined her head. "Let's call today a trial. All great actors have to try out for their parts." She nodded to the book in Sutter's hands. "Sutter, would you read a page aloud for me?"

Sutter began reading, stumbling over a few of the words in the simple primer. Callie jerked her head at Levi and stepped back from the table, out of earshot.

"They have to keep going to school after Christmas," she whispered, eyes dipping down with concern. "She can't let them off."

"If I know Rina, she won't," Levi murmured back. "Don't worry, Callie. The boys will be fine. I heard Frisco read Adam's letter. Neither of your brothers is stupid."

Her gaze remained on her brothers. "You can be smart and do poorly in school."

"And you can be brilliant and waste every opportunity given you," Levi countered. "I won't let that happen to the boys." He took her hand in promise, but the touch sent a tremor through him. Once more he wanted to hold her close, make all her dreams come true.

When all Callie wanted, all she requested, was a future for her brothers and Mica.

She let go of his hand and moved back to the table. Very likely she thought to keep an eye on the twins, but Levi caught her glancing his way from time to time as if she wasn't too sure about him, either.

After Rina had Frisco and Sutter practice arithmetic on the slate and write some words she spelled aloud, she drew Levi and Callie aside.

"Very bright young gentlemen," she said with a nod. "The biggest impediment will be their ability to sit still long enough to attend to lessons."

Callie sighed. "That's only the truth, ma'am. I don't know how to focus them unless they're playing some game."

"Make sitting a game," Rina suggested. "You could read to them—adventure stories, Biblical passages appropriate for their age like the birth of our Lord or the story of David and Goliath. Ask them questions about the work from time to time, so they listen expecting to contribute."

Levi nodded. "We'll start with the books John sent over. We can read before bed like Ma and Pa used to read to me and the others."

Callie nodded, too, but one hand had strayed to her shoulder again.

"The boys will be fine," Levi repeated after Rina had taken her leave and the twins were out bringing in the evening's firewood.

"I know," Callie said. She stood taller, as if making a decision. "How can I help with dinner?"

"I've got potatoes on the boil for a cottage pie," Levi

told her. "Drain and mash them while I get the rest ready."

They went to work.

The kitchen had seemed plenty big when Simon had designed and built it, but with Callie beside Levi, it felt downright cozy. Not that he minded.

"How'd you learn to make such good biscuits?" Callie asked as she plunged the wire masher into the potatoes.

"From Ma," Levi admitted, cutting the dried venison into smaller pieces. "She had a very light hand."

"So do you." She gave the potatoes an extra whack. "Mine always come out hard as rocks. Adam about broke a tooth once."

"You should have seen the first time Scout tried to make biscuits," he said, sliding the meat into the skillet. "They came out flat as pancakes. Of course, his mother died when he was only a few years old, so he never learned to cook until his father gave him the job when he was seven."

"He was the cook for the family at seven?" She cast him a glance, brows up.

"Not just cook. His father made him do everything—cooking, cleaning, washing. Mind you, the wash didn't happen too often and mostly consisted of Scout throwing some clothes out the back door into the lake to soak a while."

Callie grimaced. "And I thought lugging water from the creek was bad."

"His father hunted and fished at first, but later he mostly bought tinned food when he didn't spend their money on alcohol. Scout figured how to cook most anything dumped in a pan, but he never mastered biscuits."

Levi sighed, remembering the look on Scout's face. "He loved biscuits."

"What happened to him?" Callie asked, handing him the pot, potatoes fluffy. "Is he still on the gold fields trying to make his fortune? Or did he become a minister like you?"

Levi's hand felt heavy on the pot. "We had a falling out. I don't know where he is now."

Callie's hand came down on his. "I'm sorry. It's hard when someone you care about leaves you behind."

She had cause to know. Adam had gone off and never returned, leaving her with the responsibility of raising her brothers and his daughter.

He glanced her way. Heat from the stove had flushed her cheeks, and a lock of hair curled against her skin. He reached out and tucked it behind her ear. Her eyes widened, even as he felt himself leaning closer.

The door banged open.

"This better be enough," Frisco threatened, nearly invisible behind the stack of logs in his arms.

"My turn to fill the downstairs," Sutter said, teetering under his own stack.

"Thanks, boys," Levi said, wiping his palms on the towel he kept handy. He could only hope Callie would think it was the hot stove and not her presence that was making him sweat. What was he thinking, leaning in for a kiss? He was only glad that Callie went to feed Mica just then, giving his pulse a moment to return to normal.

He kept his composure through dinner and the cleanup afterward, but his heart gave a painful thump as he gathered everyone on the rug. Callie sat on one of the chairs, Mica in her lap. Ma had sat like that in the evenings, first with him in her lap, then Beth while Ma read, then with her mending, a smile playing about her lips, as one of her children read. Frisco and Sutter had agreed they could start with *A Christmas Carol*, particularly as Levi had mentioned there were ghosts in it, so Levi offered the book to Callie.

"Would you like to read first?"

Callie shook her head so sharply he knew he'd overstepped. Perhaps only the menfolk in her family had had the privilege of reading aloud. He'd known families like that.

"It's all right," he encouraged her. "You have a fine voice for reading."

She pushed his hand away. "Frisco needs the practice."

Frisco raised his head from where he and Sutter were sprawled on the rug. "Do not."

Sutter elbowed him. "Do, too."

"A shame," Levi interrupted, taking a seat closest to the lamp. "Reading aloud was an honor in my family. You knew you were important when Ma asked you to take a turn."

Sutter rose. "I'll read, preacher."

Frisco shot up. "No, me."

"How about if I start," Levi said, mindful of Rina's suggestions, "and the person who listens best gets the next turn?"

They both sat with a thump and gazed at him fixedly. He heard Callie smother a laugh. With a smile, he opened the book and started reading.

He didn't have Drew's commanding voice or James's bright wit, but Callie and her brothers listened to him as if he were a trained thespian. The twins sat on the rug, eyes blinking, faces switching from glee to concern over the plight of Ebenezer Scrooge and his clerk. Mica sucked her thumb, smiling and frowning as she took her cue from the boys. After a little while, he passed the book to Sutter, then urged him to let Frisco take a turn. He found himself watching Callie, the change in her eyes, the delicate shading of her skin. She was enjoying the book every bit as much as her brothers.

"Why don't you give Callie a turn?" he suggested to Frisco.

Callie shook her head again, rearing back in the seat so that Mica had to shift to keep her balance.

Frisco shrugged. "Won't do any good. Callie can't read."

"Bedtime." Callie surged to her feet, raising a surprised squeak from Mica. "Good night, boys."

Frisco and Sutter exchanged glances, but they climbed to their feet.

"Good night, Callie," they chorused.

"Good night, preacher," Sutter added. They hurried obediently for the stairs, but neither surrendered the book.

He was more concerned about Callie. He rose and crossed to her side, even as she started for the bedroom. "Wait. Is Frisco right? Did you never learn to read?"

Her gaze was once more defiant. "And when did I have time? There wasn't any schoolteacher wandering about Vital Creek with a primer, was there?"

"If there was a schoolteacher about, he had a pan in his hands," Levi acknowledged. "But the boys learned to read."

She shuffled on her feet. "Anna taught them. I had chores." She shot him a glance. "But I'm not stupid."

"Of course you aren't," Levi agreed. "Still, if you want to learn, Callie, now's the perfect time."

She snorted. "That would look real fine, someone like me sitting in Mrs. Wallin's school."

"Actually, I sat in Rina's school when I was eighteen. Scout, Beth and I were supposed to be her first students, but word got around quickly that there was a schoolteacher in the area, and several loggers and miners came to learn to read."

She shook her head. "I can't do it. I have to take care of Mica."

He could offer to care for the baby instead, but he had another idea. Very likely it would get him in trouble, but the thought was too delightful to forgo.

"Why don't you let me teach you?"

Chapter Ten

Oh, but this man would be the death of her. Levi's eyes were alight with eagerness. Very likely he was imagining sitting side by side as he opened the world to her through the books she'd often longed to read. She hated to douse his excitement.

"I can get a primer from Rina," he continued, as if building up steam. "I'm sure if I explained the situation…"

"No," Callie said, a shiver going through her. "I won't have you telling the others. It's bad enough you know."

He stuck out his lower lip. "Callie, it's no shame. A good many people in Seattle never learned to read or write."

A number of the prospectors had been in the same situation, as had their wives and children. She wasn't so odd there. But this was Wallin Landing, where everyone knew so much more.

"Shame enough," she said, bouncing Mica on her hip. "You don't need to teach me to read. I told you, Levi, you do right by Frisco, Sutter and Mica, and I'll be fine."

"Callie." Her name, said so soft and tender, made

her sway on her feet. Mica lay her head against Callie's shoulder with a sigh.

Levi put a hand on her arm. "Being able to read opens doors. Opportunities for employment, for learning more about our Lord through the Bible, for broadening our minds. Let me give you that."

He wanted it so badly. She could hear it in his voice, feel it in his touch. And he made her want it, too.

"All right," she said, fear causing the words to come out grudgingly. "But don't get all mopey when it doesn't work."

"It will work," he promised. "Thank you, Callie." He dipped in and pecked her on the cheek. It should have been no more than a brotherly sign of affection, yet another longing rose inside her. He stepped back from her, blinking as if blinded by the sun, then turned and nearly ran for the stairs.

Callie rubbed her finger along her cheek as she turned for the bedroom. She had a feeling this teaching was going to be harder than he thought, for another reason entirely.

True to his word, Levi started the very next day. First, though, he, Callie and Mica walked Frisco and Sutter to school. Despite their bold claims to Rina, Callie's brothers clung to her sides like mud on a gold flake as they approached the log building at the back of the main clearing.

Already a dozen children milled around the yard, girls clustered on one side, boys on the other. Most of the boys, Callie saw with relief, were dressed no better than Frisco and Sutter in their short trousers, rough calico shirts and open wool coats, and most appeared to be their age or younger. Still, they all eyed the new-comers, their games stilling, voices quieting. Frisco met their stares, head up and hands fisted.

An elegant girl with hair the color of Rina's detached herself from the group and approached Frisco and Sutter. Though fully as tall as the twins, she looked to be a year or so younger, given the roundness in her creamy cheeks. She was the finest dressed of the children, her red wool coat boasting black jet buttons and silk trim, and a rabbit fur hat rested on her curls. Mica clapped her hands together as if applauding the little beauty.

"I am Victoria," she announced, blinking sable lashes over midnight blue eyes. "You may stand with me if you like." She held out both gloved hands.

Dazed, Frisco took one hand and Sutter the other, and they wandered with her toward the school. The other children fell in behind them as Rina opened the door and welcomed them inside.

"The queen has spoken," Levi said with a smile. "Rina's daughter runs that school as much as her mother. Frisco and Sutter will be fine."

Callie could only hope he was right.

She wasn't sure why Levi followed them into the school, particularly as he thought everything was going well, but he returned quickly with a book.

Callie flushed at the sight of the primer. "You prom-ised not to tell anyone!"

"I didn't," he assured her, heading for the parsonage. "I asked for a primer so Frisco and Sutter can practice at home. Nothing says you can't use it, too."

Once back at the table, Mica propped in her chair, he sat beside Callie on the bench by the table and opened to the front of the book where letters marched proudly across the page.

"This is the alphabet," he explained, finger running down the line. "It's a list of letters. Letters come together to spell words. A word is a unique combination of letters. There's a word for everything we see, everything we do, everything we feel."

Callie nodded. "That makes sense." Mica nodded her agreement as well.

"Every letter has a particular sound," he continued, his gaze brushing hers as if determined to make her understand. "Where it gets tricky is that sometimes the sound changes depending on the letters around it."

Callie frowned. "I don't understand."

Levi pointed to the first letter. "Take *A*."

"Take a what?"

"No, no, I meant as an example. That's the letter *A*. Sometimes it sounds like that, like in away or day. But sometimes it sounds like ah, the sound you make when you stick out your tongue. Bat. Cat."

Callie threw up her hands. "Well, how are you supposed to know which is which?"

"By the letters around it. Here, let me show you." He slid closer to her, until his trousers brushed hers. Suddenly it was very hard to focus on the letters.

"This is the letter *C*," he said as if unaffected by their closeness. "It usually sounds like kuh."

"Kuh," she said.

"Right. And this is T. It sounds like Ti."

"Ti," she agreed.

Levi grinned, and she felt very clever. "Now, put them all together. What word would you have if the three letters were gathered together—*c-a-t*."

"Kuh ah ti—cat." Callie grinned. "Cat. I read a word!"

She wanted to bask in the pride shining from his eyes, perhaps lean in and press her lips to his.

Oh, no.

As he turned to next page, she edged away from him. She was here to learn to read. She didn't want to slip into admiring his eyes, the way his lips curled when he smiled.

"Let's try some words in a sentence," he said. "See here? That's the word see—*s* for suh, then *e* and *e*."

"Suh ee ee," she said dutifully.

"You know the next two words," Levi encouraged her. "Give it a try."

Callie focused on the letters. "Is it *see a cat*?"

He chuckled. "It most certainly is."

Determination pushed her chin up. She could do this. She could learn to read. Who knew what else she might achieve?

Bake biscuits.

Sew a fine seam.

Start a music school.

Fall in love with Levi Wallin.

She nearly shivered again. All were risky. She'd never mastered cooking, had rarely taken the time to sew properly, had never confessed to anyone her fool dream of making a living with her love of music.

But the last idea was the most risky of all. If she failed at the others, she risked nothing more than her pride. If she offered Levi her love, she risked her heart. She knew the pain of loss. Was she willing to take that chance now?

* * *

When Callie put her mind to it, there was no stopping her. Levi couldn't help admiring how she threw herself into learning to read. They spent an hour every morning and every afternoon at the table together, heads close together. She spent another hour with her brothers when they returned from school, listening to them read, asking them about words. She wasn't afraid to admit they knew more than she did, a fact that had Frisco and Sutter jumping in to help her, as well. Still, when Beth stopped by during reading time a couple of days later, Callie snatched up the primer and hurried for the bedroom with the excuse of checking on the sleeping Mica.

Beth watched her go with a sigh. "I'm so sorry Miss Murphy has taken me in dislike. Truly, Levi, I was only trying to help."

"I know," he told her. "Don't worry. Callie's coming around. She just needs time to accustom herself to her new life."

Beth nodded, brightening. "But, oh, Levi, just think of the fun we could have! She could help with the Christmas preparations. There's the geese to pluck, the houses and hall to decorate, not to mention the baking, and I'm trying to decide on a present for Frisco and Sutter."

Levi began to have an idea of why Callie had shied away from his sister. "Perhaps pick one of those things and ask her to help."

Beth raise a brow. "Why? She'd be good at all of them." When Levi chuckled, she shook her head. "Sorry. I had a reason for calling. James said he heard from Mr. Paul that Old Joe has been injured."

Levi sobered. "Bad?"

"Bad enough he's having trouble keeping his claim. I thought we should bring him food and comfort."

Trust his sister to think of others, even the crotchety old prospector who lived on the other side of the lake.

"I'll gather what I can. Meet me at the barn in a quarter hour."

The plan agreed, Beth hurried out. Callie stuck her head around the stairs.

"It's safe," Levi said. "She's gone."

Callie ventured out with a grimace. "I didn't want her to see me reading."

"Why? Beth would probably applaud your determination to learn."

She rubbed at her shoulder. "Maybe. But she might realize how different we are."

"Not that different," Levi countered, moving to the cupboard to see what he could take to Old Joe. "You care about family. So does she."

Callie followed him. "You fixing to cook so early?"

"Beth told me a member of the congregation has been hurt. We're going to take him food."

Callie pulled the jar of asparagus from his hand. "Choose things he won't have to cook—the applesauce, pickled beets and such."

"Good idea." Levi exchanged the jars.

She went to the stove, pulled down the bread he'd baked that morning. "Take this, too. We can make do."

"See?" Levi said, accepting the loaf from her. "You and Beth think the same way."

She shook her head. "How could we? She was raised with fine things. I was raised on promises. I can't find my footing here sometimes. You're all so perfect."

Levi set down the food. "Nothing of the kind. We each have our flaws."

She eyed him. "Like what?"

"Well, take Beth, for example. She sometimes lets her enthusiasm get the best of her."

"I noticed," she murmured.

Levi smiled. "You haven't met Simon yet, but you'll find you can cut your fingers on his sharp logic. Drew forgets he doesn't have to play the father, James never takes anything seriously and John hides himself in his books."

"All right," she said, "but their wives are perfect."

"Not at all," Levi said, looking for a cloth to cover the bread. "Drew's wife, Catherine, will dose you at the least sign of illness, Nora will mother you even when you don't need it, John's wife, Dottie, still has moments she keeps to herself in shyness and Rina sometimes falls back on her upbringing as a princess."

Callie started. "A princess? Is that why you called her daughter a queen?"

"Rina was raised by a pair of flimflam artists," Levi told her, wrapping the loaf. "They made her and everyone else think she was a princess of a small county in Europe. Suffice it to say, we all have areas of our character we must work to overcome."

She cocked her head. "Even you?"

He had to go carefully. If he couldn't confess his considerable shortcomings to his family, he certainly wasn't ready to expose them to Callie.

"Especially me," he said. "Don't see us as people who think we're better than you, Callie. We don't think that way. We're not better than you, just happier."

She scowled, reminding him of Frisco. "I'm happy."

"Are you?" He turned to her. "I remember seeing you truly happy. At Vital Creek."

She wrinkled her nose. "I don't recall too much happiness there."

Neither did he, except for a few bright moments that had involved her family. "It was early days on the strike. Your father had found some color, and he treated the whole camp to ice cream."

Her look softened, and all at once it felt like a warm sunny day at the creek. "I remember! Gap-Tooth Harding had a butter churn, and Wild Eye Jenkins had just arrived in camp with fresh cream."

Levi felt his smile growing. "Adam figured out how to hold it all in the creek coming off the ice field, and everyone took a turn cranking."

"But they started to get tired, so Mick O'Shea played his fiddle to give them the rhythm, and everyone else danced." Even her sigh sounded happy. "Those *were* good times."

And she'd had few since, he suspected. She deserved all the fun he could give her.

"The good times don't have to be over, Callie," he told her. "Christmas is coming. There will be music and laughter, food and fun, and Beth's planning a dance in the hall on Christmas Day."

"So she mentioned. A real dance." The wistfulness in her tone was unmistakable.

Levi stepped back and offered her a bow. "Miss Murphy, would you do me the honor of allowing me to escort you to the Christmas ball?"

"Ball?" Her voice squeaked. "You didn't say it was a ball."

"Dance," Levi corrected himself, unwilling to see her

retreat into fear and sadness again. "Just a dance. Nothing fancy. Farmers and loggers and miners from around Wallin Landing. Normal folks, having fun to celebrate Christmas. Will you come with me?"

She nodded, cheeks turning pink.

"Thank you." Insufferably pleased, Levi bent to pull a basket out from under the cupboard to hold the food.

"I don't know that much about dancing with someone," Callie said, fidgeting beside him. "You may have to lead me through it."

"It would be my pleasure," Levi assured her.

In truth, he was more like his sister on the dance floor—all enthusiasm. Beth had grace, but he'd been known to step on a few toes. He'd been known to trip a few entirely off their feet for that matter.

But with Callie on his arm, he thought he might fly.

Chapter Eleven

In the end, Callie decided to go with Levi and Beth, leaving Mica with Nora. After years of working much of the day outside, even Levi's spacious cabin was beginning to feel tight. And spending time with Levi's sister might help her come to terms with Beth.

Beth had enlisted the aid of one of Levi's sisters-in-law as well, in case the injured man needed medical treatment. The wife of Levi's oldest brother, Catherine Wallin was tall and slender, with pale blond hair neatly tucked back in a bun behind her head and light blue eyes. Her carriage in her fine wool coat was calm and confident. Callie knew from Levi that she ran the dispensary at the southern end of Wallin Landing, on the road to Seattle.

There was a moment of indecision as to seating. The bench of the farm wagon would only hold two. Knowing her trousers were better suited than skirts to the bed, Callie willingly climbed up into the back of the wagon. But she was surprised when Levi surrendered the reins to Catherine and joined her.

There had been plenty of room in the wagon bed for

Frisco and Sutter on the trip to Wallin Landing. The fit was more snug with Levi beside her. With the sides of the wagon rising on the left and right, it wasn't as if she could shift away. And as they set out, she found herself thankful for his warmth.

The air had turned cold. The forest was rimed with silver. Once in a while she heard the snap of a branch, saw a limb come crashing down. She hugged the basket with the food.

"Did you know Beth's a crack shot?" he asked as if trying to take her mind off their surroundings. "Second best in the family after John."

Callie glanced back over her shoulder to find Beth smiling down. "Once, but not anymore, I fear. I don't need to help with the hunting now." She gave a delicate shudder.

Callie felt for her. "Don't much like killing, either. But a body has to eat."

"I'm just glad we've expanded the farm," Catherine put in. "Nora is a genius for picking good seed."

Not a skill Callie possessed. A farmer's daughter, Anna had done all the planting at Adam's homestead. That Nora knew as much or more was another reason to admire her. In fact, it was all too easy to admire Nora. She was a rock, solid, sure of her abilities and her worth. She didn't mind getting mussed or dirty. Callie still struggled with all of Beth's lace and bows, even though they were hidden beneath a heavy wool coat at the moment.

"Callie likes to sing," Levi said when the silence grew again. "She has a lovely voice."

Warmth percolated from her toes to her top. No one had ever praised her singing. Still, she wasn't sure why he kept bringing up things like that. Was he trying to build a bridge between her and Beth?

"I love music," Beth said. "I'm hoping to have a musical surprise in time for Christmas."

A musical surprise? Once more Callie glanced back at Beth, but Levi's sister was looking out over the forest.

"A special song from Simon, perhaps?" Catherine guessed, guiding the horses around the curve of the lake.

"Better," Beth said, voice hinting of a smile.

"You convinced the Seattle band to play for the dance," Levi teased.

Beth shifted on the bench. "No, but this will make up for it. You wait and see."

Callie couldn't imagine what could be better than a real band playing, but if Beth had found it, perhaps she and Callie had more in common than she'd thought.

They reached their destination a short time later. The fellow everyone called Old Joe, his last name apparently lost in his journeys, lived in a shack on the edge of a stream feeding the lake. The sluice box told Callie what he did for a living.

"Gold or silver?" she murmured to Levi as they scooted to the tail of the wagon to climb down.

"I never was sure," he replied, offering her his hand to alight. Though she didn't need the help, she touched his fingers anyway. "He's been out here since I was a boy."

"Well, don't mention it to Frisco or Sutter," Callie cautioned. "The last thing we need is for them to offer their help."

And yet the fellow did need help. An ax lay waiting by a pile of logs that would be much needed for heat in the cold. She couldn't spot any sign of a garden as a rough voice called for them to enter on Levi's knock. Inside,

Old Joe's place wasn't much better built than Adam's, for all the prospector had had years to improve it. The single room with a dirt floor held a log bedstead, two chairs and a stump that served as a table. The man they'd come to visit was curled up under a blanket on the bed, clutching his right arm. His gray hair was wild, his beard matted. Beth looked concerned. Callie had seen worse.

Catherine went immediately to his side, setting the black bag she'd brought with her on the floor.

"Good morning, Joe," Levi said. "We heard you'd had some trouble and thought we might be able to help. You remember Mrs. Wallin and my sister. This is Miss Murphy, my ward."

Ward. No matter what Adam had written, the word sounded odd. She was too old to be anyone's ward. And a guardian should be more experienced, more fatherly, not someone who set her insides to fluttering whenever he looked her way.

"Ladies," the fellow said, trying to shift himself higher. Levi hurried to help him, and Old Joe grimaced as if the movement hurt.

"Let me have a look," Catherine said, bending closer.

"I appreciate the doctoring," the prospector said, "but I don't need any help. I'll get on just fine."

Callie glanced around. Little food on the shelves, no wood in the box. The place was all too reminiscent of the claim she'd left. Levi was right. She had needed more help than she'd been willing to confess. Old Joe was in the same situation.

Beth touched her arm, drew her back from the bed. "I don't care what he says. This place is a mess. Let's clean it up while Catherine is tending him."

Callie caught her arm before she could start. "Wait.

He won't take kindly to outright help. You have to come at it from the side."

Beth frowned, but Callie raised her voice. "Mighty cold these last few nights, don't you think?"

"I sure do, little lady," Old Joe agreed, though he kept his gaze on Catherine as she carefully felt along his arm.

"We've been using up the wood something fierce. If you have some chopped, it might be best to bring it in, just in case."

Old Joe shuddered as Catherine's fingers found a tender spot. "Good thinking."

Callie nodded to Levi, who strode to the door to fetch the wood. She could only hope he'd chop a bit more in the process.

"Seems a shame to carry this food back to Wallin Landing," Callie told Beth, careful to keep her voice casual. "I'm sure Joe wouldn't mind if we left it."

"If you think you ought," Joe allowed. He started to shrug as Beth hurried to comply, then grimaced.

Catherine frowned. "I'm going to bind that up. It looks more like a sprain and bruising rather than a break, but you aren't to use it until after Christmas."

"What?" the prospector yelped. "I can't wait till after Christmas. I got work to do."

"Nothing more important than healing that arm," Catherine insisted as Callie helped Beth stock the shelves. Out of the corners of her eyes, Callie saw the nurse pull a roll of bandage material from her bag and begin wrapping the injured arm.

Joe pulled out of reach, setting his back to the wall, left hand palm out. "I tell you, I'll be fine. I'm not an invalid. Word gets out I can't look out for myself, they'll be pounding on my door to take my claim."

He sounded like Pa, clutching his pitiful claim close until it killed him. How much could it have gained him over the years if he still lived like this? Callie's hand tightened on the last jar.

"Please," Catherine said, reaching out. "Let me help you."

"Never asked for help. I can take care of myself."

Callie whirled. "No, you can't. Not at the moment. And no one's after your claim, not with winter coming on. You need to rest up, get your arm back in good shape so you can work come the thaw."

His jaw was hard. "What do you know about sluicing?"

Now he sounded like Frisco. "More than I ever wanted," Callie told him. "I was born near Sutter's Mill, cut my teeth at the Fraser River and learned to walk on the Cariboo. I can't tell you what I would have given for neighbors kind enough to check on us in winter, make sure we had food, wood for the fire."

He held out his arm to Catherine, who swiftly continued binding it. "Reckon you're right. My apologies. Pain's got me on edge."

"Quite understandable," Beth said with a look to Callie.

Levi bumped through the door with an armload of wood.

"Mighty kind of you, pastor," Old Joe said as Levi stacked it next to the hearth. "Say, you already found a husband for your ward? I'm still looking for a bride."

Callie blinked and saw Levi doing the same.

"She's considering her options," Beth said, linking arms with Callie as if to keep her by her side. "But we'll let you know when she's made up her mind."

Old Joe blew out a breath as Catherine finished her binding. "Smart, practical gals who know something about prospecting are hard to find."

Levi grinned at Callie. "Yes, they are."

Callie shook her head. "That's because they're too smart to follow the creek. Now, what else needs to be done so you can manage on your own, Joe?"

Levi was still marveling as Catherine drove them home that afternoon. As a pastor, it wasn't uncommon for him to be called to visit the sick, injured or dying in the area. Sometimes he found it hard to offer comfort and solace when the people seemed so much older and wiser than he was. Other times, words were not enough to mend the hurt. Callie had been nothing short of brilliant in dealing with the old prospector.

Beth thought so as well. "You spoke so boldly," she told Callie, twisting in her seat beside Catherine so she could see Levi and Callie in the bed. "It was just what he needed to accept our help."

"Like knows like, I suppose," Callie said. Her gaze brushed Levi's. "And I needed some convincing to accept help."

If it was more than pride that made him smile at his part in that, he wasn't willing to admit it.

"I'm glad you convinced him, Callie," Catherine said as the horses headed north along the lake. "And I'm glad we could steer him away from the prospect of marriage."

Levi chuckled. "I remember how Old Joe proposed to you when you first came to Wallin Landing."

Catherine shuddered, but he knew she was teasing. One of Mercer's Maidens, who had come to Seattle when men outnumbered the women ten to one, she'd had more than her share of proposals before accepting his brother.

"Seems he's still looking for a wife," Beth said, chin tipping up. "But not Callie. She has her pick of grooms."

Callie shifted away from the bench. "I'm not interested in marriage."

"At least not to Old Joe," Beth said with a giggle.

"Not anyone," Callie insisted. "I got kin to raise."

He could see why she had shifted. The wagon bed felt hard, unyielding under him. He settled himself closer to Callie.

"Nothing says a husband can't help," Catherine said. "I'm sure some men would be pleased to adopt your brothers and niece."

"You haven't met Frisco and Sutter yet," Callie countered.

Levi straightened his shoulders. "They're fine lads. But all this talk of marriage is premature. Callie's only twenty."

She cast him a glance, and he couldn't understand what was going on behind those slate eyes. "Twenty-and-one come spring."

"Having held a great deal of responsibility for some years, I've heard," Catherine reminded him.

Beth swiveled to face Callie. "I'll think on it. There are so many eligible bachelors in the area. I'm sure one will suit you."

"Beth," Levi warned.

Callie put a hand on his arm, and he glanced at her in surprise. Surely she wasn't going to indulge Beth in this. Callie was too busy, as she'd mentioned. She had better things to do.

And she was his.

The feeling wrapped around his heart even as he tried to push it away. Yes, she was his to protect. So were her brothers and Mica. That was what he'd promised when they'd agreed to be partners. He wouldn't allow himself to feel more.

Beside him, Callie swung around to look Beth in the eye. "I'm not interested in courting. I know you're trying to help, and I appreciate that you care. But if we're to be friends, you have to be willing to see my side of things."

Beth stared at her, then her head started bobbing. "Yes, of course. I agree completely. We can wait on courting. There's Christmas to get through first, in any event. And, truth be told, I'm not all that interested in courting, either."

Levi's shoulders relaxed. "Good. So there will be no more matchmaking."

Catherine laughed. "Oh, Levi, you know none of us could ever promise that."

Both Callie and Beth blushed.

"Don't worry," Levi murmured to Callie as Beth faced front again. "I won't let them push you into anything."

"Neither will I," she assured him. Then she cast him a sidelong glance as she reseated herself. "But I noticed you didn't say anything about courting. I expect a preacher has to marry."

"Perhaps," he allowed. "But I'm not interested, either."

Callie cocked her head. "Why?"

Levi made himself shrug. "Same reason as you. I have two boys and a baby to raise while pastoring a church."

"A wife could help," she pointed out, echoing Catherine's sentiments.

Very likely. In fact, he could picture the lady, reading over his sermons and suggesting ways to improve them, going with him to visit the sick, singing as she moved about the cabin, slate-colored eyes soft.

"I'm fine with things the way they are," he said and sent up a prayer to hold onto that thought. He might not be ready to see Callie courting, but he surely wasn't ready to be a husband.

Chapter Twelve

So Levi didn't want to wed. The matter troubled Callie as Catherine drove them back to Wallin Landing. She couldn't very well fault his logic, especially since it matched part of her own. She just couldn't understand why she felt so disappointed.

As if to prove he was too busy to court, he was away most of the next day. He rode to town to pick up materials for the Sunday school he was planning to start after Christmas, then he holed up in the church working on what he would say come Sunday. She kept herself busy, as well. She poured over fashion magazines with Beth, took Mica to visit Nora and even emboldened herself to make the acquaintance of John's wife, Dottie, and their son Peter, who was a few months older than Mica. The two babies made quite a contrast. Blond Peter tended to be serious, studying people before reacting. Mica laughed and smiled indiscriminately.

"I hope they'll be good friends growing up," Dottie told Callie, her hair as blond as her son's. "And I hope we will be, too."

Callie was beginning to hope so, as well. Perhaps she

could fit in at Wallin Landing. Perhaps she, her brothers and Mica had finally found a home.

She wasn't sure what to expect when Sunday rolled around. She knew that was the day ministers generally preached, but the only service she'd ever attended had been in a tent on a gold rush camp. That preacher had explained how God had sent His Son to die for everyone's sins, but she'd gotten the impression God wasn't much pleased with people in general. Certainly the minister didn't like them, for he'd marched up and down the aisle shaking his finger at the miners and predicting their downfall if they didn't repent.

Still, she was a little surprised when Levi worked with her brothers to haul buckets of water to the stove Saturday night so they could each take a bath in the tin washtub. Seems ministers took cleanliness seriously. Levi and her brothers waited upstairs until she was finished, and she and Mica waited in the bedroom until they were finished. And when Levi came downstairs the next morning, he was dressed in a suit of dark blue wool that fitted his lean form, emphasizing his shoulders. She glanced down at her usual shirt and trousers.

"Should I wear Ma's dress to church?" she asked.

Levi smiled. "God doesn't care how you dress, only that you come to see Him."

"We're gonna see God?" Sutter asked as he and Frisco hopped down the stairs.

"No, stupid," Frisco said. "Nobody sees God. He's way up in the sky."

Sutter frowned.

"Actually, God is right here with us now," Levi told them. "You may not see Him, but you can feel Him inside and sense what He wants you to do."

Now both her brothers were frowning, but they went to the table for breakfast without arguing. Callie slipped away to change into her mother's dress. Levi may think God approved of everyone, but she wasn't so sure.

Shortly after breakfast, he led them down the breezeway and in the side door of the church. Unlike the time they had looked in previously, now everything was neat. And full. People crowded the benches, gazes turned expectantly to Levi. Callie would have preferred to sit at the rear, but that would mean walking past all those people. She and her brothers settled in the front row instead, Mica on her lap. She tried not to think about the number of gazes on their backs.

As Levi went up onto the raised platform, another tall man with the same sharp cheekbones as him came to the front and set a violin under his chin.

"Look, Callie," Frisco said. "He's got a fiddle."

Callie hushed him, but the murmur that went through the church was more kind than censorious.

The man, who Callie guessed must be Levi's older brother and Nora's husband, Simon, played two songs. Everyone in the church seemed to know the words, because several dozen voices from high to low joined in. Callie caught on to the refrain after the first verse and added her voice to theirs. There was something strong, something powerful about so many people singing together. She felt as if the bubbles from a sarsaparilla were lifting her off her feet.

After the music, Simon sat down and a man she didn't recognize—dark hair, broad shoulders, strong chin—stood up and read from the Bible. Like Levi and Simon, he wore a suit, but she didn't see any resemblance to the Wallins. Someone from the area, perhaps. He had a confident smile, and when he came down from the platform he winked at her as he passed. Mica waved back happily.

Well!

"You know him?" Sutter whispered as Frisco frowned after the fellow.

Callie shook her head.

Other men came forward to pass around the little velvet purses, and Callie realized they were for collecting money. Perhaps that was how Levi was paid. She hoped the congregation was generous.

Finally Levi stepped up to the podium. The light from the lamps overhead set his golden hair gleaming.

"Look, Callie," Sutter cried. "It's the preacher." He waved.

Callie wanted to sink under the bench.

"Good morning, Sutter," Levi said with a smile as another murmur ran through the crowd. He glanced out at the church. "Good morning, everyone. I'm glad to see you today."

Callie waited for his look to turn stern, his voice to raise. She wasn't sure what fault he'd find in the seemingly good folk of Wallin Landing, but he'd spent hours working on this talk. Surely he had something he wanted to say.

"I've been thinking a lot about traveling lately," he started. "Many of you know I sought my fortune on the gold fields. I met a lot of men there who were travelers, always looking ahead to the next big strike."

Frisco and Sutter were still beside her, listening. Mica's gaze was fixed on Levi, too. Callie could understand why. There was a glow about him, as if a fire was burning inside him, warming all who came near.

"As we move through the Advent season, we read

about a number of travelers. Mary and Joseph traveled to Bethlehem to be counted in the census decreed by the Roman Empire. The wise men from the east followed a star to find the newborn King. Travelers have a goal, a destination in mind and a dream of what they'll accomplish when they arrive."

A fool dream. It seemed even important folk in the Bible had them. Yet were those dreams as foolish as her father's and brother's? She'd heard the story of the Christ child, told around campfires or in crowded hotel rooms at Christmas. Mary and Joseph had wanted to raise a baby, just as she was raising Mica. The wise men had wanted to find someone more impressive.

She was a traveler, too. She'd journeyed up the West Coast and inland as far as Vital Creek. Her only goal had been to survive and make sure Frisco, Sutter and Mica did all right. Now they were safe at Wallin Landing, with every opportunity for a bright future. Could she start dreaming of more?

Levi found it easier than usual to preach that morning. Oftentimes when he stood up, one look at his congregation reminded him that more than half the people in the room had known him since he was a boy. Would they listen to anything he had to say? He'd been trained to speak formally, forcefully, following the sermons laid out in the church manual. But he couldn't help falling back on the more informal discussions he'd heard growing up. Even so, he sometimes wondered whether someone like him had anything worthwhile to share with this community.

Today, he'd felt confident in the message he brought

and his ability to bring it, and that had a great deal to do with Callie and her family in the front row.

"So this week," he concluded after speaking for some minutes, "I challenge you to think about your own journey. Where are you traveling? What's your destination? And what do you hope to accomplish? Ask the Lord to give you wisdom to seek Him as we continue through this Advent season. Shall we pray?"

He led them through the final prayer, gave the benediction and climbed down from the pulpit as his congregation rose to take their leave.

Sutter and Frisco ran to meet him as he stepped off the altar.

"That was really good, preacher," Frisco said. "But I like the fiddler the best."

"Though you talked good, too," Sutter told him.

"Thank you," Levi said as Callie joined them, Mica in her arms. She nodded her agreement to her brothers' praise, but her gaze was unfocused, as if she was seeing something other than the church.

"All the Wallins generally spend Sunday together," he explained to them. "One family may visit another, and everyone gathers at the main house for dinner and games afterward."

"Can we go?" Sutter begged.

Both boys watched him for the answer. He heard Callie suck in a breath and knew she must be thinking the same thing he was.

This was the first time they'd sought his permission instead of hers.

"Callie?" he asked.

She nodded again. "It's a fine idea."

"Yay!" Sutter ran for the door as if ready to go right then.

"He said dinner," Frisco reminded him, loping after his twin. "That's hours away."

Sutter paused in the act of opening the door. "Oh."

"In the meantime," Levi put in smoothly, "I'll show you that fishing hole I mentioned. You still owe James a fish, if I remember correctly."

Both boys brightened, but the voice that answered came from his left.

"That's a fine idea, pastor. You take the lads fishing, and I'll keep Miss Murphy company."

Levi turned with Callie to eye the big logger who had come up to them. Harry Yeager was the second man on Drew's logging crew, after Levi's brother. Tall and muscular, with wavy brown hair and deep brown eyes, he had volunteered to be one of the deacons at the new church.

Now he smiled down at Callie as if discovering a rose blooming in winter. "I'm Harry Yeager, Miss Murphy. Pleased to meet you and eager to learn more about you."

Callie hefted Mica. "Nothing to know. And I have Mica to keep me company."

The baby batted her lashes and blew bubbles at Harry.

"And very fine company I'm sure she is," the logger said. "But I imagine she might be a little thin on conversation."

"Don't much need conversation, either," Callie replied.

Was she being contrary on purpose? Couldn't she see Harry was intent on furthering their acquaintance?

Levi could. Funny—he'd always rather liked the bold

and brash logger. Now he wanted to order him from the church.

"Callie and Mica are coming fishing with us, Harry," he said. "But thanks for the offer. Everyone has been very kind about welcoming them to Wallin Landing."

"Just helping a sister traveler, pastor," Harry said. He winked to Callie, then turned to saunter down the aisle.

"Does he have something wrong with his eye that way he keeps winking?" Callie asked as she headed for the side door after her brothers.

Levi kept himself from smiling. "You never know. Let's get everyone bundled and go fishing."

She didn't protest, so he hoped she'd forgiven him for his high-handedness in including her and Mica in the outing.

If anything, the air was even colder than it had been, so the trout weren't inclined to bite, even at the spot on the south side of the promontory, where he, his brothers and Scout had always fished. As it was, Sutter caught the only fish. It was so small Levi insisted that he throw it back.

"But I caught him," Sutter protested, clutching the string with the wiggling fish close. "He's mine."

"He'll taste much better after he's had a chance to grow," Levi promised him, managing to detach the fish from the hook.

"Taste?" Sutter stared at him as Levi released the fish into the waters of the lake. "You *eat* the fish you catch?"

"What else do you think we do with them, silly?" Frisco jibed.

Sutter's face fell. "I thought he'd be a pet."

"You don't have pets on a farm," Frisco told him, turning away. "Mary says animals here have to work."

Mary had obviously had that discussion with her father, Drew. Levi had certainly heard the sentiment from his oldest brother over the years.

"I think a pet is a fine idea," he told the boys. "I'll ask around and see if anyone has a dog with puppies expected in the spring."

Frisco and Sutter grinned at each other before running ahead.

"That went smoother than I'd feared," Levi said, watching them.

"You're doing better with them," Callie agreed as she walked beside him, Mica in her arms. "You just have to know when to stand your ground."

"And when to allow life to teach the lesson," Levi replied. "Would Sutter have learned more if I let him eat the bony thing?"

"He wouldn't have eaten it. He'd have tried to keep the poor fish in a pail of water. It's better this way. The fish is free, and Sutter can brag he was the only one to catch one."

There was that. Sutter needed more encouragement, he'd noticed, while Frisco had to be reined in once in a while. It was a delicate balance, one that Callie seemed to have mastered.

Now if only he could find the key to working beside her.

Beth had told Levi she planned dinner for five, so he took Callie and the other Murphys over to the house a quarter hour earlier. Everyone supplied something for the meal. He was carrying four dozen biscuits along with a jug of apple cider a neighbor had given him.

Callie walked beside him, stiff. She kept tugging at

her coat as if concerned about the shirt and trousers she'd changed into before they'd gone fishing. Mica peered from one face to another as if waiting to see who would smile first. Sutter and Frisco seemed the most eager for the get-together.

Levi was used to the circus, but Callie clung to his side when they entered the house. In truth, his parents' house was quickly outgrowing the family. Drew and Catherine had three children; so did James and Rina. Simon and Nora had two, and John and Dottie had one. Harry and the other two members of the logging crew were also invited. Adding Callie, her brothers and Mica made the big room feel all the more snug.

And busy. Dottie and Catherine were ferrying bowls from the kitchen, stepping around a wrestling match that spanned the room and seemed to involve all the boys, most of his brothers, the logging crew, a few of the girls and Beth. Rina, her daughter Victoria and Nora with Peter and two of the toddlers were milling about the edges as if they couldn't decide whether to join in or order everyone out. Before Levi could even think, Sutter and Frisco detached themselves from his side and dove in.

Harry appeared out of the crowd. "Miss Murphy, may I take your coat?"

Callie flinched away from his outstretched arms. "Why? What would you want with my coat?"

Harry opened his mouth and shut it again.

Beth bustled up to them, hair hanging down one side of her face and cheeks pink. "I'm so glad you're here. Levi, take the biscuits to the kitchen and pour the cider."

"I'd be happy to find you a seat, Miss Murphy," Harry said, recovering.

With a distracted frown, Callie nodded.

Levi didn't like leaving her alone with a near stranger, but it was best not to argue with Beth. He hurried toward the kitchen, managing to snag John's arm on the way.

"Pour the cider," he told his brother, dropping the biscuits on the sideboard and leaning around John to keep an eye on Callie.

"Glad to be of help," John said. "After all, you'll have to fend off Tom and Dickie, too."

He was right. Harry had positioned Callie and Mica in Ma's old bentwood rocker by the hearth, and already the other two members of his brother's logging crew, Thomas Convers and Dickie Morgan, were bearing down on her. Levi had to remember that Seattle was still lacking in female companionship. Any unmarried lady was bound to be besieged.

And when that lady was as pretty as Callie...

He shoved the jug of cider at his brother and hurried back into the fray.

"Do you like fish, Miss Murphy?" dark-haired Tom was saying. "I can bring you a dozen a day."

"No, thank you," Callie said, adjusting the collar on Mica's gown. "Sutter would only want to make them pets."

Tom frowned.

"That's a nice baby," the younger Dickie ventured, straw-colored hair sticking out in all directions as he kept his distance. "She's almost as pretty as you."

Callie regarded him. "Do you need spectacles, Mr. Morgan?"

Dickie stepped farther back as if she'd wounded him.

Levi didn't know whether to help the poor fellow or shout a hallelujah that Callie didn't recognize their attempts at courtship. Callie had more important things to do—learning to read, tending Mica, spending time with him. Callie had made it clear she couldn't abide matchmaking. And when the time came for her to court…

He was in trouble. Because no man, especially him, would ever measure up to the husband Callie deserved.

Chapter Thirteen

Callie glanced at Levi as they walked home from Sunday's dinner with his family. His brother James had shown Sutter and Frisco how to whistle, and their shrill notes drifted back to her as the twins ran ahead up the hill.

Levi smiled, carrying a drowsy Mica in his arms. For a moment, Callie allowed herself to remember how it had felt to rest her head against his shoulder.

"Was that a sigh?" he asked. "Is something bothering you?"

Callie hurriedly looked away. "No. I just keep thinking about your talk this morning."

He lifted Mica higher, so her little head cuddled against him. "My sermon? Did I say something to confuse you?"

"You made me wonder," Callie allowed as they reached the house. "What's my destination?"

His smile deepened. "Wherever you want."

Easy to say, not easy to know. Callie frowned at him, but he was turning toward her brothers.

"Time for bed, boys," he called.

"Why?" Frisco asked.

Levi looked taken aback.

"School tomorrow," Callie told them. "You want to be ready for studying."

Frisco and Sutter exchanged glances. "The play," Sutter said, and Frisco nodded. As one, they headed for the stairs.

"That was easy," Levi said, recovering himself.

"Too easy," Callie told him. "I'd watch them if I were you."

"Will do." He handed her Mica, then stepped back. "And Callie, I truly believe you could do anything you put your mind to. All you have to do is decide." With a nod, he turned for the stairs.

Callie carried Mica into the bedroom, propped the baby on the bed where she curled up on the quilt, then went to the chest. About to shove it over the door, she paused. All she had to do was decide, he said. Decide to learn, to dream. Decide to trust him and his family. Decide to love.

She left the chest at the foot of the bed.

The next week, she did her best to give as she had been given. She sat dutifully beside Levi at the table as she practiced her reading. She learned new letters and words every day and warmed at his smile. She worked with Dottie to shelve more books in the new library, Mica and Peter playing on the rug in the middle. She and Beth washed clothes, including her mother's quilt and Levi's shirt. She helped Beth make chains out of strips of red and green paper to use for Christmas decorations.

She and Levi took the twins fishing again and managed to catch a trout big enough to suit James. She'd never seen her brothers stand so tall as when they delivered it. She also laid out the red-and-green plaid fabric so Nora could cut out the pieces for the new dress she was making for Callie. It was to have little black buttons all down the bodice and ruffles at the high neck, just under her chin.

"It will flatter your face," Nora promised, working with the shears. "And the fitted bodice will call attention to your figure."

Callie almost told her to stop right there. She hadn't worn anything fitted since she was fifteen. Then she remembered she was safe here. There was no need to hide herself anymore.

Even from the likes of Harry Yeager.

He came by early in the week just as she was overseeing the twins cleaning up after dinner. Levi had gone to fetch something from the church, and Mica was in her chair, banging on the table with a wooden spoon, grinning at each smack.

"I thought I could chop some wood for you, Miss Murphy," he said when she answered his knock.

"Sorry," she said. "That's Frisco and Sutter's job."

"Oh." He shifted on his feet, then glanced at her, head cocked so that a lock of brown hair fell across his brow. "Then maybe you'd like to walk to the lake with me. It's beautiful in the moonlight."

Callie glanced around him at the gathering dusk. "Should be dark of the moon tonight and mighty cold. Not a good time for a stroll."

He puffed out a breath. "Then maybe I could come in and visit a spell."

"I have chores," Callie told him. "Good night." She shut the door, turned around and found Levi grinning at her from the door to the breezeway.

"What's so funny?" she demanded. "I suppose I should have been a lady and invited him in. Did you see the size of him? He'd probably eat all our food."

Levi crossed to her side. "We're in no danger of running out of food, Callie, so please invite anyone you like to visit. I just found it amusing that Harry is trying so hard to show you he likes you, and you won't let him."

Callie shook her head. "You're wrong. A handsome fellow like that wouldn't chase after me. He's looking for something. I'd sure like to know what."

Levi hurried to help her brothers finish the cleaning.

Still, when both Tom Convers and Dickie Morgan showed up at the door the next day, she began to suspect Levi was right. And that confused her all the more. It wasn't like when the miners at Vital Creek had first noticed she was female. The looks in their eyes had made her feel as if she'd fallen onto the muddy creek bottom. Harry, Tom and Dickie were more respectful, admiring even. But why would they so much as look at her with the beautiful Beth around?

She said as much to Nora one morning as they sat sewing in the parsonage while the older children were at school and the little ones played together. "I'm nothing special."

Nora smiled, taking a careful stitch. "I disagree with you, Callie. I think you're quite special indeed."

Callie blushed. "So is Beth, and she's unmarried."

"Ah, but Beth is related to their employer. That might make a fellow think twice."

"I certainly wouldn't want Drew Wallin angry with me." Callie focused on the seam. Her stitches were nearly as small and neat as Nora's. "But if they're as proper as they've been to me, I don't see why they can't court her."

"I believe Beth made it clear she isn't interested."

"So have I," Callie insisted. "But they keep coming around like mosquitoes in the spring."

Nora raised her dark brows. "I hope they aren't that bad. I think you're not giving yourself enough credit. I can see why they'd be interested in you."

Callie snorted. "And I haven't even put on your new dress yet."

"It takes more than a new dress to interest a fellow," she said, pulling the thread tight. "I made myself all kinds of fancy dresses, and very few gentlemen showed the least interest."

Callie glanced at her friend. A little gray had wormed its way into the black hair, but it wouldn't have been there eight years ago, when Callie had heard Nora and Simon had married. After having two children, Nora might be a little plumper than she had been then. Still, she was a handsome woman now and one of the sweetest Callie had ever met.

She stabbed her needle into the fabric. "Maybe those men needed spectacles."

Nora's smile deepened, until it lit her gray eyes. "Perhaps. But I was so certain no gentleman I'd want would ever want me that I asked Simon to marry me."

"Did you?" Callie regarded her with new respect. "He must have said yes, because you're his wife."

"He agreed, but only because I brought one hundred and sixty acres with me. As his wife, I could file a claim for land he needed."

Callie wrinkled her nose. "He married you for the land?"

Nora nodded. "But somewhere along the way, he fell

in love with me. It was more than I ever dreamed possible, and all I could ever want."

She'd never seen so much joy. It was shining from Nora's eyes, glowing from her round cheeks. It almost made Callie want to fall in love, too.

She pulled the thread taut. "Well, from what I see, most of the land in this area has been claimed, so Harry and the others can't be after me for it."

"No," Nora admitted. "They can't."

Callie blinked. "Then that must mean they really like me."

Nora nodded with a giggle that made the children raise their heads and laugh, too.

"So," Nora said, leaning closer to Callie, "which one do you like?"

A face came immediately to mind—strong cheekbones, golden curls, deep blue eyes. Callie busied herself sewing.

"None of them," she told Nora. "I suppose I better let them know it if they haven't guessed already."

And make sure they didn't guess where her real feelings lay.

Levi finally tacked the last of Beth's chains to the wall of the hall and climbed down from the ladder. His sister turned in a circle as if counting the swags of red and green paper, the little cones made from pictures cut from her precious magazines, waiting to be filled with candy, nuts and raisins on the big night.

"Very festive," Levi told her, taking the ladder to the big pantry that opened off one end of the long room with its windows looking out on the forest. "You and Callie did a fine job with the decorations."

"And we're not done yet," Beth replied, pausing as she turned. "I want a wreath on every wall, the Christmas tree in the corner there and a kissing bough near the top of the room in front of the stage."

Levi shook his head. "A kissing bough?"

He must have sounded as doubtful as he felt for Beth wagged a finger at him.

"I thought you'd be all for it. Don't tell me that now you're a minister you're against kisses in public places."

"Not at all," Levi said, heading for the lantern they had lit to brighten the space on the gloomy day. "But the married couples don't need the excuse, and the unmarried couples don't need the encouragement."

"Callie does," Beth insisted, following him.

Levi stopped, hand on the brass ring at the top of the lantern. "Callie has no use for a kissing bough."

"Of course she does! Haven't you noticed Harry, Tom and Dickie buzzing about her like bees to pollen?"

Levi snatched up the lantern. "Making cakes of themselves, more like. You heard her when we went to visit Old Joe. Callie isn't interested in courting."

"I know," Beth said as she followed him to the door. "It's clear she doesn't fancy Tom, Dick or Harry. But that doesn't mean we can't find her a match."

He felt as if his sister had punched him in the chest. "No matchmaking, Beth. You promised."

Beth lifted her skirts and scurried along beside him, as much to keep up with him as to escape the cold, he suspected. "I most certainly did not. I said I'd wait until after Christmas, but why wait when it's such a romantic time of year?"

Was he the only one in the family who hadn't taken their father's adventure novels seriously? "Callie won't thank you for this," he told his sister as they reached the parsonage.

Beth's face puckered. "But I only want her to be happy. What about Mr. Pentercast, the new fellow who's been talking to James about opening a livery to the north?"

Levi cast her a glance as they entered. He knew that look on his sister's face. Few people could ever win an argument with Beth. He was just glad Callie had taken Mica to visit Nora so she was spared his sister's attempts at matchmaking.

"Pentercast came to see me last week," Levi said, setting the lantern on the table. "He has a sweetheart traveling from Georgia to marry him and asked if I'd perform the ceremony."

"That handsome Mr. Everard in town. I adore his English accent."

"So do most of the ladies, I hear," Levi warned her.

"Mr. Cropper who recently joined the sheriff's office?"

He tried to picture the gregarious redhead with Callie and failed. But then, he was having a hard time seeing anyone with Callie.

Anyone but him.

"I doubt they'd have much in common," he said. "Let her find her own way, Beth."

Beth slumped. "Well, I'll keep thinking." She came to give Levi a hug, and he allowed himself to absorb the love it represented.

Suddenly, Beth pulled back. "Oh, Levi, I know who would be perfect for Callie."

Not again. Levi started to protest, but she grabbed his arm.

"You."

A jolt shot through him. Levi disengaged from her, stepping back. "No."

Beth pursued him, face eager. "Yes, you! I don't know why I didn't see it before. She's already comfortable with you, looks to you for support and encouragement."

"I'm her guardian," Levi reminded her, backing away. "She's supposed to look to me for support and encouragement."

Beth waved a hand. "It's more than that. She's prickly with everyone else, but not with you."

"I assure you, she's just as prickly with me, perhaps even more so."

"Really?" Beth clasped her hands. "Oh, Levi, you know what that means? She likes you!"

He could not follow her logic. "I'd say she tolerates me. We agreed to partner to raise the twins and Mica. That's all."

"So, she trusts you with what she finds most precious— her family." Beth lowered her hands. "I call that love."

"I call it survival," Levi argued. "You can't appreciate the life she's led, Beth. You can't understand how she thinks, how she feels."

"But you do," Beth insisted. "That's clear as day. Admit it, Levi. You admire her."

"Of course I admire her. She's taken care of Frisco and Sutter with little help from her older brother that I can tell. She's raising Mica. She's had to shoulder burdens few men could handle."

"And too many women have had to bear," Beth agreed. "All the more reason she deserves someone at her side through life."

"A partner," Levi said.

"A husband," Beth countered.

Levi bent to put his eyes on a level with his sister's, dark blue meeting dark blue. "I'm not going to marry Callie Murphy."

"Oh!" Beth stamped her foot as he straightened. "Why do you all have to be so pigheaded? Catherine was perfect for Drew—everyone could see it, but he was worried about taking on another person after Pa told him to care for all of us."

"He couldn't see we were grown," Levi remembered.

"Simon's logic got in the way of love," she continued, obviously warming to her theme, "and James and John seemed to think they weren't good enough to marry, which was utter nonsense." She put her hands on her hips. "So, what's your excuse? Too busy being a minister to manage a family? You already have one, Levi. And you're doing a fine job. Why can't you open your heart a little more?"

Because his heart had shriveled the day he'd betrayed his best friend. Because it would take a lifetime to atone. Because Callie deserved better.

"Perhaps," Levi said to his sister, "you should think about finding a husband of your own and stop trying to find one for Callie."

Beth's face tightened. "Why do I need a husband when I have five brothers to tell me what to do? I'm just about ready to wash my hands of you, Levi Wallin."

Levi turned away before she could see that her words had scored. "You have ample reason to do so. Let's leave it at that."

Chapter Fourteen

Callie met Beth on the path up the hill as she was returning with Mica from Nora's. Beth's lavender skirts whipped about her legs and lightning flashed from her dark blue eyes.

"My brother is the most stubborn, annoying fellow," she declared as they drew close. "I begin to believe you could do better." She stomped past before Callie could disagree with her.

"What did you say to Beth?" she asked as soon as she entered the parsonage. Levi was sitting at the table, Bible open, paper in front of him and pen in hand. He frowned as he looked up.

"What did she say to *you*?"

"Only that you were stubborn and annoying," Callie supplied, going to set Mica in her chair. The baby waved at Levi, and his frown eased.

"I'd think you'd agree," he said, rocking the pen in his fingers.

"Stubborn, certainly," Callie said, shucking off her coat. "Annoying, occasionally. But kind and helpful and forgiving, too."

"Those who had been forgiven much should be the first to forgive," he murmured, gaze returning to the Bible, and she thought he was repeating something he'd read.

She hung her coat on a peg beside the door, brought Mica a wooden spoon, then came to slide in beside him on the bench. She could pick out most of the words on the page, but a few escaped her. He seemed to be reading about a son who had left home. She looked to what he'd written on his paper. "What's a prodigal?"

He pulled the paper a little closer as if to keep her from seeing what else he'd written. "Someone who turns his back on everything he knows and goes away, then regrets it later and comes home."

"Must be hard," Callie said, gaze returning to the Bible. "You're used to a certain way of life, but you think there's something better over the next hill. Sooner or later you have to learn the truth and come home."

He was staring at her. "That's it exactly. How did you know?"

Callie shrugged. "It's the way Pa and Adam behaved. It's the story of most every prospector I've ever known. Only some of them never come home."

She had been thinking of her family, but his shoulders slumped as if he felt her pain. "No, some never do," he murmured, smoothing the thin pages of the Bible.

"At least Adam tried to shake off the gold fever," Callie told him. "He'd claim he wanted to settle down to farm, make a good effort. But sooner or later he'd meet another prospector or hear about a strike. Then he'd fill his pack, promising to be back. Only this last time, he didn't keep that promise, either."

Mica brought her spoon down on the table with a mighty whack as if just as frustrated by the pattern.

He set aside the pen and pressed his hand over Callie's on the table. "I'm sorry, Callie. Sorry that he disappointed you. Sorry that he left you. All I can promise is that I'm not going anywhere."

She wished she could believe that. "Even preachers get assigned to new churches. You might be needed in another town, another territory."

"Then I'd take you and the boys and Mica with me," he said. "We're partners, remember?"

She remembered, but a part of her was beginning to want more.

She couldn't tell him, couldn't bear to see sadness or, worse, pity in his eyes. Besides, who was she to know whether these growing feelings were anything more than the fever that had gripped her father and brother?

She didn't act on those feelings most of the next week. Even when they all attended church that Sunday, she fancied she looked no more interested in Levi's sermon than anyone else in the congregation. Besides, with her, her brothers and Mica seated on the front row, nobody could see her face to know if she looked moony.

She had expected Levi to talk about being a prodigal, the story he had been studying in the Bible, but he spoke about how angels visited Joseph in dreams to tell him it was right and good to marry Mary. She didn't remember most of her dreams, but she didn't think angels had ever come to tell her what to do.

"Did that ever happen to you?" she asked Levi as they left the church after services. Frisco and Sutter were chasing Levi's nephews around the yard, and Beth was cooing at Mica as she rocked the little girl in her arms.

He shook his head. "No angel ever brought me a message. But God has ways of getting His point across."

Callie frowned. "Like what?"

He stopped, gaze going out over his departing congregation. "The miracles in nature, a word from a trusted friend, the quiet answer to a prayer."

"And you know what He wants then," she pressed.

He nodded, gaze returning to hers. The sadness she'd seen on occasion had been replaced with something else, something satisfied, peaceful. "I know what He wants for my life. I don't presume to know what He wants for others."

Callie drew in a breath. "Then maybe I should ask Him about my life. Excuse me."

She hurried away before he could question her.

She probably could have prayed right there. Levi certainly had no trouble speaking to God aloud in front of others, at mealtimes, during service. But she had never talked to God before. The first time ought to be private. She wanted to make sure she did it right.

She bypassed the church, where a few people were still gathered, and headed down the hill. She avoided the main clearing, having no interest in sharing her thoughts with the other Wallins, and struck out on a path through the forest. The moss was hard under her boots. She could hear it crunching. A bird darted past, most likely frightened by the sound.

Callie sighed, trying to gather her thoughts, which seemed as jumbled as the contents of James's store. She had said she didn't want a husband, didn't want to watch another man dream fool dreams while his family suffered. Levi Wallin might not be running off to pan, but how could she know he wouldn't dream of more? She was tired of moving, tired of not knowing where her head would be resting a month from now, tired of wondering how she'd find food when winter came.

But he was such a good partner, watching over her brothers and Mica, helping her learn to read. Was it his kindness that was making her start to dream as well?

She stopped in the path, glanced in all directions. The woods had fallen silent. Pa had said that meant there was a predator in the woods. She thought it might be her. She closed her eyes, drew in a breath, let the cold of the air pierce her lungs.

God, Almighty One. From what I've seen and heard here at Wallin Landing, You want me to talk to You. I'm sorry to ask questions my first time, but I don't know what to do. I find myself wanting to be part of this place, this family. I want to be more to Levi than a partner. Is that foolish?

Levi had said God would answer. Maybe there'd be some bolt of lightning. She cracked open an eye. The woods remained silent, wrapped in winter's chill. Nothing looked or sounded the least bit different. And still she felt conflicted.

Callie closed her eyes again.

Am I doing this wrong? I read in the Bible that I'm supposed to talk without a lot of highfalutin words. Maybe You could just tell me what You want. Is this place meant to be home? Am I meant to be Levi's wife?

Something touched her face, soft, like the brush of a finger. Callie opened her eyes again. Snow drifted down, thick and tufty, like goose feathers on the air. It reminded her of the last time she'd seen Vital Creek as they had been forced south for the winter, the last time she, Adam, Pa and the twins had been a family.

Was this her answer? Did God mean she'd be forced to leave Wallin Landing like they'd left Vital Creek, or was He saying she'd finally found a family again?

Inside the parsonage, Levi listened to Frisco and Sutter bickering, but his mind was far away. Even though he'd preached on something appropriate to the Advent season, he kept thinking about the story of the prodigal son. He knew himself to be a prodigal, returned home by the grace of God. But the things he'd done while he'd been away continued to haunt him. He could see Scout's wide, panicked eyes, hear his friend's cries that he was innocent as the prospectors surrounded him. How did a man ever make up for betraying his best friend? He felt as if he'd fallen in mud and no amount of scrubbing would ever wash him clean.

Mica gabbled at him from his lap, and he forced a smile. "You'll make better choices," he assured her.

Silence was his only answer.

His head jerked up. The twins were nowhere in sight, and he heard no thuds from outside that would have assured him they were chopping wood.

"I don't suppose you know where they went," he said to Mica.

She looked at the ceiling even as a thump echoed overhead. Rising, Levi went to set the baby in her chair at the table, then loped for the stairs.

The loft looked empty the first time he glanced around, but two of the pallets were bumpier than usual, the quilts piled up over the pillows as if someone was sleeping under them. Napping, on a Sunday afternoon? He didn't believe it for a moment.

"What a shame," he said aloud. "I was thinking

about asking Frisco and Sutter to help me churn some ice cream. They must have been tired from all that hard work studying for the theatrical."

"No, we aren't," Sutter said, popping out from beside the hearth. "I'll help you churn, preacher."

Levi sat on his bed. "Maybe you could call me Levi."

Frisco followed his brother out of hiding. "Callie won't like it. She says we have to call men mister or sir."

"Or by what they do," Sutter reminded him. "Like being a preacher."

Levi was too young to be their pa, and he wouldn't have felt comfortable having them call him that. Being a father was a serious role. Even Drew had nearly buckled under the responsibility.

"How about uncle?" he suggested.

"Uncle Levi," Frisco said as if trying out the appellation. "I like it."

"Me, too," Sutter said. "Can we go churn ice cream now, Uncle Levi?"

Levi rose. "Shortly. First, I want to know why you decided to hide this afternoon."

Two gazes met. As if he saw something in his brother's eyes, Frisco nodded.

"You got to promise not to tell Callie, pre—Uncle Levi," he said solemnly.

"Callie and I are partners," Levi told him. "It's not right to hide things from your partner."

"Even if it's a surprise?" Sutter pressed.

Levi cocked his head. "What kind of surprise?"

In answer, the boys beckoned him closer to the hearth. Against the stone, where the chimney shadowed a small section of the loft, was a pile of something. Levi squatted to get a better look.

"Feathers?" he asked.

"Shh!" Sutter warned. "She might hear you."

Levi was fairly sure Callie was still out for her walk, though he didn't understand why she'd wanted to leave in the first place. Something told him he was the cause of her agitation. He just didn't know what he'd done.

"All right," he whispered. "Why feathers?"

"Miss Beth said she'd help us make a hat for Callie for Christmas," Frisco explained.

"A real one," Sutter put in. "All fancy-like. Callie never gets fancy things. We thought she deserved it."

Levi put out a hand to him. "You're right. She does. I'll keep quiet about the feathers. Just see that you look for them outside. No need to tug them out of your pillows."

"How did you know?" Frisco demanded.

Levi straightened. "I was a lad like you not that long ago. Very likely anything you could think to try, I already did and lived to regret it."

Downstairs he heard a door shut.

"Frisco? Sutter?" Callie's voice drifted up the stairs. "Who's minding Mica?"

"I think you just found something else to regret, Uncle Levi," Sutter said.

But he couldn't regret learning about the boys' surprise for Callie. He was pleased to know they'd thought about getting their sister something for Christmas. Yet it made him think. What could he give Callie and the boys to make their first Christmas at Wallin Landing special?

He should have known his sister would have an opinion on the matter. Beth had clearly remained focused on her matchmaking, for she drew him aside as soon as he, Callie, the twins and Mica arrived for dinner that afternoon.

"James says you haven't picked out a Christmas present for Callie," she whispered as they stood near the hearth.

Levi glanced to where his irrepressible older brother was playing a game of fox and hens with all the children old enough to run around in a circle. "I've been thinking."

Beth clasped her hands. "I can help. I have so many ideas. A heart-shaped brooch, perhaps, with a lock of your hair."

Levi grimaced. "She'd run screaming for the hills."

Beth dropped her hands, frowning. "Why? It's a perfectly romantic gesture."

"Did someone say romance?" Catherine swept up to them. "Has Callie settled on one of the crew, then?"

"No," Levi said, then nearly grimaced again as Nora and two of the toddlers looked his way.

Catherine frowned. "Are you sure? Harry seems most attentive."

Even now the big logger was making funny faces that set Mica to giggling in Callie's arms.

Levi's skin prickled. "She isn't courting. You know that, Catherine."

Catherine drew herself up. "Well, we can fix that. I'll suggest to Harry that he invite her to the Christmas dance."

Callie must have noticed Levi's gaze on her, for she left Harry to cross to his side.

"Everything all right?" she asked him. "You look rather fierce."

"Yes," Beth said with a giggle. "He does, doesn't he?"

Catherine eyed him. "Are you feeling unwell, Levi? I'm sure I have something that would help."

"No," he said, taking a step back. Despite his intentions, he slipped an arm about Callie's waist, saw her brows go up. "And Callie will not be attending the Christmas dance with Harry or anyone else you might suggest."

Beth's face fell. "Why not?"

"Because," Levi said, watching color climb in Callie's cheeks, "Callie promised to attend with me."

Chapter Fifteen

Callie thought another young miss would be delighted with the way Beth clasped her hands and grinned at Levi's announcement. Catherine smiled knowingly, and even Mica applauded as she turned from one smiling face to the next. But Callie wasn't fooled. The look in Beth's eyes meant trouble. Beth didn't understand Callie and Levi were just partners. His sister was set on matchmaking, despite Callie's earlier protests.

"Oh, Levi, that's wonderful," Beth said. "Nora can make a ball gown."

Callie hefted Mica closer. "I don't need a ball gown."

"Of course you do. And I can fix your hair, maybe in the Greek style, like in the November issue of *Godey's*."

Callie widened her stance. "My hair is fine."

Beth rubbed her hands together. "Now, about the jewelry…"

"No," Callie said. "No jewelry. No ball gown. No fancy hair. I'm not going courting, remember?"

Beth's mouth snapped shut, and she hurried for the kitchen. Looking contrite, most likely for her part in the attempted matchmaking, Catherine excused herself, as well.

Callie sighed. "I hurt your sister's feelings again."

Levi shrugged. "She overstepped. I'm not sure what else would have stopped her. She seems compelled to play matchmaker. But she wants the best for those she cares about. None of us can help it if our vision doesn't align with hers."

"So what do you do?" Callie asked.

"We take her aside, explain how we feel about the matter."

"Does that help?"

Levi grinned. "Sometimes."

Callie handed Mica to him. "Then I'll try." She turned for the kitchen.

Beth was stirring the stew, movements brisk. The color in her cheeks suggested that more than the heat of the stove was involved.

"I came to apologize," Callie told her. "You keep trying to help."

Beth sniffed, head down and spoon moving. "You don't want my help. I understand."

Callie went to take down the dishes she knew the Wallins used for Sunday dinner. "I'm not sure you do. Let me explain. Ma died when I was twelve, Pa when I was sixteen. I've had to be responsible for everyone in my family. When you step in without asking, you show me you think I'm not doing well enough on my own." Callie turned to face her. "You're saying I'm not good enough."

"Oh, Callie!" Beth dropped her spoon and ran to enfold her in a hug. "I beg your pardon. I never meant to imply you weren't perfect just the way you are."

"I'm not perfect," Callie said as Beth pulled away. "I'm just doing the best I can."

"Everyone can see that," Beth assured her. "We admire you for it."

Admired her? All the fine men and women of Wallin Landing? Callie ducked her head. "Thank you. Just realize I have a hard time accepting help."

Beth frowned. "Even from Levi?"

Especially from Levi, but Callie refused to confess as much to his sister. "He's done enough for us already. You've all done too much."

"We're family," Beth said, chin coming up. "Family helps each other."

Beth's eyes, so like her brother's, were bright, her smile determined. "You really believe that?" Callie asked.

Beth nodded. "And I believe something else, as well. Despite his protests, Levi is starting to care for you."

She knew it! "You stop playing matchmaker," Callie scolded.

"Why? I'm fairly good at it, having had a hand in all my brothers' courtships." She leaned closer. "What are you planning to get him for Christmas?"

Callie felt as if a rock had settled in her stomach. "Must I get him something for Christmas?"

Beth leaned back. "No. Generally, all the adults work together to make sure Father Christmas brings something for each of the children. Husbands and wives exchange gifts, of course, and children make something for their parents. Which is Levi to you?"

"None of those things," Callie told her. "We're partners. He's certainly not getting me anything for Christmas."

Beth raised a brow. "Are you sure about that?"

In truth, she wasn't. There had been times Levi withdrew by himself. She'd assumed he was working on preacher things—visiting the less fortunate, making notes for his next sermon, tending to the church. But what if he was making her something for Christmas? Shouldn't she do the same? Not that she had all that many skills. Still, he'd done so much for her and her family.

"If I was to get him something," Callie murmured, brushing out a wrinkle in her dress, "what would it be?"

Beth, of course, had all kinds of ideas, from the costly to the impractical. A saddle for his horse? Where would she get the money? A pin made from her braided hair? Who'd want that? Her dismay must have been written on her face, for Beth sputtered to a stop.

"I'm sorry, Callie," she said. "There I go again, telling you what to do. I'm sure Levi would be delighted with whatever you give him. Why, he always said the best present he ever received was a tin harmonica. He played that thing for hours. He must have lost it on his trip north, because I've never seen it since he's returned. But if he could be happy with such a simple present, you needn't feel compelled to get something fancier."

Which was a good thing, as the few coins she had left from Adam might not be enough even for a simple harmonica.

Yet the idea remained on her mind the next few days. She'd managed to avoid committing to a new dress or hairstyle for the dance or admitting that her feelings for Levi were also growing, though Nora, Catherine and Beth asked her about the matter as she helped them finish the costumes for the school play. She was thinking things over as she started back to the parsonage.

Sunday's snow had been fleeting, and now a few flakes drifted down from the sky, landing on Mica's lashes and making her blink as she tried to focus on them.

A harmonica. Music. Something treasured lost on the gold fields. It seemed so fitting. Would James have one in that crowded store of his?

She was halfway up the hill when Zachariah Turnpeth, one of the prospectors who had visited her cabin before she moved to Wallin Landing, stepped out of the woods.

His heavy coat and trousers were stiff with cold, his boots crusted with mud to the tops. Fingers poked through the knit of his gloves. He nodded politely enough.

"Miss Callie, sorry to trouble you. We never did find a way to head south, but we're hoping we can soon. Might you have some place we could stay the night?"

His partner was close behind, pack grasped in each hand.

Callie frowned. "What happened to your horses?"

Zachariah shifted from foot to foot as Willard joined them. "Well, we were running out of money…"

So they'd sold the poor things. Small wonder they hadn't made it south. And now winter was closing in.

Just then, the schoolhouse door burst open, and children flowed out into the clearing. Frisco and Sutter ran to Callie's side.

"We have dress rehearsal tomorrow," Frisco announced, heedless of their visitors.

"That's the last practice," Sutter informed her. "We don't really have to wear dresses."

"Except Davy," Frisco confided. "He plays an angel."

Sutter shushed him. "You're not supposed to tell!"

As Frisco looked daggers at him, the prospectors laughed.

"Sounds like you two are fitting in just fine," Zachariah said.

Sutter blinked, then elbowed his brother. "Look, Frisco. It's Mr. Turnpeth and Mr. Young."

Zachariah smiled at the boys, though Willard was too busy rubbing his arms as if trying to stave off the cold.

"Good to see you, boys," Zachariah said. "And your sister and little Mica, too. Any plans to go panning when the weather turns?"

Frisco and Sutter's eyes lit.

"No," Callie said, as much to answer the man as to silence her brother's hopes. "And we'll have to ask about you staying the night. We're living with friends."

"Uncle Levi will say yes," Frisco predicted.

"He's a minister," Sutter explained. "He has to be nice to folks. God told him."

Callie wasn't so sure about that. And she couldn't shake the feeling that something was wrong.

"I'd like to meet this uncle of yours," Zachariah said, reaching for his pack. "Can you give me his direction?"

Sutter pointed up the hill. "Here he comes now."

Strangers were rare enough at Wallin Landing, even with James's store, that Levi lengthened his stride when he spotted Callie and the boys with two men he didn't recognize. Their packs said they were travelers. Where could they be heading with winter closing in?

Sutter ran to meet him. "Prospectors came by," he reported, falling in next to Levi and scurrying to keep up. "They knew our pa."

As he drew abreast of the men, he could see the pan

affixed to each pack. He aligned himself next to Callie. She took a step closer as if needing his support.

"Friends of yours?" he asked.

She shrugged as if she wasn't sure. "They came by the claim the day you arrived. They say they knew Pa and Adam."

The closest man stuck out his hand and introduced himself and his partner. "We were hoping to beg a room for the night."

Sutter perked up. "Like Mary and Joseph. Only we got room at the inn."

Levi smiled at him before turning to the two men and shaking Zachariah's hand. "Levi Wallin. I'm the pastor of the church. You're welcome to stay in the hall tonight, and Callie and I can cook you dinner and then breakfast in the morning."

"Much obliged," Zachariah said as he drew back his hand. "And I'm glad to see Fred's children and Adam's little girl in such a nice place. You've done Adam proud. He was a good man."

"Smart, too," his partner said. "Smarter than us."

He almost made it sound like a complaint. Zachariah must have thought so as well, for he stepped in front of his friend as if to keep him from saying more.

"We're glad to accept your offer, pastor. Mighty cold in these woods the last few nights. If you could show us the hall?"

Levi led them up the hill, while Callie and Mica headed for the parsonage. Frisco and Sutter peppered the prospectors with questions as their visitors laid their packs down with a clatter and clank. Levi sent the boys for firewood for the hearth.

"Looks like you're fixing to have a party," Zachariah

said, glancing around at the chains and cones Beth and Callie had made.

"A Christmas dance," Levi explained. "Do you two have somewhere to be for Christmas?"

The two men exchanged glances, reminding him of Frisco and Sutter.

"We have business in the area," Zachariah said. "I'm hoping to have it resolved by Christmas. But thank you for your concern, Pastor."

Callie had her back up again that night as Zachariah and Willard ate dinner with them. Frisco and Sutter had arranged themselves on either side of the prospectors, sharing stories about gold rush camps they'd known.

"Adam was going to strike it rich," Frisco bragged as they finished the stew Levi had made. "He had a place all picked out."

Both men perked up at that.

"And he never sent back any money to show for it," Callie countered, rising from the table.

Levi rose, as well. His look to Frisco and Sutter had them on their feet, too. Mica crowed as if she was proud of them.

Zachariah scrambled up and nudged his partner.

"What's the to-do?" Willard grumbled, shoving back from the table.

"Didn't your ma teach you any manners?" Zachariah demanded. "You stand up when a lady stands."

"What lady?" Willard asked with a perplexed frown.

"That's what I said," Frisco told him. "It's just Callie."

Callie headed for the stove, but not before Levi saw that her cheeks were pinking.

"Your sister deserves the same respect as any other lady," Levi informed her brothers.

"Are we gonna have to stand when Mica does, too?" Frisco challenged.

"When she's old enough to be called a lady," Levi said with a smile to the baby.

"Oh, sit down," Callie said, bringing the pan to the table.

They all obeyed.

She served the apple pandowdy around, to the praise of the prospectors.

"Haven't had anything so good since your brother left camp," Zachariah declared. "He was one dedicated prospector. Takes a strong man to keep panning when the color won't come." He turned to Levi. "What about you, Pastor? Didn't I hear you used to follow the creek?"

How did he know? Nothing about Levi's clothes or demeanor showed he'd once held gold more precious than family or friends. Still, he refused to lie now.

"My partner and I had a claim at Vital Creek," he told him, reaching to move his cup out of the way of Mica's inquisitive fingers. "Didn't amount to much, I'm sad to say."

"Never too late to try again," Zachariah commiserated.

Callie held up her spoon. "Anyone want another helping?"

Willard ignored her offer, leaning forward to meet Levi's gaze. "I reckon you must have some idea where you'd want to try next."

Was he looking for divine guidance? If God was going to give him a message, it wouldn't be about where to start panning for gold. "Sorry, gents," Levi told them.

"I don't think much about striking it rich anymore. You might say I pan for men now."

They both frowned. So did Frisco and Sutter.

"How do you pan for men?" Sutter wanted to know.

"It's like that story he read us from the Bible," Callie put in, returning to her seat. "Jesus started asking men to follow Him. He told some fishermen they'd be fishers of men."

Why was it she always understood what was in his heart? "That's it exactly. Whatever gifts I had in life, I use them for God now."

Willard puffed out a sigh as if highly disappointed.

"That's real noble," Zachariah hurried to assure Levi. "But it seems to me that if you know the best place to pan, Pastor, and aren't going to use it, you're honor-bound to share."

They were both watching him, more eager than most of his congregation during a particularly uplifting sermon.

What do I tell them, Lord? Their souls are worth so much more than the gold they seek.

A verse came immediately to mind.

"For what shall it profit a man, if he shall gain the whole world, yet lose his own soul?" Levi quoted.

Willard's face turned red. He shoved back from the table, making Mica squeak in surprise. "Thanks for the food and room for the night. At least that's something."

Zachariah rose. "That's a great deal, you oaf." He nodded to Levi and Callie. "Pastor, Miss Callie. Don't worry about us in the morning. We'll pack up and get out of your way."

Feeling heavy, Levi walked them to the door.

"I didn't mean to imply there was anything wrong

with prospecting," he told them. "But when the search for gold becomes everything to you, it's time to stop."

Zachariah nodded, but Willard leaned closer, eyes narrowed.

"Easy for you to say," he hissed. "You got a nice house, a job that don't take much work. You don't deserve it. You might fool Callie and her brothers, but you don't fool me. I heard what you did at Vital Creek. Callie and the boys wouldn't look at you so sweetly if they knew you was nothing but a low-down claim jumper."

Chapter Sixteen

Frisco and Sutter were bickering again, but Callie paid them only half a mind. She was watching Levi and the prospectors at the door. Having the pair extol the glories of panning to her brothers was bad enough. She wasn't about to have them awaken the hunger in Levi.

She saw Willard's sneer before Levi blanched. They hadn't much liked his remark that faith was more important than gold. Very likely Willard had lashed out. She rose to intervene.

"Mighty cold out tonight," she said as she approached the trio. "You need extra quilts?"

Willard clamped his mouth around whatever else he had been going to say.

"We'll be fine, ma'am," his partner said, grabbing Willard's arm and tugging him out the door. "Thank you again for your hospitality." They disappeared into the night.

Levi shut out the blast of cold.

"I don't like them," Callie said. "They better be gone in the morning and nothing missing. Frisco, Sutter, go find the hatchets and bring them inside."

"Ah, Callie," Frisco said, slipping off the bench. "They ain't gonna steal nothing."

"They aren't going to steal anything," Sutter corrected him. "Remember what Mrs. Wallin said? *Ain't* ain't a word."

"Sure it's a word," Frisco protested. "It's just not a word she likes."

"Git!" Callie ordered them.

They shoved their arms into their coats and went.

"I suppose you're going to tell me they're fine fellows, too," she said to Levi, going to set the wash pan on the sideboard.

"I don't think they'll steal," he allowed. He walked toward her slowly, stiffly, as if he'd aged in the last few minutes. Fear curled like smoke around her.

"Do you miss it?" she asked, straightening from the sideboard. "The excitement of the camps?"

"Sometimes I miss the camaraderie," he admitted, going to gather the pots from the stove. "Nothing like sitting around a fire with a dozen friends, celebrating, commiserating."

Callie sighed. "There were some good times. You've helped me see that. But for every nugget found, there's a life lost, days wasted, people left behind. That cost is too high."

"Agreed." The single word held so much pain that she crossed to his side.

"I won't regret you never struck it rich," she told him, fighting the need to smooth those curls off his brow. "If you had, you wouldn't have come for me and Frisco, Sutter and Mica. You wouldn't be the man you are today."

"That's true enough." He glanced toward the door.

"But why does it take a tragedy to get through to people? I'd like to spare Zachariah and Willard that."

Callie put a hand on his arm. "That's real kind of you, but some folks need a tree to fall on them before they pay any mind to the important things in life."

"Yes, they do." His gaze returned to her, shadowed. "Callie, there's something you should know…"

Frisco and Sutter bumped through the side door just then, lugging the hatchets. Her brothers' heads were white, making them look like little old miners.

Frisco shook off the snow with a shudder. "Coming down hard."

Sutter dropped his hatchet on the floor. "Snow's not hard, silly. It's soft as a feather."

"It will be hard enough when I make a snowball and hit you in the head," Frisco threatened.

"Boys!" Callie went to fetch a towel. "Wipe yourselves off before you get water all over the floor." She tossed them the towel and returned to Levi's side. "I'm sorry. What were you saying?"

"Nothing," he said, watching the boys. "It's old news that has no bearing on my life today. Let's get this cleaned up."

Zachariah and Willard were gone the next morning. Callie checked the hall, including the pantry, but nothing seemed to be missing. Still, she watched Levi and her brothers the next few days, ready to fight any sign of gold fever. Levi seemed quieter than usual, but he went about his duties, worked with her on her reading and helped with the Christmas preparations readily enough. She even found time to slip down to the store and purchase the harmonica for him, though his brother also tried to interest her in something more romantic. As for Frisco and Sutter, preparing for the school play consumed all their time, until it was the night of the big event.

Beth had warned her everyone came dressed as if they were going to a fancy theatre, so Callie donned her mother's gown and put a bow in Mica's hair. The baby kept reaching up to finger the long end of the ribbon, beaming as if she knew she was even prettier than usual.

Frisco and Sutter had gone ahead to the hall to get ready, so Levi was the only one in the house when Callie and Mica came out of the bedroom. He was wearing his Sunday suit, the dark blue fabric matching his eyes. She dropped her gaze before he could notice her admiring the way it called attention to the breadth of his shoulders.

He offered her his arm. "May I have the honor of escorting you, Miss Murphy?"

So formal. As if she was a grand lady. Callie put her nose in the air, and Mica copied her. "You may, Mr. Wallin."

He led her to the wall, then helped her into her coat. Even the worn buckskin couldn't make her feel less like a lady tonight.

The hall did not disappoint. Lanterns here and there cast an amber light, leaving corners mysteriously shadowed. The raised platform at the top of the room held a manger filled with hay, and the wall behind it had been draped with dark fabric on which tiny sequins glittered like stars in the light. Benches had been brought from the various houses to allow seating for the parents and other family members of each child, as well as for neighbors who'd come to see the spectacle. Callie was so used to sitting at the front of the church that she was a little surprised when Levi took her and Mica to a bench a few rows back. She was just glad she could see around the people in front of her.

She recognized Nora and Simon, Dottie and John, Catherine and Drew, Beth and James as they came in and found seats for themselves and the younger Wallin children.

"That's why you wanted us to sit back," she murmured to Levi. "So the little ones could see their brothers and sisters."

"And cousins. Some of the neighbors have children, too. I thought Mica might be a little young to care what she could see."

He was right. Mica spent most of her time cooing at the people nearest them, all of whom looked back with fond smiles.

Just then Rina stepped to the front of the hall, purple dress splendid in the simple surroundings. Voices quieted, people leaned forward to hear her speak.

"Thank you all for coming," she said, voice carrying. "Our students have worked hard on this theatrical. I hope you will give them your full attention. Now, without further ado, we bring you *The Gift of Christmas*."

She backed against the side wall to polite applause. Mica was the last one to stop clapping.

As the hall quieted once more, from the left side of the stage, Sutter appeared with Victoria. Both wore robes belted with rope, towels draping their heads. The little girl was carrying Peter, who was fully half her size. She helped him climb into the manger where he stared at the crowd solemnly. Mica waved at him.

Callie was more interested in her brother, pale in his costume.

"We have traveled far from Nazareth," Sutter said, gaze on the baby. "But there was no room at the inn."

"What a gift that we could rest in this stable," Victoria said. She knelt beside Peter and patted him. He wiggled as if the manger was too tight.

Five children came in from the right, all dressed in long white tunics with fir garlands on their heads and pasteboard wings at their backs. She recognized Mary, Drew's daughter, and her brother Davy among them.

"Our gift to the newborn king is praise," Drew's daughter said.

"We come to proclaim His birth and peace to all on whom His favor rests," Davy added.

"We have told the shepherds the Good News," another child said. "They will be here soon."

"I was supposed to talk first!" the fourth complained.

The other girl hung her head. "Sorry."

"Say it," Davy hissed.

The little girl drew herself up. "Glory to God in the highest." She spread her tunic and curtsied.

"Let us all sing," Davy said. *"Angels from the realms of glory, wing your way through all the earth."*

The song echoed through the hall, voices joining on all sides, underscored by Drew's deep bass. This was what a host of heaven must have sounded like—pure, clean, filled with awe and hope. Callie met Levi's gaze, and the warmth of his smile made gooseflesh pimple her arms. She hugged Mica closer.

As the song ended, the shepherds came in from the other side, led by Frisco. Callie could hardly wait to hear what her other brother would say.

He pointed toward the manger. "Baby Jesus is trying to escape."

Sure enough, Peter was halfway out of the manger. Victoria nudged him back in. He frowned at her.

Frisco cleared his throat and struck a pose, chin up and feet planted. "We shepherds bring the Prince of Peace all our devotion."

Pride surged through her. Those were her brothers up there. Again she looked to Levi and saw that he was watching Frisco and Sutter with just the same amount of pride.

"We heard the angels' call and left our fields and flocks to answer," another of the shepherds said.

Just as Levi had left the gold fields to heed God's call. She reached out her free hand and gave his a squeeze. A smile played about his lips.

"There He is, just as the angels said," a third put in, nodding to the manger.

"He's escaping again!" Frisco warned.

Dottie moved out of her seat and went to join Victoria by the manger.

"Who are you going to play, Aunt Dottie?" Victoria asked.

Dottie colored. "Baby Jesus's nanny."

A murmur of laughter ran through the crowd, but the children all seemed to accept that. Rina was rubbing the bridge of her nose as if she felt a headache coming on. Callie wasn't sure why. This was better than any play she'd ever watched.

The fourth shepherd stomped her foot. "It's *my* turn!"

"You're right," Frisco said. "Everyone be quiet so Jenna can speak."

The cast fell silent. Everyone in the audience waited expectantly.

The little girl turned red and wrung her hands. "I forgot!"

"Praise God who..." a woman who was likely her mother urged from the benches.

Jenna blew out a breath. "Praise God who revealed Himself to such as us."

"Good work!" the man beside her mother called.

"I did it." Jenna wiggled her relief.

"Now can we sing?" the last shepherd asked with obvious relief.

"While shepherds watched their flocks by night, all seated on the ground," Frisco started. *"The angel of the Lord came down and glory shone around."*

Once again the audience joined in, singing until Callie's heart swelled and she thought the walls of the hall might tremble. She kept her hand firmly in Levi's.

As the song faded, she sat taller and craned her neck, eager for the next part of the play. Three more students came from the left. Their robes were richer, with touches of velvet and fur. All three wore gold paper crowns on their heads.

"We three kings give of our riches," the first said, setting a gold-colored box by the manger. Peter reached for it, and Dottie nudged it a little farther away.

"We saw His star rise in the East and followed it here to Wallin Landing," the second said, laying down a cutglass bottle that glittered like a jewel.

"Bethlehem," Frisco corrected him.

"Oh, right, Bethlehem. I always get that wrong."

Some parent groaned.

"Won't you help us sing?" the third asked, setting down a small, potted plant. *"We three kings of Orient are / bearing gifts we traverse afar."*

She'd heard the song in Vancouver and San Francisco. Maybe it was because it featured gold, but the miners had loved belting it out. Her voice added to the wave that crested through the hall, bringing praise, joy. Levi let go of her hand, but slipped his arm about her shoulders. She had no need to be anywhere else.

"What wonderful gifts to welcome our son," Sutter said. He looked out into the audience. "What gift will you give to welcome Jesus this Christmas?"

"I think He'd like one more song," Victoria said. *"Silent night, holy night."*

Around Callie, voices were raised, solemnly, thoughtfully. Callie let the sound roll over her, touch her heart. But Sutter's words lingered through the melody.

From what she was learning, Jesus had only asked for one thing: love. What gift could she give the man who had welcomed her, her brothers and Mica into his home and his heart?

Levi rose with the others for a standing ovation. He couldn't have been prouder of Frisco and Sutter. He knew from experience how hard it could be to stand in front of people and speak. He'd nearly forgotten his line the last time he'd been in one of Rina's plays, and he'd been eighteen at the time.

"That was so good," Callie said beside him. Her eyes were still shining, her cheeks glowing, as if she'd been the one to perform. The touch of her hand, the feel of her beside him, had made every moment more precious. He almost didn't want it to end. But he knew his duty now.

"Yes, it was," he agreed. "Let's collect our actors and congratulate them."

Most of the audience had the same idea. The stage

was mobbed with reuniting families. Sutter and Frisco fought their way to Levi and Callie.

"Did you see me, Callie?" Sutter asked, eyes bright. "I was Joseph."

"I was the head shepherd," Frisco bragged. "I had to make sure the other shepherds knew what to do."

"So I noticed," Levi assured them. He put an arm about each boy. "You were both marvelous."

"That was such a good play," Callie kept repeating as if she'd never seen anything finer. "How'd you know what to say, what to sing?"

The boys launched into a complicated story about how Rina had come up with the lines, how they'd practiced, who'd struggled and how they'd helped each other. Levi found himself watching Callie. She nodded along with the story, exclaimed over the troubles and complimented them on their triumphs. Such a simple thing as a school play with all its flaws and imperfections, and she was in awe. What else could he do to make her life happier?

He thought about it the next few days as they all finished preparing for Christmas. The play had concluded school until the new year, so Sutter and Frisco were free to do other things. Levi had been concerned that the boys might chafe at being inside, but they threw themselves into the Christmas work, stringing popcorn for garlands and helping Beth make wreaths for the hall and the church. He was fairly sure part of the time they spent with Beth they were making Callie's hat with the feathers they'd collected.

All the more reason for him to find her something, as well.

As Christmas Eve approached, he went to seek his

brother's advice. The store on the shores of Lake Union seemed emptier than Levi remembered as he entered. Some of the shelves were bare, and he could see a great deal more of the planks of the floor as he crossed to his brother, who stood behind the counter as if looking for his last friend.

"Happy Christmas Adam," James greeted him. Levi knew he'd have to explain the greeting to Frisco and Sutter, if Beth hadn't already. It was a family custom to call the twenty-third of December Christmas Adam, because it was the day before Christmas Eve, and Adam had come before Eve.

Levi nodded to James now, glancing around again. "Happy Christmas Adam to you, too. Is everything all right?"

James leaned on the counter as if weary. "See for yourself. Between the cold weather making it difficult to reach Seattle and the coming of Christmas, I've been cleaned out."

Levi frowned. "Isn't that good?"

James grinned, straightening. "Excellent. It will make for a very merry Christmas for my family."

"I'd like my family to feel the merriment, as well." He leaned closer, then chided himself. There wasn't anyone else in the store. He didn't have to speak confidentially. It wasn't as if Callie could hear him up in the parsonage.

"Ah," James said. "Well, I can tell you the twins have been eyeing the steel fishhooks over there."

"I'll take them," Levi said. "And I was thinking about a sled."

James's lean face lit. "Excellent idea. I have one left. It's yours. And for Callie?"

There lay the rub. Levi shook his head. "I have no idea. She doesn't like dress goods and ribbons and such."

"A natural beauty who needs no adornment," James agreed. He rearranged a display of taffy on the counter. "Still, perhaps an accessory—handkerchief, shawl, wedding ring?"

Levi groaned. "Not you, too?"

James spread his hands. "What can I say? I'm a hopeless romantic. But even Simon thinks it's logical."

Had his brothers been discussing him and Callie? "Simon doesn't know all the facts."

James nodded knowingly. "I thought I noticed her eating with her mouth open. I could never marry a woman like that, no matter how pretty and spunky."

"She eats perfectly well, as you know," Levi told him.

James leaned his arms on the counter. "Then she must snore. I suppose you can hear her through the floor of the loft."

"I don't hear a peep out of her and Mica."

James straightened. "Then why the hesitation? Marry the girl!"

Levi felt the strain in his smile. "I'm just here for a Christmas present, and you aren't helping."

James sighed. "All right, but I still say she'd prefer a wedding ring to anything else I have to offer."

"I'm surprised you have a ring at all," Levi countered. "How many can you need out here?"

"Six," James told him. "One for Harry, Tom, Dickie, Beth and you."

"That's five."

"One as a spare," James said. "You never know when Scout will return home."

Levi very much doubted Scout would ever return to

Wallin Landing, but he couldn't bring himself to tell his brother that.

"What happened between you and Scout?" James asked quietly.

Was Levi that transparent? "Enough that he never wants to lay eyes on me again."

"I doubt that," James said. "You two got into a lot of scuffles when you were boys. You always made up in a few hours at most."

"This was more than a scuffle," Levi assured him. "Suffice it to say I nearly cost Scout his life."

James paled. "That bad?"

Levi nodded. "Worse. And if Callie ever learned the truth, it wouldn't matter what I get her for Christmas. She'd never speak to me again as long as I lived."

"Then you have to tell her," James said.

Levi raised a brow. "That's mad, even for you."

"You're not the only one who's been in a scrape or two," James reminded him. "Think about it. How much better to hear from you than someone else?"

Zachariah and Willard came to mind. His blood had been ice when Callie had approached as they'd confessed they knew about his past. One of the miners involved must have broken his promise to Thaddeus and told the story. What would he have done if Willard had told her?

"I've tried," he admitted to his brother. "It's hard enough reliving it, much less watching someone you care about realize how craven you are."

James wiggled his eyebrows. "It seems you do care."

"I'm not ready to talk about that, either," Levi told him. "So you and Beth and the others can stop asking, at least until Christmas is over."

Chapter Seventeen

It was Christmas Eve. Callie knew because Frisco and Sutter woke her early to tell her so. She'd been dreaming of white feathers drifting from the sky when she heard the door open, and suddenly two bodies bounced onto the bed with her.

"It's Christmas Eve," Frisco informed her as if she should have been up and moving by now.

Sutter nodded, wiggling on the bed as if appreciating the springs for the first time. "Yesterday was Christmas Adam, and Adam comes before Eve. Miss Beth said so."

"And that means we have to hang our stockings," Frisco finished. They both gazed at her expectantly.

Callie smothered a yawn as she peered over the side of the bed at Mica, sleeping soundly in her cradle. "Why would we hang our stockings? Do we wash on Christmas Eve?"

Frisco and Sutter looked horrified at the very idea.

"We hang our stockings on the mantel because Father Christmas is coming," Levi called from the other room. "Leave your sister alone, boys. I've got cocoa."

Grinning, her brothers jumped off the bed and ran out.

Father Christmas. She remembered the shenanigans at the camps surrounding the name—lumps of coal stuck in boots, men running through camp pelting each other with oranges. It was all nonsense, but as apparently the Wallin family thought Father Christmas fun, she supposed she should let Frisco and Sutter enjoy the myth, as well.

They weren't the only ones anticipating, she saw after she dressed, woke and changed Mica and came out of her room. Levi had just finished nailing his stocking to the mantel. Sutter's and Frisco's hung next to it.

Levi shot her a grin. "Bring me two of yours for you and Mica. I'll hang them, as well."

"You take this seriously," she accused.

He drew himself up. "Christmas is a solemn occasion, madam. As minister to this community, it is my duty to uphold tradition."

He didn't fool her. She could see the twinkle in his eyes. She set Mica in her chair and went to fetch a stocking for each of them.

He had porridge on the table when she came back, and her brothers were already gulping it down while Levi fed Mica.

"What's the hurry?" Callie asked, joining them.

"It's Christmas Eve," Frisco reminded her, sounding a bit exasperated that she would have to ask.

"So I heard," Callie informed him. "But bolting breakfast isn't going to make Father Christmas come any faster."

There was a knock on the door.

"He's here!" Sutter shouted, running to answer.

"Father Christmas doesn't come until night, silly," Frisco said, but he followed as if to make sure.

Beth was standing on the stoop. A heavy wool coat bundled her figure, the fur-lined hood pulled up around her face. Her breath fogged the air. "Good morning! Happy Christmas Eve."

"Father Christmas is coming," Sutter told her.

"So he is," Beth agreed with a smile. "In the meantime, we need help with a different kind of delivery."

Levi frowned, but the boys wiggled to see around her. Callie went to join them.

A wagon was trundling up the hill in the snow. The driver reined in the horses in front of the church. Squeezing past Beth, Sutter ran to see them.

The driver, an older man with a grizzled chin, hopped down. "The invoice said you'd have men here to do the unloading." He looked pointedly at the boys.

"Plenty of men," Beth assured him. She glanced at Callie. "May I put your brothers to work?"

Callie eyed the bulky, blanket-wrapped item on the back of the wagon. "I'm not sure they can carry that."

"Very likely not," Beth agreed. She called Sutter back. "Put your coats on, boys. Frisco can run up to the farm and ask Simon to help us. Sutter will go fetch James from the store. John should be here shortly. He will have seen this go past on the road."

"But what is it?" Callie asked as the boys ran to do Beth's bidding.

Levi brought Callie her coat and pulled his on. "What have you done, Beth?"

Beth grinned. "You'll see."

Just then, John came striding up the hill. "I saw the wagon. Is that it?"

Beth nodded, rubbing her mittened hands together. "Oh, I can hardly wait."

Her excitement was contagious. Callie exchanged glances with Levi and saw him grin, as well. But neither Beth nor John would say anything further until Simon and James arrived to help, having sent the twins up to stay with Nora.

"It's heavy," John advised, jumping up into the bed of the wagon. "And a little fragile. But we can move it with the right leverage."

As Callie watched, Mica snuggling closer and Beth calling suggestions, the four men maneuvered Beth's surprise down from the wagon. Callie's gaze kept straying to Levi. He was so strong, so sure. He must have noticed her looking his way, for he stood a little taller.

"You don't have to carry it all by yourself to impress your lady," John teased him. "There are three more of us, you know."

James straightened. "You can carry my side anytime. My lady's not here."

Callie blushed and thought she saw pink working its way into Levi's cheeks. Still, all the men were sweating by the time they shuffled the thing into the church and set it against the wall.

John stepped back and wiped his brow. "Beth, would you like to do the honors?" He pulled a knife from his belt and handed it to her to cut the twine holding the blanket in place.

Beaming, his sister moved forward and snapped the twine, pulling off the blanket with a flourish. Callie took in the black lacquered sides, the gold paint outlining the name. Fingers tingling, she pressed closer and ran a hand along the smooth wood. Mica's eyes were wide.

"A piano," Simon said, face lifting.

"Egg money must be better than I thought," James put in, rubbing his chin.

Beth blushed. "I used part of my inheritance from Ma. A real church needs a real piano."

Callie glanced at Levi. The tent used for church meetings at Vital Creek had never boasted a piano. Her mind boggled just thinking of carrying the thing up the wild mountain passes. But, oh, to have such an instrument here!

"It will certainly add something to the music," Simon was saying.

"And when I affix wheels to the bottom," John said, "we can move it over to the hall to play for dances."

Levi touched Callie's arm. Very likely he was trying to remind her about the upcoming dance, but all she could see was the piano.

"And Rina's theatricals," James said.

"You're forgetting one thing," Levi said. "No one knows how to play it."

No one? Again her fingers tingled. Was this truly meant for her? Was this the answer to her prayer?

Thank You, Lord. Here's how I can contribute to Wallin Landing.

Beth stepped away from the instrument, head coming up. "Simon can play. He's musical."

Simon shook his head. "I play the violin. There's a world of difference between a stringed instrument and a percussion one."

"Not that he couldn't learn," James said as Beth glared at Simon.

Callie opened the case, and her heart nearly jumped from her chest and onto the keys. It had been so long. What if she'd forgotten?

Mica glanced from the ivory keys to Callie and back, as if wondering the same thing.

John scratched his chin. "I thought you had someone ready to play, Beth, or I would never have helped you pick this out from the catalog."

James put a hand to his back. "Or sprained ourselves carrying it in."

"Beth, this had to have been a huge expense," Levi said. "Can you return it? Sell it to someone in Seattle?"

That did it. She couldn't lose that piano. Callie sidled up to Levi. "Hold Mica."

He took the baby, gaze on his sister.

Beth raised her chin. "I won't return it. We need a piano. I've wanted one since Simon designed the church. If we must, I'll learn to play. It might take a while, and I'm not sure who could teach me, but…"

Callie brought her fingers down on the keys, a thrill running through her as the music flowed from her touch. In Levi's arms, Mica clapped her hands along.

Everyone turned. She could feel them staring at her and almost faltered. Who was she to play a piano in church? Yet something rose higher inside her with each note. This was what she was meant to do.

"Get on board, children," James sang as she hit the chorus. "Get on board, children. Get on board, children. There's room for many and more."

"You can play!" Beth was fairly hopping on her feet. "How marvelous! Oh, how marvelous!" She threw her arms around Callie and hugged, halting Callie's efforts.

Once more pride was shining from Levi's eyes as he moved to join her. Simon, John and James came along, as well.

"It's a bit out of tune," Simon said, head cocked.

"Only to be expected from the jostling it must have taken aboard ship on the way here."

Callie rested her hands in her lap to keep them from leaping back upon the keys.

"Beautiful," Levi said, and he sounded as if he meant more than her playing.

"I see we'll need to lay in a stock of sheet music," John said.

"Oh, *Godey's* has some," Beth told him. "All the latest songs. I have months' worth."

Callie rose, glancing from one face to the next, enthusiasm dipping. "What's sheet music?"

Beth stared at her. "You mean you play entirely from memory?"

Callie shrugged. "I hear it, I can play it."

"Where did you learn?" Levi asked, still with that look as if he'd discovered she could fly.

"We lived over a dance hall in Vancouver one winter," Callie told them all. "I talked the piano player into showing me how to play. Pretty soon I was as good as he was. I used to earn money playing."

James laughed as he clapped Beth on the shoulder. "Behold your virtuoso, sister."

Was that praise or criticism? Levi must have noticed her confusion, for he stepped closer. "My brother means we are blessed to have someone of your talent to play the piano for us."

Talent? She glanced around to find them all smiling and nodding. They believed her good enough to play in church.

They believed in her.

She thought she might bust a button off her suspenders.

"Will you play for Christmas service, Callie?" Beth asked.

Callie nodded, throat too tight to speak.

Levi handed Mica to Beth and turned to Callie. His smile was soft, his look warm. She felt it, too, something more than the music, more than their partnership, more than Christmas. Before she knew what he was about, he pressed a kiss to her cheek.

Joy sparkled in the air, brighter than snowflakes. If she turned her head, she could kiss him back. Maybe he'd put his arms around her, hold her close, tell her that his kindness had grown beyond expectations.

Maybe her present from Levi for Christmas would be the gift of love.

Levi had meant the kiss as no more than a response to the moment, but the touch of his lips to Callie's cheek raised such a tumult of emotion in him that he froze. She had stopped playing moments ago, yet it seemed he still heard a melody in his heart.

James cleared his throat. "Ah, Christmas. How I love thee, eh, Levi?"

Levi couldn't come up with a response, especially with Callie gazing at him that way.

"Drew must have brought in the Christmas tree into the hall by now," Beth said. "Let's go see." She took Mica and led the others out, giving Callie a grin as she passed.

Callie's cheeks were pink, as if the touch of his lips had painted them. "Thank you," she murmured, "for everything. James is right. Christmas can be special."

He tucked her hand in his arm. "It's all the more special with you here. You play so well. Why didn't you tell me?"

She shrugged, gaze on her boots. "It didn't really matter. There wasn't a piano to play—until now."

"Is there anything else you haven't told me?" he teased. "Some other hidden talent I should know about?"

Her blush deepened, and she met his gaze with a smile. "Not me. You?"

Scout's face flashed through his mind. Levi kept his smile in place. "Nothing that matters. Let's go see that tree." He led her out the door.

Before he'd left for the north, his family used to bring in a Yule log. Beth had told him they had decided a few years ago to celebrate with a tree instead. Drew had brought in the perfect specimen, a cone of a fir seven feet tall. He'd erected it in a corner of the hall, just as Beth had planned. The area around the tree was now a beehive of activity, though not enough to take Levi's mind off Callie beside him.

Each family had made a different set of decorations, all orchestrated by Beth. Dottie pointed out the wooden star to Peter as John climbed the ladder to place it at the top of the tree. Simon's children had cut snowflakes from paper, and he lifted first one child and then another to sprinkle the ornaments about.

Drew's children had dipped candles; Catherine and Drew were helping them seat the tapers in tin clips on the branches. James's family had made tiny crowns of gold paper. James kept trying them on, to Seth's giggle and Victoria's frown. Beth, Harry, Tom and Dickie were busy placing bright red apples here and there among the greenery, while, at Beth's hip, Mica tried to grab them back.

Frisco and Sutter had evidently come down with Nora, for they were getting tangled up in their popcorn strings, which Beth must have carried from the main house. Levi led Callie to them.

"Like this," he said, showing them how to loop the strings from branch to branch around the tree. The boys set to work with a will.

Beth came around the tree and drew Levi and Callie back from it.

"We have a small problem," she murmured, Mica in her arms. "I stored some of the presents from Father Christmas in the pantry this morning, and someone's been through them."

Callie stiffened. Levi sighed. "Frisco and Sutter were so excited. I suppose they couldn't wait." He glanced to where Drew and Simon each had one of the twins up on their shoulders to finish the popcorn garland at the top of the tree.

Callie followed his gaze and frowned. "How did they know where to look?"

Beth threw up a hand. "How did Levi and I know where to look? Ma hid them in a different place each year, and we usually found them anyway."

He remembered. Once he'd figured out that Father Christmas was really Drew and Ma, he'd felt rather smug knowing what he was getting before he went to peer into his stocking.

"But you were expecting the presents," Callie protested. "This is all new to my brothers. I think they truly believe some stranger is going to bring them gifts tonight."

Now Beth frowned. "Then who could have sorted through the presents? All the children have been out of school since the theatrical, but everyone has worked hard to keep them busy."

"Let's leave it for now," Levi said. "There was no harm done."

Beth nodded, frown easing. "Very well. I best go help the others." She hurried to rejoin the family around the tree, taking Mica with her.

Callie stepped in front of Levi as if to keep him from following his sister. "If you truly think Frisco and Sutter are guilty, you can't coddle them again."

Levi raised a brow. "I thought we agreed they were innocent."

"My brothers?" She shook her head. "I was hopeful, until I heard Beth's explanation. All the other children are accounted for. Who else could it be?" She waved a hand to encompass his whole family. "You can't tell me one of your brothers did it."

Levi smiled. "I imagine James peeked a time or two before I was born, but as everyone likely bought the gifts at his store, he wouldn't have to this time. Drew would have been too upright, Simon probably stopped believing in Father Christmas when he was six. John would have been too good to cheat. I know it wasn't me, and Beth and my sisters-in-law would have had no need."

Callie cocked her head to look up at him. "What about me? I might have burned with curiosity."

"Up until this morning," he said, "I'm not sure you thought Father Christmas was even coming."

She sighed. "Which means it has to be Frisco and Sutter. You can't let them get away with it."

Levi shrugged. "Why not? As I said, no harm done."

"But they cheated," Callie protested. "You know as well as I do how that could turn out."

Levi felt as if someone had dumped snow on his head. "What do you mean?"

His stomach cramped as he waited to hear her denounce his actions at Vital Creek. But Callie merely shook her head.

"You must have seen what happens when one partner cheats another," she told him. "Anger, lashing out and worse. Why, I've known men to kill when they thought their claims were taken from them."

So had he, and he'd been the one to take it.

"This isn't a claim, Callie," he said. "It's just two boys who couldn't wait to see their Christmas presents."

"Christmas presents today, mining claims tomorrow," she insisted, hands on her hips. "They have to understand that keeping your word means something. Pa never taught them that. Neither did Adam. They kept promising life would be better. It only got worse."

She turned away, but not before he saw the tears shining in her eyes. He felt as if his own heart was breaking. He drew her farther from the others, gathered her close.

"I know how strong the lure of gold can be, Callie," he murmured. "We won't let Frisco and Sutter follow that path, but right now, they're just boys. They'll make mistakes, and so will we. The important thing is to forgive, learn from those mistakes and become better."

She rested her head against his chest, and he only wanted to keep holding her like this, sheltering her from every loss.

"But if they don't know they've made a mistake," she murmured, "how will they learn from it?"

Levi started at the truth of her statement. Was that his problem? Had Ma and the rest of his family looked the other way so many times, thinking they were being kind to their littlest brother, that he'd failed to develop the character necessary to withstand the promise of the gold fields? He might have made different choices if he had been held accountable more often, yet he found it hard to blame them for his choices. He knew right from wrong. So should the boys.

"All right," he told Callie. "We'll speak to them this afternoon." He leaned back to gaze into her face. Hope gleamed in her tear-filled eyes. Was he mad to see something more?

"Don't cry, Callie," he said. "All I want is for you and the boys to have a happy Christmas. Let's see what we can do about that."

Chapter Eighteen

When Levi looked at her that way, Callie found it hard to believe it could be anything but a happy Christmas. He made her dream of the impossible—peace, joy, love. How easy to just bask in the glow, but she had a duty to her brothers. If the twins had disturbed the Christmas presents, they had to be held accountable. Frisco and Sutter had to grow into finer men than their father or brother, men who understood the value of family over riches, men who kept their promises. She couldn't lose anyone else to the gold fields.

She wasn't sure what was going to happen after the tree was decorated, but Levi's family stayed together most of the afternoon playing games and singing carols. Whenever the opportunity arose, Levi cradled her hand in his. He was careful to explain things to her quietly, so she understood the traditions, like the fact that the candles, standing tall and proud among the greenery, remained unlit. That spectacle, Levi told her, was for Christmas Day.

Each of the men slipped out from time to time, often with something bundled under his coat. As they usually returned with more wood for the hearth or a treat for the children, Callie paid them little mind. It was late in the afternoon, as the shadows lengthened, when Beth clapped her hands to get everyone's attention.

"Time to head for home," she said, smiling at Peter, who was drowsing in Dottie's arms. Mica had her head against Callie's shoulder, as well. "We'll regroup in the morning for services."

"And the dance tomorrow night," James declared, giving Rina a twirl with one hand over her head. His wife smiled at him while Victoria stood watchful. Callie caught Levi's eye and smiled, as well. A real dance!

As the Wallins gathered up their children and left, Levi led Callie, Mica and the boys across the yard to the parsonage.

He paused at the door, face solemn. He was going to talk to her brothers at last. Callie stood taller.

"Boys, I have some bad news," he said, looking from face to face. "It seems Father Christmas stored some of his presents in the hall. I understand someone pawed through the pack and mixed things up."

Frisco and Sutter's brows shot skyward.

"Who?" Frisco demanded. "He ought to be ashamed of himself."

"Can we help Father Christmas sort them out?" Sutter wanted to know.

Levi met Callie's gaze, clearly as confused as she was. She'd been so sure her brothers were the guilty ones, but Frisco and Sutter were simply not that good at acting. Could they be innocent after all?

Levi seemed to think so, for he laid his hands on her brothers' shoulders. "I believe things have been settled.

I just wanted you to be aware in case you found something odd in your stocking."

The boys nodded and slipped past him into the house.

Levi paused with Callie at his side. "I don't understand. Did I describe it too vaguely?"

"No," Callie murmured, watching her brothers take off their coats and hang them beside the door. "They sounded too concerned to be guilty. You've seen how Frisco acts when he's caught, blustering out an excuse. This was something different."

In her arms, Mica wiggled as if she didn't understand, either.

Levi shook his head. "Maybe Beth was wrong. Maybe someone else in the family went through the presents looking for something."

Callie could only hope he was right. If her brothers were innocent, accusing them outright was a sure way to hurt them.

She carried Mica into the parsonage, Levi closing the door behind them. But instead of starting supper, he headed for the side door. Odd. The wood box was full. With a shrug, Callie turned for the stove herself.

A cry from Sutter and Frisco had her whirling. Her brothers were running for the hearth, where all five stockings bulged.

Father Christmas had come earlier than expected.

She set Mica in her chair and hurried for her room.

"Callie!" Sutter called. "Come back! You have to see what you got."

Callie grabbed the harmonica from where she'd hidden it in her mother's pack and rushed back to the hearth. The boys had removed their stockings and carried them to the rug to dump them out. She had a feeling there'd be two more socks to darn by the haste in which they'd pulled the socks from the nails. She went to slide the harmonica into Levi's stocking, then ventured over to her brothers as Mica raised her hand and grunted in her chair, begging to be picked up again.

Though they'd each received an orange and a handkerchief, the other gifts held more interest.

"Look, Callie." Sutter lifted a steel fishhook. "I'll catch lots of fish with this, and they won't wiggle off."

"Very nice," she said with a smile.

Frisco held up a pocket knife. "And I can make tinder with this, so you won't have to work so hard to light the fire."

Callie put an arm around each of them. "Did any sister ever have such thoughtful brothers?"

Sutter pulled away to hop to his feet. "Let's see what Mica got." He ran for her stocking.

Callie straightened to go help him take down the stocking more carefully. Both boys followed her to the table, where Sutter placed the stocking in front of the baby. Mica patted it, smiling at them all.

"You got to open it," Frisco told her. "Here, I'll show you."

"Let me," Sutter protested, reaching for it, as well.

"I'll open it," Callie said, suiting word to action. Inside was a wooden rattle and a rag doll with a sew-on face that smiled as broadly as Mica did.

"Baby stuff," Frisco said with a sniff.

Sutter frowned. "What did you expect? She's a baby."

Mica seemed happy enough with her gifts. She took up the rattle and shook it, giggling at the noise. Then she bonked it down on the rag doll.

Callie picked up the doll. "Maybe we'll save this for later."

Levi pushed through the door just then. "I told you Father Christmas was all mixed up. Look what he left by the woodpile."

He held out a sled. The center panel was painted red with gilt outlining a winter scene, the runners made of metal. It was far prettier than the sturdy variety she'd seen prospectors and their mules pull up north.

Sutter and Frisco ran to him as Levi winked at her.

"That must be for me," Frisco said, holding out his hands.

Sutter elbowed him. "No, me."

"I'm fairly sure it was meant for all of us," Levi said. "It's plenty long to hold you two and Mica. Maybe even Callie."

Callie moved closer, eyeing the sled. "I'm not getting on that. I've seen them tip over too many times."

"Not this one," Levi assured her. "See boys, how the runners curve at the front and back? That's for stability and speed."

Frisco laid hold of it. "Let's try it now."

Sutter nodded, fairly dancing on his feet.

Someone needed to remember what was important. "We should start dinner first," Callie reminded them.

Her brothers turned on her. "But Callie!" they chorused.

Levi gave her a pleading look. "But Callie."

How was she to answer that? They were mad, the lot of them. It was cold. It was getting dark. There were chores to be done. They would only come back wet and worn.

But the sled did look like it would go really fast. How fast? Only one way to find out.

"All right," she said, setting them all to grinning. "But only until the light fades. Now, go bundle up."

Her brothers ran to comply.

Levi closed the distance between them. "Thank you."

She jerked her head toward the hearth. "You haven't looked in your stocking."

He chuckled. "Very likely it's coal."

"You haven't been that naughty," Callie said with a smile.

He raised a brow as if he wasn't too sure about that, but he leaned the sled against the wall and crossed to the hearth. She could hardly stand still as he pulled out the harmonica.

"What's this?" he asked, face splitting in a grin.

Arms still only half in their coats, Frisco and Sutter skidded across the floor to his side.

"Father Christmas sure got mixed up," Frisco said. "That was probably meant to be mine."

"No, mine," Sutter said, eyes shining.

Callie crossed to Levi. "No, it's Levi's," she told them firmly. "He had one when he was a boy, and he lost it. Father Christmas just brought it back."

Frisco and Sutter deflated.

Levi had been fingering the silver filigree on the instrument. Now he lifted it to his lips. Music, low and mournful, weaved through the room. It brought back memories of huddling around a fire, knowing she was safe with her mother and father, even as the wolves called from the wood. Once more gooseflesh pimpled her arms.

When he finished, Mica clapped her hands and wiggled as if asking for more. Callie knew just how she felt. She would have requested another tune, but Levi slid the harmonica into his pocket.

"I'll have to thank Father Christmas when I see him," he said, glancing at Callie with a smile.

She returned his smile, warm inside.

"Can we go?" Frisco demanded, shrugging into his coat and heading for the door.

Sutter glanced at the hearth. "But Callie hasn't looked in her stocking."

Now, that probably did contain coal given how she'd behaved when she'd first arrived at Wallin Landing. "It can wait," Callie said.

"Nonsense," Levi said. "*We* can wait." His look to her brothers defied them to say otherwise.

"Why don't you get Mica ready?" Callie told the twins. "That way we won't be delayed further."

They hurried to find Mica's wrap.

Callie approached the stocking. She knew Father Christmas hadn't filled it. Very likely Levi or one of his brothers had. That must be why they'd kept leaving the hall, to fill all the stockings. Levi's brothers wouldn't give her coal, no matter how she'd vexed them. But what would they think to give her?

She took the stocking down carefully and peered inside. Like her brothers, she'd received an orange and a handkerchief with her initials embroidered on one corner. Beth's work, most likely. But something else pressed against the stocking. She put her hand in and drew out a tiny brass key.

"You find it fits this," Levi murmured. He went to the cupboard and pulled a box from behind the flour sack. Made of polished wood, it was about the size of her hand. Levi took the key and inserted it in the opening on the front, then twisted it round and round. She could hear something grinding inside with each movement.

Her brothers wandered closer. "What is it?" Sutter asked.

"Open the lid," Levi told Callie.

A tingle running through her, she did as he asked.

Inside lay a brass cylinder next to a fine-toothed steel comb, all covered with glass. Immediately the cylinder started rotating, and high tinkling music flowed. Callie stared at it in wonder.

"The song is called 'The Blue Danube,'" Levi told her. "It will keep playing as long as you wind up the box."

Sutter stuck out his lip as if impressed. Frisco shook his head. "More music?"

As if there could ever be enough! Callie touched the smooth wood, feeling as if the melody was writing itself on her heart.

"Do you like it?" Levi asked.

Callie tore her gaze away. "Like it? I love it! I've never heard of anything more marvelous. Don't you see, Levi? Father Christmas gave me my very own orchestra!"

The day might have been cold, but Levi felt warm inside as he, Callie, Mica and the boys took the sled for its first run. He wasn't sure why he was so relieved his presents had been well received. The boys had seemed pleased with the fishhooks, but the way Callie had lit up to the sound of the music box made him want to puff out his chest.

Now he led her and her family to the edge of the hill, where the path sloped down to the main clearing. As Callie held a squirming Mica, he positioned the sled, then nodded to Frisco and Sutter to climb on. Once the boys had scrambled into place, he pulled back slightly.

"One, two," he started.

"Three!" Frisco shouted, and Levi pushed.

They shot down the hill. He had barely straightened before they had reached the bottom and spun to a stop. Leaping off the sled, they looked up at him expectantly.

Levi motioned with his gloved hand. "Well, bring it back up. You ride it, you carry it back. Those are the rules."

They each grabbed a curved end of a runner to drag the sled back up.

Callie shook her head. "They're going to wear themselves out."

Levi shot her a grin. "We should be so fortunate."

Her chuckle made him feel even warmer.

But while he enjoyed having her beside him, watching the boys' excitement, he wanted to try something else.

"Care for a turn?" he asked Callie as he positioned the sled for another run.

She shook her head, stepping back. "I'm not putting Mica on that."

Levi nodded to Frisco and Sutter, who climbed back aboard, then he shoved them to start. Their delighted squeals echoed back up the hill.

Levi straightened. "I wasn't asking about Mica. I was asking about you."

Callie eyed her brothers, who were hurrying back up with the sled. "I don't know. What if it tips over?"

"Then we'll fall in the snow," Levi said with a shrug.

She raised a brow. *"We?"*

"Did you think I was going to wait much longer for a turn?" he teased.

Callie handed Mica to Sutter as he came abreast. "Hold her. I'm going down with Levi."

Sutter's eyes widened.

Frisco held the sled in place as Levi helped Callie settle near the front. Then he climbed on behind her, legs straddling hers, chest pressed against her back, arms braced beside her. Her body was tense, but he hoped that meant she was as excited as he was to give it a try.

"Push," he told Frisco, rocking forward to help the boy.

Frisco shoved, and the sled was away.

Wind whipped past Levi's cheeks as they flew down the hill. The trees, the snow, everything became a blur, until it was only him and Callie, dashing through the snow. Her laughter tickled his chest as she shouted against the air. He wrapped his arms around her and hung on.

The sled spun to a stop at the bottom of the hill. For a moment, he just held her, resting his cheek against the top of her head. His chest was heaving, but not from any exertion. He didn't want to move.

But she shifted against him, and he knew he had to get up. Climbing off, he offered her his hand to rise. She scrambled up, eyes shining, cheeks red. There was nothing for it. He pulled her close and kissed her.

And all at once the sled seemed tame. Even the thrill of finding a nugget in the stream was nothing compared to the feel of Callie in his arms. This was what he'd been seeking all his life, this exhilaration, this joy.

Callie pulled back to stare at him, and he couldn't tell whether she was shocked or delighted.

"Hey!" Frisco's call echoed down the hill. "You got to bring it back. Those are the rules."

The rules. The rules said Levi was a minister; Callie was his ward. The rules said he was to treat her like a sister. But there was nothing brotherly about the emotions singing through him. He was only glad his back was turned to the twins so they most likely didn't know what he and Callie were doing.

"We should go," he murmured, gathering up the sled.

She didn't argue with him as he started up the hill. But she didn't suggest going down the hill again, either. In fact, a short while later, she took Mica and returned to the house. He could only hope he hadn't offended her.

The boys wanted to keep sledding, and it seemed to Levi to be the wisest course of action. Certainly he needed some time for his blood to cool. He stayed out with the boys until they could barely see each other in the twilight. Sutter heaved a happy sigh as they headed for the parsonage at last.

"Father Christmas sure knows what to get a boy," Callie's brother said as he entered the house.

Frisco caught Levi's arm to keep him from following. His face in the light from the door was troubled.

"Do you think Father Christmas might have gotten mixed up on the sled, Uncle Levi?" he murmured. "Davy told me he wanted one real bad. Maybe this was supposed to be his instead of mine and Sutter's."

Levi was fairly sure each of his brothers had purchased a sled for their families, with the possible exception of John, who was capable of making his own when Peter was old enough. "You'll have to ask Davy tomorrow to be certain," he told the boy, "but I think this was meant for you."

"Really?" Hope kindled in Frisco's blue-gray eyes.

"Me and Sutter never had anything so nice. I thought maybe it was a mistake."

"No mistake," Levi assured him, throat tightening. "Take the sled around back for safekeeping. I'll be in in a moment."

Frisco hefted the sled and carried it through the breezeway.

Levi straightened and walked out into the twilight.

Is that the lesson You've been trying to teach me, Lord? Do I believe deep down I don't deserve anything nice? Have I felt empty so long I can't accept it's possible to be full again?

The moon was rising, plump and nearly round. The silver light glowed on the snow, brightening everything. Callie had brightened his world. Like Frisco, he hadn't expected anything and had been given a priceless gift. He wouldn't take it for granted.

And that meant he would have to tell her the truth, even if it cost him everything.

Chapter Nineteen

Christmas morning passed in a haze for Callie. She gave Frisco, Sutter and Mica the caps Nora had helped her make. Mica kept trying to tug the wool off her hair. Her brothers ducked their heads as if embarrassed, but they wore the caps when they all went out sledding, where they discovered that Davy and the other Wallin children also had sleds to race against. Beth brought over the red-and-green plaid dress Nora had made for Callie, and she wore it to church, feeling as if she fit in with the festivities. She and Simon played "We Three Kings" together, as it was the only Christmas song she knew well enough, and the whole congregation sang along.

But every time she had a moment to think, she thought of Levi.

His smile when she'd listened to the wonderful music box for the first time.

His delight in watching her brothers sled.

The feel of him behind and around her as they'd sped down the slope.

The sweet pressure of his lips against hers.

She'd been afraid of falling off the sled. Instead, she was falling in love, with a preacher no less!

She still did her best not to show it. He had enough on his hands what with leading worship, dealing with her overly excited brothers and supporting his family. Besides, she didn't want to give Beth any ammunition.

Levi's sister was clearly the chief instigator of Christmas. She gathered up everyone and made sure they arrived for worship on time, then chivied them all to the main house afterward for a Christmas dinner. Callie had never seen such food. But Beth wasn't done yet. She organized games for the children, activities for the adults. She was like a bee, buzzing through clover.

And Callie was fairly certain she was behind the hat Frisco and Sutter presented her for Christmas. The little oval was made of stiffened black velvet and trimmed with mallard feathers that turned iridescent when they caught the light. It looked rather fetching on her hair, even if it was the most impractical thing she'd ever seen for keeping the rain off.

But Beth's crowning achievement by far was the kissing bough.

They all repaired to the hall after dinner, and Beth handed each of her brothers a taper so they could light the candles on the Christmas tree, to oohs and aahs of appreciation. Then she had Drew hang the bough near the top of the room with similar fanfare. The bundle of fir branches was entwined with white satin ribbons and dotted with red apples. Beth swiftly stationed each of the married couples under it for a kiss, and she kept eyeing Levi as if calculating how she could maneuver him to the right spot. Callie stayed as far from the device as possible. The last time Levi had kissed her, she'd nearly swooned from the delight. She wasn't about to go into raptures in front of his whole family.

She was helping Beth lay cloths on makeshift tables for the food at the dance that night, waiting her turn on a game, Mica safe in Catherine's arms, when the door of the hall opened and a man stepped inside. He shook snow off his shoulders as he removed his broad-brimmed black hat. Callie recognized the lawman who had questioned her in Seattle.

Levi strode to meet him. "Deputy McCormick. Merry Christmas."

Beth set about rearranging the linens stacked on the table, back to the door. Callie was more interested in what had brought the deputy out this way.

"Pastor," he drawled to Levi. Then he nodded about the room. "Wallin family all. Sorry to interrupt."

Levi clapped him on the shoulder. "No interruption. You're welcome to join us."

Some of the others called their support.

The lawman's smile was tight. "Just wanted a word with you and Miss Murphy."

Her? Callie startled, and Beth looked at her askance.

"Excuse me," Callie murmured before hurrying to Levi's side.

"Is something wrong, Hart?" Levi asked, taking Callie's hand as she drew near. His touch sent a shiver through her, but she didn't think Levi noticed as the deputy glanced between them, eyes the color of a well-used shotgun.

"I've ridden out Columbia way several times now, looking for those men you spotted. Never came across them."

"Then they must have had business elsewhere," Levi said.

Callie nodded her agreement, shoulders relaxing. It had been nearly a month, after all.

"Maybe," the deputy allowed. "But yesterday I rode as far as the Murphy cabin. Found it all tore up."

Callie stiffened. "What! It's still ours until the state hears about Adam's death."

Levi's eyes were narrowed. "Animals?"

"Not that I could tell," Deputy McCormick said. "No scat and no scratch marks. Whoever was inside was looking for something. The table was overturned, floorboards pried up and loose rocks in the hearth pulled out."

Callie made a face. "That was stupid. We never had much. We sure wouldn't have left it behind."

"Just thought you should know, ma'am," he said with a nod. "I'll leave you two to celebrate the season."

She couldn't seem to move, but Levi caught the lawman's arm. "Join us, Hart. There's plenty of food and a dance tonight."

The deputy pulled back to slip his hat on his short-cropped dark hair. "I'm on duty today so the sheriff can be home with his family. I best keep riding."

"At least let us send you with some food," Levi insisted. Turning, he called across the hall. "Beth! Can you bring the deputy a bag of those cookies we brought up here?"

McCormick backed toward the door. "There's no need."

"Nonsense." Levi went to help his sister.

Callie eyed the deputy. He was shifting from foot to foot as if he couldn't wait to get out into the snow. It seemed gold wasn't the only thing that drew men.

Beth came up with a cookie and held it out stiffly to the deputy. "Here you go. Safe travels."

Where was the generous Beth Callie had come to admire? Surely she didn't begrudge the man a few cookies.

He hastily removed his hat again and inclined his head, though his gaze never left Beth's face. "Thank you, ma'am, and merry Christmas."

Beth thawed. "Merry Christmas to you, too, Deputy."

Levi had come up behind her. Now he grinned, pointing above their heads. "And look who got caught under the kissing bough this time, Beth."

Beth and the deputy glanced up, faces blanching. Then they scrambled away from each other. The lawman backed for the door as if he didn't trust any of them not to draw on him if he took his eyes off them. The door slammed shut behind him.

"Time for another game!" Beth declared, dashing back to the rest of her family with just as much determination.

"Why does Beth dislike him?" Callie asked Levi.

Levi was watching his sister. "I don't know. Beth used to think him a fine fellow, even made cow eyes at him when she was a girl. I wonder what changed."

So did Callie, but she had no chance to ask her friend as the afternoon progressed. All the Wallins stayed together, enjoying the fellowship, until the shadows lengthened outside once more. Then one by one the families walked back to their homes to prepare for the dance that night. An older couple who were neighbors were coming to care for the children. Callie had barely reached the door of the parsonage before Beth swooped in beside her.

"Oh, no, you don't," she proclaimed. "All the ladies are getting ready at my cabin. You are coming with me."

"But Mica," Callie protested. "Frisco and Sutter."

Levi smiled. "I'll see to them. You go and have fun."

She wasn't sure how much fun it would be watching the others getting dressed. After all, she was already wearing the nicest dress she'd ever owned. But she'd seen how hard Beth had worked to make Christmas special. If she could help Levi's sister now, she would.

Callie touched Beth's arm. "All right, but first, come inside with me. I have something for you."

Beth's eyes lit, and she followed Callie into the parsonage. Callie led her to the bedroom and went to her mother's pack. Beth smiled down at the chest at the foot of the bed.

"I remember when Drew carved this for Levi."

Callie glanced up. "Your brother made that?"

Beth nodded. "Pa carved one for him, Simon and James when they turned twelve. He passed away when John was ten. Drew carved the chests for the rest of us. The salmon is perfect for Levi. They travel far to the sea, you know, but they always come back to where they were born."

"I guess salmon are prodigals, too," Callie said, fingers closing around what she was seeking.

Beth was looking at her oddly as Callie rose, and something inside her fluttered as she held out her mother's comb.

"Merry Christmas, Beth," she said.

Beth took it, gazed down at it. Callie could scarcely breathe.

"It's beautiful," Beth murmured. She flung her arms around Callie and hugged. "Thank you!"

"It was Ma's," Callie confessed, leaning back. "Pa got

it for her the first time he found some gold. It's from the inside of a shell." What, was she babbling now?

Beth stroked the iridescence. "Are you sure you want to part with it?"

Suddenly, she was. "Yes. I want to wish my dearest friend a merry Christmas."

Tears sparkled in Beth's deep blue eyes. "Oh, Callie. I'm so glad we're friends." She reached out and seized Callie's hand. "Now, come on! I have a surprise for you, too."

Beth should have been exhausted after all her exertions. Instead, she hummed to herself as she led Callie down the hill and around the main cabin to the path through the woods to her house. It was a neat little cabin, with boxes under the windows and a wide front porch, where a lamp was burning. Beth climbed the stairs and opened the door.

All of Levi's sisters-in-law were clustered near the hearth, their skirts so full Callie could hardly make out the table behind them. Gowned in shiny taffeta and soft velvet, they had lace draping their shoulders and hems. She could almost hear her father's voice. Such fine clothes. All that was missing was the big house and servants.

"You're already dressed," Callie said with a look to Beth, who dimpled.

"Surprise," Nora said with a smile.

"We are here to help you dress," Catherine explained.

"Something special for your first Christmas with us," Dottie agreed.

"There's nothing like feeling yourself a princess," Rina put in, "if only for a little while."

A princess? They separated to give her a clear view of

the table. On it lay a dress of lustrous blue that glowed in the lamplight. Midnight blue velvet made a diamond pattern along the hem and V-neck. Callie wandered closer, put out a hand to touch the soft fabric, then pulled back. This was for her? "I couldn't."

"You can," Beth insisted. "We all pitched in to sew it for you, based on Nora's measurements. And there's more."

Callie didn't know whether to feel like a princess or a doll as they helped her out of the plaid dress and into the blue. Catherine produced slippers to match, bending to help Callie try them on. The dainty satin shoes were only the slightest bit loose. Rina tucked pearl-studded combs into Callie's hair. Beth draped a white wool shawl over her shoulders. Seeing herself in Beth's looking glass, Callie could hardly believe her eyes.

"I'm beautiful," she said, staring at the reflection.

The others gathered around her, smiling their agreement.

"Yes, you are," Beth said, dusting a stray hair off Callie's shoulder. "But you were already. We just shined up the silver."

Callie whirled and hugged her tight. "Thank you."

They all murmured their delight as she embraced them in turn.

Beth hurried to change as well, then they all set out. Callie wore her boots as far as the hall, careful to keep the hem of the dress from touching the ground. Once inside, Beth directed her to the back of the room, where benches had been set up, and Callie changed into her new slippers. Her fingers were shaking again as the room grew more crowded with all the Wallins and their friends and neighbors.

Beth caught her arm. "There's Levi. Come on."

She was glad for Beth's insistence, for she couldn't seem to make her slippers move. They felt so light on her feet after the heavy boots, yet each step was like walking through wet snow. What would he think of her now?

She was only a few feet away when he spotted her. He froze, staring. Callie stopped, swallowed. Then he smiled, and she knew whatever Beth and the others had done, it had been worth the price.

For the first time in her life, she felt beautiful inside and out, and she wasn't afraid to show it.

Levi couldn't take his eyes off Callie. The dress outlined her figure, brought color to her cheeks. Her hair gleamed as brightly as the pearls holding it back. He hardly knew he had moved until he found himself standing right in front of her. She gazed up at him as if searching for something in his face. Anyone looking at him would know he was besotted.

"Ahem."

Beth stood beside them, foot tapping under her pink skirts. She pointed over Levi's head. He didn't need to glance up to know he and Callie were standing under the kissing bough.

"Merry Christmas, Callie," he murmured, bending to brush his lips against her cheek. She trembled as he pulled away, and a similar tremor shook him.

"Well?" Beth demanded, hands on hips. "What are you waiting for? Go and dance."

Bemused, he took Callie's arm and led her out onto the floor.

For the first time since he'd spotted her, she faltered. "I don't know how to dance, remember?" she murmured, glancing around as if she thought the lack was spelled out on her forehead for all to notice.

"Of course you do," Levi said, hand on her waist. "I'm sure you danced a time or two at Vital Creek."

"That was different," she insisted. "It was just a bunch of sourdoughs hopping around the creek bank. This is fancy."

"Not so fancy." He spun her around, and he thought he saw a smile threatening on her pink lips. "Most folks here never took lessons from a dance master."

Her eyes widened until they reflected the blue of her dress. "You mean a man will come teach you how to dance?"

"More likely you learn by watching your mother and father or older brother and sister. I did. And this is just a waltz. Listen. I think you'll recognize the tune."

She blinked, and a smile won free. "'The Blue Danube'!"

Levi twirled her around the floor. "Exactly. I asked Simon to play it."

She floated along with him, light as a feather in his arms. "Thank you. This is all marvelous. I just have one question."

"Ask it," Levi said, willing to give her anything in that moment.

Callie gazed up at him. "What's a Danube?"

Levi laughed. "I have no idea. We'll ask Simon or John tomorrow."

She spun through the music with him, and he didn't step on her toes once. The next dance would have a caller. All he and Callie had to do was listen and do what he said. He wasn't sure who Beth had recruited to call the dances, but he wasn't surprised when Drew stood up beside Simon and his fiddle at the head of the room.

"Claim your sweetheart," Drew ordered in his deep voice. "I want two lines right down the middle. Let's have a reel."

His family and neighbors lined up, women on one side, men on the other. Callie was sandwiched between Beth, who was partnering Tom, and Rina, who was partnering James. Levi knew the two women wouldn't let her put her foot wrong.

Indeed, as the dance progressed, Callie became ever more sure of herself, her movements smooth, her smile wide. She picked up Drew's calls easily, skipped about with more enthusiasm than half the women on the floor. When she had to wait, she grasped her blue skirts and swished them back and forth to the music. All Levi could do was grin.

He wasn't the only one. Harry, Tom and even tongue-tied Dickie renewed their pursuit. Harry and Tom were doomed to disappointment, though she did favor Dickie with a dance.

"She's the belle of the ball," Beth said beside Levi with a happy sigh as they watched the couple. "I knew she would be."

"No doubt," Levi said as Dickie tripped and Callie propped him up with an encouraging look that made his round face turn even redder.

"You're sweet on her, aren't you?" Beth accused.

No sense denying it when his feelings must be written on his face. "Yes, but don't get your hopes up, Beth. She may not feel the same way."

Beth shook her head. "It's plain as day she cares for

you, Levi." She sidled closer. "Tonight would be the perfect time to propose."

He must have hesitated too long before answering, for she nudged him. "Come on, Levi. What do you have to lose?"

Everything.

He was just glad the dance ended then, and Harry and Tom closed around Beth, allowing Levi to make his escape.

Dickie was stammering his thanks to Callie when Levi approached.

"You did real well," she assured the shy logger. "Try asking Beth. I think she'll say yes."

Dickie lowered his gaze to his boots. "Oh, I couldn't."

Levi grinned at him. "A minister I knew used to say that a gentleman must pick himself up to move forward."

Callie met his gaze. "So I hear."

What was she suggesting? It wasn't shyness that made him think twice about revealing his feelings.

Dickie shuffled his feet. "You don't understand, Pastor. Your sister is pretty and nice and really smart. I don't know if she'd ever look at the likes of me."

Callie put out her hand to him. "It's easy to see your own faults, but everyone has them. You have to focus on your strengths. You're kind to everyone, you're a hard worker from what I hear and you sing real pretty in church."

The tops of Dickie's ears were turning red under his short-cropped hair. "Thank you, Miss Murphy. Maybe you could tell that to Miss Beth."

"Maybe you should show her," Callie said, withdrawing her hand. "Better yet, believe it yourself. You're a fine fellow, Mr. Morgan. Don't forget that."

"Thank you, ma'am." Dickie wandered off looking thoughtful.

Levi shook his head. "Good advice, Callie. I think he needed to hear it."

"So did I," Callie murmured. She started to put her hand on her shoulder and seemed to think better of it. "When you brought us here, all I could see was how different I was. Now I know there's nothing wrong with being different, so long as you use that difference to benefit others."

"Weighty thoughts, Miss Murphy," he said, impressed. "Perhaps you should give the next sermon."

"That's your job," she countered. "Mine's to look out for Frisco, Sutter and Mica, and to see how else I can help at Wallin Landing. Maybe some concerts to start."

Levi raised a brow. "Concerts?"

She nodded. "We have some real musical talent. Simon and his violin. You and your harmonica. I don't know if you can tell up at the front of the church, but Dickie and Dottie have fine voices."

"And you on the piano. I think it's a great idea. One of the reasons John wanted to start a library was so folks could have access to culture."

She glanced up and smiled. "Oh, look. Simon's done with his break. Can we dance some more?"

"I thought you'd never ask." Levi offered her his arm.

Around them, others were getting ready, too. James had taken Drew's place as caller, and Levi could only hope his flamboyant older brother wouldn't try anything funny. Rina had consented to partner Harry, and Dickie, grinning so widely his face broadened, was escorting Beth onto the floor. The way to the refreshment table stood open, giving Levi a clear view for a moment.

Perhaps that was why he spotted Zachariah and Willard filling their pockets with food.

The music started, and he went through the steps of the dance, trying to catch another glimpse of the pair. They should have headed south days ago. Why were they still in Wallin Landing? It was possible a neighbor had taken them in for the winter, offering board for work. But why would they need to steal food, then? Or had they been too proud to ask for help this time after how they'd parted from Levi?

When the music ended, he seized Callie's hand and drew her aside. "Did you notice our prospector friends among the crowd?"

She glanced around "No. I figured they were long gone."

Levi followed her gaze, but saw only friends and family. "I'm certain they were by the refreshment table when we started dancing again. I don't like the thought of anyone out in this cold."

She nodded. "We both know the damage it can do to a body. We'll go out and look for them tomorrow, let them know they're welcome to stay in the warmth."

It was the best he could do at the moment. But he couldn't help wondering if there was more to the story of Zachariah and Willard than misplaced pride.

Chapter Twenty

Callie floated back to the parsonage after the dance, for all she'd swapped her pretty slippers for boots. Beth had said to leave the cleanup until tomorrow. It was just as well. Callie wasn't sure she'd be much good. She couldn't stop thinking about the evening. She'd danced every round, mostly with Levi. Beth said that meant he had serious intentions.

She cast him a glance as he walked beside her the short distance between the hall and the door of the house. The snow had started falling again, harder this time, and already she could see it sparkling in his hair like stars. Was he truly thinking about marriage?

He opened the door, letting her go before him into the house. They'd kept the stove and hearth banked; the room felt warm after the chill of the snow.

"I'll fetch the boys and Mica from the main house," he promised.

Callie caught his arm before he could leave. "Thank you, Levi, for everything." She stood on tiptoe and pressed a kiss against his cheek, feeling the beginnings of stubble. His arms stole around her, held her against him a moment, and her heart started beating faster. He was going to kiss her again. She knew it. Her lips were pursing in anticipation.

But he released her and hurried back out into the snow.

Callie sighed as she closed the door, then headed for the bedroom to change before her brothers or Mica could accidentally damage the beautiful dress. She couldn't help giving one last twirl, the skirts belling out around her. Beth seemed so certain Levi loved Callie. Why did he wait to proclaim his love? Did he hope she'd tell him her feelings first? She had insisted she didn't want to court. Perhaps he hesitated because he was as worried as Dickie she might not return his love. Perhaps he thought his case hopeless and was content to pine away at her side.

Perhaps she'd been listening to Beth too much.

She had her coat on over her nightgown for warmth and modesty when Levi returned with her brothers and Mica. The baby went readily to Callie's arms, head down and thumb in mouth. Even the boys trudged for the loft with a murmur of "Merry Christmas."

"Looks like someone finally tired them out," Callie marveled.

"They aren't the only ones," Levi murmured. "Someone danced my feet off." He gave her a wink before heading after her brothers.

She should be tired as well, but as she lay in bed, scenes of the day played out in her mind. Frisco and Sutter racing down the hill. Beth and the deputy caught under the kissing bough. All the Wallin ladies making her look like a princess. Levi dancing, and dancing, holding her in his arms and looking at her as if his heart would burst.

And she made up her mind to tell him how she felt at the first opportunity.

Callie woke to Mica's happy gurgle, then dressed quickly in the cold. It must have been earlier than usual, because no light gleamed around the curtain. And there was the oddest sound, as if a dozen women were sighing over and over, just beyond the house. Callie bundled up Mica and went to peer out the window.

All she saw was white, swirling wildly past the glass. The hall, the church, were invisible. It was as if the entire world had disappeared.

Fear stabbed her. Hugging Mica close, she hurried out into the main room.

"Blizzard," she said to Levi, who was standing by the stove.

He turned to her. Though he smiled as if to reassure her, she saw the lines of tension fanning out from his eyes. "I heard it come up early this morning. I've already warned the boys not to open a window or door or go outside. So long as we stay put, we'll be fine."

She wanted to believe him. Her brothers came thudding down the stairs.

"Did you see it, Callie?" Sutter wanted to know.

"You can't see it," Frisco told him. "It's nothing but white."

"And it's nothing to sneeze at," Levi reminded them, bringing two steaming cups to the table. "But thanks to you two, we're all set. We have plenty of wood for the fire and the stove, and plenty of food and water. We just have to wait it out."

His matter-of-fact approach calmed her. Callie set Mica in her chair and went to pour herself a cup of cocoa.

"How long do we have to stay inside?" Sutter asked, holding his cup with both hands as if to warm himself. A cowlick stood up at the back of his head. Callie smoothed it down as she passed.

"It could be hours," Levi admitted with a smile to Callie as she came up beside him. "It could be all day."

Both of her brothers groaned.

"It won't be so bad," Callie told them, pausing to take a sip of the silky chocolate. "You can do some chores. We can read."

"But the sled," Sutter protested.

"Just think how much snow the storm will leave behind," Levi said.

"It was getting rutted with everyone coming to the dance," Frisco allowed. He elbowed Sutter. "I get to be in front the next time we go down."

Sutter's face darkened. "It was my turn to go first."

This could be a long storm. Callie turned to Levi. "Let's get breakfast on the table."

The next few hours, she and Levi worked side by side to keep her brothers peacefully occupied, singing songs, playing the harmonica and the music box, reading and drawing. Frisco and Sutter ran to the window every few minutes at first, anticipating how high the snow would pile and how fast the sled would go. But as the snow started to mount, they shifted about, complaining.

"When will it be over?" Frisco asked.

"Won't it ever stop snowing?" Sutter lamented.

Even Mica turned to grumbling, banging her new rattle on the table before pushing the toy away completely.

"How about popping some corn?" Levi suggested.

Frisco kicked at the wall under the window. "We already strung enough, and Christmas is over."

"Not for stringing," Levi told him. "For eating."

The boys perked up.

That kept them busy for a little longer. Callie put Mica down for a nap, then listened to the corn popping in the kettle. As her brothers fairly hopped in front of the stove, she tried not to think about the cold just outside, snatching at the house with greedy fingers.

Her brothers' fingers were just as greedy. The twins hardly waited until Levi poured melted butter on the tufts of yellow. Then he motioned them and Callie to carry the bowls over to the rug. Why was it a smile from him made the world a better place?

"Let's play a game," he said. "It's called Two Truths and a Tall Tale."

Callie hadn't heard of the game before. Neither had her brothers, it seemed, for Frisco and Sutter frowned as they munched their corn.

"How's it work?" Frisco asked.

"I'll tell you three things," Levi explained. "Two will be true, and one will be farfetched. Whoever guesses which is the tall tale wins that round and gets to go next."

Sutter sat higher. "I'll play."

Frisco eyed Levi. "Me, too. I'm good at spotting the truth."

Levi's look turned serious. "My name is Levi Wallin. My middle name is Aloysius. And I made a fortune panning gold."

"That's easy," Frisco bragged. "Nobody's named A-lo-wish-us."

Levi smiled. "Actually, that was the truth. My pa

gave me that name from the old country. The tall tale is that I made any money panning. I came home with less than when I left."

So had Pa and Adam. Count on Levi to remind her brothers of that. Frisco pouted, most likely to have guessed wrong, but Sutter nodded at Levi.

"Try another."

"All right," Levi said with a smile to Callie. "I am a pastor. I am six-and-twenty years old. And I play the fiddle as well as my brother Simon."

"Do not!" Frisco cried.

Levi grinned. "Right you are. I can play the harmonica, but I never learned to play the fiddle. Our pa taught Simon when I was a baby. And then Pa died."

Sutter looked impressed, likely that Simon had learned so young. How sad, though, that Levi had had so little time with his father. She hadn't enjoyed being carted from one camp to the next, but at least they'd all been together most of the time.

"My turn," Frisco announced. He frowned for a moment, then his brow cleared. "My name is San Francisco Murphy. I have a twin brother named Sutter, and I was the most important shepherd in the Christmas play."

Now Sutter frowned. "But all three of those are true."

"No, they ain't," Frisco said with a grin.

Callie decided not to correct him on the word. She nudged Sutter's leg with her foot. "Your name isn't just Sutter."

Sutter scrambled to his feet, nearly oversetting his popcorn bowl. "That's right! I'm Sutter's Mill Murphy."

Frisco nodded. "Your turn."

Sutter sat down. "No, it should be Callie's turn. She guessed first."

"Very generous of you," Levi said with a smile. "So, Callie, what are your two truths and a tall tale?"

Callie eyed him, an audacious thought bubbling up. She'd wanted to have a moment alone with him since last night, but the blizzard would make that impossible, perhaps for days. Could she speak her mind in front of her brothers and Mica? They'd likely find out soon enough. She simply couldn't hide her feelings much longer.

She drew in a breath. "My name is California Murphy. I've lived in eight gold rush camps, and I'm in love with Levi Wallin."

Frisco and Sutter immediately began arguing about how many camps they'd lived in, completely accepting Callie's outrageous statement about loving him as the truth. Levi could only stare at her. She met his gaze boldly, though color was creeping into her cheeks. Had she meant that?

"Nine!" Sutter yelled in triumph. "We lived in nine camps."

"And you probably lived in more before we were born," Frisco agreed. "My turn."

"Mine," Sutter argued. "I said it first."

"After I told you."

"Did not!"

"Did, too!"

Levi shook himself. "Boys! Go see how high the snow is now."

With a scowl at each other, Frisco and Sutter rose and headed for the window.

Levi moved to the chair closest to Callie, leaning over to speak for her ears alone. "Was that the truth?"

She nodded, gaze on her fingers rubbing at a spot on

her trousers. "I thought you should know, in case you felt the same way."

He did. It had been building since the moment he'd seen her again, standing with a baby in her arms, laundry at her feet and the sun in her hair. Beneath the tough exterior she hid behind, she was soft as new-fallen snow. He only wished he had the right to offer her his heart.

"Half way up the window," Sutter reported, returning to the rug.

"And it's still blowing," Frisco added, joining him.

"Might for a while yet," Levi told them, wrestling with his conscience. "Ma told me the first year they arrived in Seattle it blew for three days straight."

Frisco and Sutter looked horrified.

Overhead, something creaked. All the Murphys stared at the ceiling, their faces washing white. Levi wasn't sure what had frightened them, until Callie recovered.

"This isn't a tent, boys," she told her brothers, gaze falling to theirs. "Levi's house is built nice and strong. The roof won't collapse."

So that was their concern. "Not with that pitch," Levi promised. "The snow can only build up so high before it slides right off. Before it's over, the drifts could reach the eaves. You boys will have to help me dig a path out from the door."

"And we can sled off the roof," Sutter realized.

Frisco grinned.

Levi got them busy building a fort from the chairs and quilt from Callie's bed. Callie went to feed and change the recently woken Mica, but she kept glancing in his direction. He hadn't answered her, and she knew it. Every moment he remained silent, her doubt would grow. She deserved better.

When the boys started bickering again, Levi pulled down the quilt and bundled them on the rug.

"I have a story for you," he said, feeling as if the cold from the snow had seeped into his bones.

"Like *A Christmas Carol*?" Sutter wanted to know.

"Maybe not as good," Levi allowed, rubbing his palms on his trousers. "And I'm not sure about the ending. But I can tell you it started here at Wallin Landing."

The boys settled at his feet, pulling up the quilt around themselves. Callie set Mica on her lap, head cocked as if she wasn't sure what he was about.

"A good seven years ago," Levi said, "there were two young men, best friends."

"Like me and Sutter," Frisco said, earning him a grin from his brother.

"That's right," Levi agreed. "They were determined to make their fortunes, so they gathered a stake and set off for the northern gold fields."

Sutter wiggled up to his knees. "Which strike? Cassiar?"

"Wild Horse Creek?" Frisco guessed.

"Vital Creek," Levi told them, avoiding Cassie's look.

"We were there," Sutter said, sitting back down again.

"I know you were," Levi said. "These two friends filed a claim at the other end of the camp from your father's. They knew they were going to strike it rich. They'd come home with gold spilling out of their pockets, and everyone would respect them."

Frisco and Sutter sighed as if they could imagine it.

"Fool's dream," Callie spit out. Mica shifted in her lap to look up at her with concern.

Levi nodded. "It certainly was. After weeks of panning, they had little to show for it, even though the claims on either side of them were doing well. Worse, their supplies were gone, and only one of the miners in the area was kind enough to share. So, desperate to find gold, one of the friends did what no prospector can ever forgive. He moved the claim markers."

Callie gasped, the sound like a knife in his heart. Frisco and Sutter were staring at him.

"But that's not fair," Sutter protested.

"The other fellows staked that claim," Frisco agreed. "It was their gold."

"Yes," Levi said, "it was. The other prospectors realized what had happened before his friend did. But they didn't know which friend to blame. They came across the other friend first, the innocent one. He told them he didn't know anything about the claim markers being moved, but they wouldn't listen. They took him down to the stream and got out a rope to string him up."

Sutter was on his feet. "But he didn't do it!"

Frisco frowned at him. "It's just a story."

Sutter glanced from his brother to Levi. "Is it, Uncle Levi? Is it just a story?"

Levi shook his head, gaze moving from Sutter to Callie, who was hunched around Mica. "It's a story, Sutter, but it's not a tall tale. You see, the innocent one was my friend Scout. And the guilty one, the one who was so desperate to strike it rich he broke the law, was me."

"That's not true!" Sutter shouted. "You're nice. You wouldn't let your friend die for something you did."

"I nearly did," Levi said, shame clogging his throat. "I was so scared of what I'd done, of what they might do to me if they knew. But I couldn't see Scout swing for it. I stepped forward and admitted my guilt to the lot of them."

Sutter sank back down again. "What happened?"

Callie was whiter than the snow swirling outside. "Did they leave Scout be?"

Levi swallowed, remembering. "They didn't want to believe he hadn't been involved. He was my partner, after all. He had to have known. They stripped off his shirt, beat him something fierce. Two of them held me so I couldn't stop them. Then they put the noose around my neck."

Even now, he felt the rasp of hemp, heard the jeers all over again. Only this time, he couldn't close his eyes against it. This time, it was a part of him.

"I thought I was going to die," he admitted, knowing every gaze was on him. "But another man came along, drawn by the noise. I think God pointed him in the direction. Thaddeus Bilgin was a preacher, come to minister to those in the camps. He talked them out of killing me, promised I'd make up for what I'd done. I started by giving our claim to the men I'd wronged. They found gold on it within the week."

"Figures," Frisco muttered.

"What happened to Scout?" Sutter asked.

"The minister and I nursed him, but as soon as he could walk, he left Vital Creek. I never laid eyes on him again."

Sutter's face twisted. "He must have been awful mad at you."

The lump in Levi's throat grew larger. "He has every right. I nearly got him killed. I was supposed to be his friend, to look out for him."

"But you made up for it," Sutter protested. "You tried to make things right."

"I am still trying," Levi said. "I will go to my grave trying to be a better man than I was that day at Vital Creek."

As if the parsonage was as disappointed with him as they all were, it gave a mighty creak.

"Frisco, Sutter," Callie said. "Go check on the loft."

Her brothers jumped up and ran for the stairs. As soon as they were out of earshot, Callie rose and came to Levi's side. She looked bowed, as if carrying Mica was suddenly too heavy for her.

"Thank you for the truth," she said. "I understand now. You never cared about me or the boys or Mica. You're trying to make up for what you did at Vital Creek. You can't give me your heart, because you lost it on the gold fields, just like Pa and Adam."

Chapter Twenty-One

Callie had hurt when Ma and then Pa had died, when Anna had breathed her last, when she'd heard that Adam would never come home. That hurt was as bad as the pain that wrapped around her now. She'd believed that Levi was different, better than the men she'd known on the gold fields. Now she knew he'd been worse. She'd thought he truly cared about her. Now she saw he cared more about comforting his conscience. He was as lost to her as if he had gone north to pan.

His face was shuttered, as if he would hide the ugliness he'd just confessed. "I stand by our partnership, Callie. I will do right by you and the boys and Mica."

Callie pulled Mica close. "Doesn't matter. I took care of them before you came along with your fool dream of making us a family. I can take care of them again. That's one good thing to come out of this. All of you at Wallin Landing have shown me I have something to offer. As soon as the snow thaws, I'll find a way to move my family out of the parsonage."

He recoiled as if she'd struck him. Perhaps she had. At the moment, she wanted to grab him by the shoul-

ders and give him a good shake. She could forgive his
past, could see that he was trying to make amends. That
wasn't the problem. The boys, his family had all reached
out to him. She'd been ready to hand him her heart. He
couldn't see the light of their love because he was too
focused on the dark of the past.

Somehow, they made it through the rest of the day.
The wind blew so hard the house moaned, until even
Mica whimpered as she cuddled close to Callie. Snow
came down the chimney, setting the fire to popping and
hissing. Levi, Frisco and Sutter kept stirring the wood
around and adding dry tinder to keep things burning.
The wind drove the snow through the smallest cracks—
under the front door, beside the bedroom window and
through the shutters in the loft. Levi had the twins drag
down the pallets and quilts to keep them from soaking
up the moisture. Callie used every spare cloth mopping
and drying.

She wasn't sure of the time when Levi suggested they
go to bed, but no one argued. He'd had the boys set up
space for themselves on the rug in the main room, the
one dry spot left besides her bed and Mica's cradle. She
left them all to settle before retiring herself, putting the
pillow over her head to hide the sounds of the storm.

But the storm still raged inside her. Levi had told
her once that the important thing was to learn from a
mistake and move on. That was what he had been trying to do. Could she forgive him from keeping the truth
from her? Of course. He'd become a better man, just as
he'd vowed. Did she believe he would help her and her
family? Certainly. He was still trying to atone. But she
couldn't believe that he'd be willing to risk his heart in

loving her. It was as if he'd walled off a part of himself
that day at Vital Creek. The bigger question was, was
she willing to risk being in love with him?

Prayer came easier this time.

*Almighty God, I may not always understand what You
want from me. But You put a lot of stock in love, that's
clear enough. We're supposed to love even our enemies.
That must mean we're called to love even if the other
person feels differently.*

She sighed under the covers, wiggling to stay warm.
It didn't matter if Levi never returned her love. She loved
him. Though she'd threatened to leave as soon as the
storm ended, she couldn't go through with it. She had
agreed to be his partner. She'd keep that promise and
work hard to make it grow into more, for both their
sakes. Peace stole over her, more warming than the covers, as she finally fell asleep.

She woke, sensing something wrong. Removing the
pillow from her ear, she sat up, listening. There was a
hush to the house, the only sound the soft murmur of
Mica sleeping.

Was it over?

Callie climbed from the bed, mindful of the fresh pile
of melting snow beside her window. White covered the
glass. She couldn't catch so much as a peek of the outside world. And everything was so quiet.

She drew the quilt off the bed and bundled herself in
it before opening the door. Frisco, Sutter and Levi were
three lumps under the quilts on the floor. She tiptoed
into the room, then stopped, arrested by the sight. Levi's
golden lashes fanned his cheeks. His curls tumbled about
his face. That was the man she loved. She couldn't seem
to move to wake him.

As if he felt her watching, he opened his eyes, the deep blue pulling her in.

"Callie?" he asked.

She put her finger to her lips, then tipped her head toward the window. Rising and wrapping the quilt around himself, he moved to her side.

"I think it's over," she whispered. "Can you see?"

Frisco and Sutter opened sleepy eyes as Levi followed Callie to the window.

This window was more sheltered. The snow was higher than her head, but she caught a glimpse of blue at the top. Was that the sky?

Levi had to stand on tiptoe to peer out. "It's stopped snowing," he reported as Frisco and Sutter came up to them, yawning and rubbing their eyes. "The trees are still, so the wind's died down. We made it through."

She wrapped her arms around his waist, laid her head against his chest. "Thank God."

"Thank the good Lord," Levi echoed. Slowly, as if he feared rejection, his arms wrapped around her.

She allowed herself to be held, warm through and through.

"Can I see?" Frisco begged, tugging on Levi's arm.

Callie almost sighed as Levi released her. He lifted first Frisco and then Sutter to look out. A gurgle from the bedroom told her Mica was awake. When she went to dress and returned with the baby, Frisco and Sutter were at the table while Levi began heating breakfast.

"Can we go sledding?" Frisco wanted to know.

"First we have to dig out," Callie reminded him as she joined them.

"And soon," Levi said with a look her way. "It's Sunday."

She stared at him. "You don't think anyone will come through this."

They came.

Drew arrived first, Catherine in his arms, rope across his broad chest tied to a sled behind carrying their three children. Harry, Tom and Dickie followed on snowshoes. James came by sleigh, bringing his family and Beth. He made a second run to fetch John, Dottie and Peter. Simon and Nora were the last to arrive, Simon breaking a trail with his long legs and the others following like ducklings. Nora carried his violin while Fleet pulled a sled with the youngest children bundled on it. Once freed of his duties, the dog seemed delighted to run about the area while they went into the church.

Callie was almost afraid to see the inside after the snow that had driven itself into the parsonage, but the Wallins had built the church snug and sure. Snow had pushed under the front door, leaving a puddle that Nora immediately began wiping up. The others pitched in to help, talking of huddling in the dark, waiting out the storm, while the children planned the sledding and snow forts and snowball fights to come. Callie even asked John about the mysterious word *Danube* and learned it was a river on the Continent. In the meantime, neighbors began trickling in, including Old Joe. They came on skis, snowshoes and sleighs, until the church was nearly as full as on Christmas.

Callie had never felt more thankful than when she played the opening hymn in her mother's dress, a song Ma had taught her to sing. The others must have felt the same, for voices rang against the rafters, filling the church with joy. Levi echoed her feelings when he stepped up to the pulpit.

"I cannot tell you how thankful I am to see you all here," he said, gaze moving about the room. "That was some storm."

A murmur rippled through the church as couples exchanged glances and children nodded agreement.

"I don't know about you," he continued, "but there were a few moments when I thought I just might meet my Maker. And as I lay on the floor last night beside Frisco and Sutter..."

Her brothers perked up on either side of her. So did Mica.

"...I was reminded of a psalm. Let me read part of it to you." He opened his Bible.

"Bless the Lord, O my soul: and all that is within me, bless His holy name. Bless the Lord, O my soul, and forget not all His benefits: who forgiveth all thine iniquities; who healeth all thy diseases; who redeemeth thy life from destruction; who crowneth thee with loving kindness and tender mercies."

He looked up at the congregation. "He certainly did that last night. We have all been saved from destruction. But I sometimes forget there's more to this psalm. Listen." He bent to the Bible again.

"He hath not dealt with us after our sins; nor rewarded us according to our iniquities. For as the heaven is high above the earth, so great is His mercy toward them that fear Him. As far as the east is from the west, so far hath He removed our transgressions from us."

Callie wasn't sure where his sermon was headed, but she couldn't look away as he raised his head and turned toward her.

"Frisco," he said, and her brother sat bolt upright.

"Yes, sir," he said.

"What happens if you just keep traveling north, all the way to the pole and down?"

Frisco frowned a minute, then brightened. "Why, you start heading south."

Levi nodded. "Very good. Sutter?"

Sutter was fairly wiggling to be given a chance. "Yes, Uncle Levi?"

Callie caught smiles from those closest to her at her brother's enthusiasm.

"What happens when you go east as far as you can, all the way to our nation's capital in Washington, DC, and across the Atlantic?"

Sutter snapped a nod. "You just keep going east. East is always east of you."

"That's right." Levi looked out over the congregation again. "The psalmist could have said north from south, which is a long way. But, as Frisco just pointed out, north and south eventually meet. East and west never do. That means that when God forgives our transgressions, we'll never meet them again. It's over. Done. We are new creations."

His gaze speared Callie. "Yet so many times, we cling to our past. We know it helped shape who we are."

That was true enough. She wouldn't be so determined if Pa hadn't died and left her and her brothers orphaned. Levi might not be the man she loved if he hadn't lived through the events at Vital Creek.

"We forget God offers us a chance," he continued. "Our sins are forgiven. They no longer shackle us. We need to remember that, and behave accordingly. I know I have some work to do in that area. If you're in the same situation, I'll be praying for you." He nodded to Harry, who came up to lead the final prayer.

Callie knew she should bow her head, but her gaze seemed permanently fixed on Levi. His head was bent, his lips moving silently. Could he apply that lesson to himself? Was he willing to let the past go?

Could they truly have a future, together?

She shifted on her feet as the service ended, eager and afraid to ask. But Levi went to the back of the church, talked with each member of his congregation as they were leaving. Frisco and Sutter made a beeline for Davy, no doubt confirming plans on where and when to sled. Callie sighed as Beth bustled up to her.

"We're all going to meet at the main house for dinner," she said. "I don't care how much it snows. It's Sunday." She winked at Callie. "And I don't care how much Drew and Simon talk about digging out barns and sheds or cleaning the hall. From what I hear, all the animals are safe and fed. Today, we play in the snow." She rubbed her hands together as if she couldn't wait.

Neither could Frisco and Sutter. The next time Callie looked for them, they'd disappeared.

"They must have gone back to the parsonage," she told Levi as they left the church together at last, Mica on her hip. "You mark my words—that sled will be gone from the breezeway."

He slid his hand over hers, cradling her fingers as they walked. "I can't blame them. They've been cooped up for the last day."

Mindful of the demands that her brothers could make as soon as she and Levi reached the parsonage, Callie slowed, tugging on his hand to get him to stop beside her. He raised his brows in inquiry.

"Your sermon," she said, searching his face. "You said God forgives our mistakes and we should too. Does that mean you're ready to let go of what happened at Vital Creek?"

He glanced out at the snow piled up against the buildings. "I don't think I'll ever forget what happened. I slept little last night, it was so much on my mind."

Callie dropped her gaze, weight settling over her even as Mica rested her head against her shoulder. "I've spent a lot of time thinking about the past—Pa's promises, Adam's failures. I've come to see it doesn't do me any good. I can't change their choices. I have to move on, live my own life."

"There's a difference," he murmured, fingers tightening on hers. "You suffered for their mistakes. You can offer forgiveness. Scout suffered for mine."

Callie raised her gaze. His cheeks looked hollowed, as if they reflected what he felt inside. "You suffered for it, too. You have to forgive yourself. Can you do that?"

He drew in a breath, and she held hers, waiting. On her hip, Mica heaved a sigh.

Levi's lips curved up. "Yes, I can. Because of you." He bent and caressed her mouth with his. Love and devotion flowed from his kiss. Even though her eyes were closed, she thought she could see forever.

Mica laughed, pushing against his chest and Callie's.

Callie laughed too as he pulled away with a grin. "Come on. Beth says we're going to have some fun in the snow."

"The twins won't want to miss that," he predicted. "We'd better locate them and the sled."

But when they reached the parsonage, the sled was still propped against the inside wall of the breezeway.

"Should I open the door?" Levi teased. "Who knows what they've been up to."

"Only one way to find out," Callie said, pulling her hand from his to open the door.

The parsonage was quiet as they stepped inside. She felt as if snow trickled down her back.

Levi must have felt the same sense of foreboding, for he started for the stairs. "I'll check the loft."

Callie's gaze lit on a piece of paper propped against the lamp on the table. "Don't bother. Looks like they left a note."

As Levi crossed to her side, she set Mica in her chair, then picked up the letter. Her brothers had never informed her of their intentions before, but maybe they were just showing off their new writing skills. Her gaze ran over the words, and her stomach dropped.

"Callie?" Levi's voice seemed to come from miles away. "What is it?"

Callie almost wished she'd never learned to read so she wouldn't have seen the brash words on the note. "Frisco and Sutter," she told him, shiver running through her, "they've been kidnapped. If we don't tell the kidnappers by noon tomorrow where Adam struck it rich, we'll never see my brothers again."

A hole seemed to yawn beneath him. Levi put a hand on the table to steady himself.

"Who'd be fool enough to think Adam had found gold?" Callie demanded. Her head jerked up, and she met his gaze, blanching. "What will the kidnappers do when they figure out we have nothing to give them?"

Levi took the note from her tight fingers and scanned the wording. They demanded a note be left on the big stump near the road leading to Seattle by noon tomorrow. The letters were printed large, in pencil and marked out and smeared in places as if the writer had been unsure of the spelling.

"Could this be a joke?" he asked. "Could Frisco or Sutter have written this to tease us?"

Callie shook her head. "I saw their letters when they were practicing for school. They didn't write this."

She was shaking, in fear or anger, he wasn't sure. He gathered her close nonetheless, held her sheltered in his arms. "It will be all right, Callie. We'll get them back. I promise."

She shifted in his arms, and he waited for her to denounce him. Who was he to make such a promise? Instead, she snuggled closer. "I believe you, Levi."

His heart nearly flew from his chest. She and the boys were his to protect. He would never let them down.

Drawing in a breath, she pulled back from him. "What do we do? We can't tell the kidnappers where Adam found gold. He didn't strike it rich. We would have heard."

"Maybe." Thoughts swirled through his mind, sliding neatly into place like gears locking on a shaft. "Or maybe someone didn't want us to know."

Callie frowned. "Who do you mean?"

"I don't think the prospectors who brought me Adam's things knew," Levi said, thinking back. "They told me someone else had handed them everything. I thought it was because the men who had buried Adam didn't want to come this far south before returning to the gold fields."

Callie nodded. "Makes sense. They would have wanted to keep panning as long as possible."

"But what if they did come this far?" Levi pressed. "Remember the two riders we saw the day we left for Wallin Landing, the destruction Deputy McCormick found in your cabin? Someone was looking for something."

"The mess in the church when we first arrived," she said, eyes lighting.

"And Beth said someone had pawed through the Christmas presents."

Callie shook her head. "Frisco and Sutter were innocent after all. Someone came down from the gold fields to search for word of Adam's strike."

As if she agreed, Mica struck the table with her palm and grinned at the noise.

"And I think I know who." Levi met Callie's gaze. "Zachariah and Willard asked all kinds of questions about Adam. They were at the Christmas dance."

Callie shivered again. "We were going to help them, and then the blizzard struck and we had no chance. But if they were camping out, they'd be in trouble. No one could have survived that blizzard in a tent."

"Maybe they aren't staying in a tent. There are plenty of sheds and barns in the area. If they kept out of sight, the owner might not have realized they were there."

Callie rubbed her arm as if the chill just wouldn't leave her. He knew the feeling.

"Then that's where they're holding Frisco and Sutter," she said. "In some shack near Wallin Landing."

"Very likely," Levi agreed. "Only with this snow, it won't be easy to get out and locate it."

"The snow!" Callie ran to the window. Already the sun was melting the cold, dropping the level against the glass. Levi could see the way between the house, church and hall, well trampled now by foot and hoof.

She whirled to face him. "Wherever they went, they

left tracks. We might not be able to see them close to the house, but the farther away we go…"

"…the more obvious they'll be," Levi finished. He strode for the door. "I'll fetch my brothers and Harry and the crew. We can spread out in all directions."

Callie dashed to his side. "Wait! I'm coming with you."

He would have liked nothing better than to have her at his side, but Mica was waving at him from her chair as if just as determined to go with them. "You can't, Callie. Someone has to protect Mica. She could be in danger, too. She's Adam's daughter."

Callie hesitated, glancing at the little girl, who waved at her as well, smiling as happily as always.

"Frisco and Sutter are strong and smart," Levi murmured. "They might even be able to escape their kidnappers. Mica depends on you."

"All right," Callie said, voice laced with reluctance. "I'll stay. But I'm going to look through Adam's things again, just in case there's something about a new claim."

Levi nodded. "I'll ask Beth to stay with you."

Callie raised her chin. "Good. Between the two of us, no one will touch Mica."

So brave, so determined. How could he not love this woman? Levi bent, pressed a kiss against her forehead. He wanted to gather her close again, keep her safe. But Frisco and Sutter needed him more. He grabbed his coat and gloves, opened the door and dashed out into the cold.

Chapter Twenty-Two

Callie wanted to run to the window, press her nose against the glass, watch Levi until she couldn't see him anymore. But the snow was too high. For the first time, she felt trapped.

She made herself turn and smile at Mica, who babbled her delight at the attention.

"Let's see what your pa left you," Callie said, heading for the bedroom.

She had Adam's meager possessions spread out on the table when Beth arrived. Hanging her coat on the hook by the door, Levi's sister propped a rifle beside the table next to where Callie had set hers, in easy reach.

"I am so sorry," she told Callie, midnight blue eyes troubled. "But Levi and the others will find Frisco and Sutter. We don't let anyone hurt family."

Family. Callie felt the same way about the Wallins. Funny how that had changed over Christmas.

"Thank you," she told Beth. "Will you help me with Adam's things? The kidnappers seem to think he found gold. I doubt it, but if he did there might be a sign of it in his belongings."

Beth set to work with a will. They went through every pocket, opened every flask and canister. Callie felt along seams for secret compartments.

"A nickel and a button," Beth said with a shake of her head, eying their plunder. "It doesn't look as if your brother was ready to come back wealthy."

Callie sighed. "I could have told the kidnappers that. When Adam had money, he found a way to send it home." She picked up the note Frisco had read to her, smoothed out the wrinkles her little brother's hand had made. "He might even have written to tell us. There's nothing about it on this note, and these were his last words."

Beth came around the table and laid a hand on Callie's shoulder as if in support.

Callie blinked, reading the words herself for the first time.

I think I'm done for.

Don't worry. I asked Levi Wallin to take care of you.

Levi had fulfilled Adam's request and more. He'd given her a home, made her part of his family, reawakened her faith. Adam might not have realized it, but he'd made his siblings and daughter rich indeed.

She smoothed the paper further. She'd keep this for Mica to read when she was old enough. She could imagine the girl sounding out the words, realizing how much her father had loved her.

Why wouldn't those wrinkles even out?

With a frown, she lay down the letter, pressed it flat to the table, peered closer.

"What is it, Callie?" Beth asked, bending to look as well.

Callie focused past the letters, noticing lines, curves,

the mark of an X scratched into the paper. She glanced up at Beth.

"It's a map. Maybe Adam found something after all."

Levi paused in the snowy wood, wiping a hand across his forehead. Harry came up beside him to do the same.

"We'll find them," the big logger assured him. "There's only so many places they could be in this cold."

Levi nodded, afraid to speak his thoughts aloud. Drew and Simon had gone north, James and John west. Dickie and Tom were searching along the lake. Levi and Harry had headed south, but so far the only trail he'd seen had been the one he and Harry were making.

The morning's respite of sun had given way to dark clouds and a chill wind that froze the top of the snow, making their steps crunch. No animal moved among the trees. In such harsh conditions, it would be hard for two grown men to keep themselves alive and fed. Would Zachariah and Willard find it too difficult to take care of Frisco and Sutter? Would they leave the boys in the snow?

Levi shivered, and it had nothing to do with the chill.

Harry drew a flask from inside his heavy coat. "Hot cider," he said, handing it to Levi. "Leastwise, it was hot when Miss Beth poured it in."

It was tepid now, despite its position near Harry's chest, but Levi took a swig before handing it back to the logger.

Harry wiped off the neck, then took a drink himself. Pocketing the flask again, he glanced around. "What do you think? Should we try Paul's? His barn is big enough to hide a regiment."

Their neighbor Mr. Paul kept a herd of dairy cattle. At least the beasts' body heat would help warm the barn.

"Let's go." Levi pushed off.

He and Harry slogged through the snow for hours, until he could hardly lift his feet and his toes were numb. The Paul outbuildings proved empty of human habitation, as did the sheds of the homestead beyond that. The only tracks in the woods were from animals, and they were few and far between, as if even the denizens of the forest were wise enough to stay in their homes.

Harry fell silent as they trudged back to Wallin Landing in the gathering gloom. Drew, Simon, James, John, Tom and Dickie were nearly as glum as they reported no sightings.

"It makes no sense," John, their best tracker, insisted. "They didn't fly away from the parsonage. They must have left some mark."

"It's too dark now," Drew said. "We'll try again in the morning." He lay a hand on Levi's shoulder. "I'm sorry. Tell Callie we won't give up."

Levi thanked them all, then left to climb the hill. Each step felt heavy, and not just because he was cold and tired.

He'd have to tell Callie he'd failed.

Callie and Beth looked up as he opened the door. They were seated on chairs, Mica playing on the rug at their feet. She gurgled a welcome and scrunched up her nose at him.

Callie came straight to his side. "What happened? Did you find anything?"

Even as she spoke, she was helping him off with his stiff coat. Beth hurried to the stove to put water on to boil.

"Nothing," he said, sinking onto the bench by the

262 His Frontier Christmas Family

table. He bent and fumbled with his boot laces, but they were crusted with snow, and his fingers were stiffer than his coat.

Callie crouched beside him, skirts pooling on the floor. "You're nearly frozen clean through. Let me help."

He didn't have the strength to protest. She worked at the laces, then pulled off his boots. When she started on the socks, Levi put out a hand.

"I can do this," he murmured.

She glanced up at him. "So can I, but very well." She rose. "It's all right, Levi. You might not have found the twins yet, but Beth and I discovered something."

"A treasure map," Beth agreed.

Levi paused in the act of rolling the sodden wool off his feet. "A treasure map?"

Callie nodded. "Adam left it. He scratched a map on the letter he sent home. That's what Zachariah and Willard must have been looking for. That's what we can trade for Frisco and Sutter."

Callie brought him the letter, angling it to the lamp. The lines fell in sharp relief. Levi leaned closer, pulse quickening. "He had to have found gold, perhaps a sizeable strike." His gaze roamed the paper, trying to align the markings to any place he had traveled. What he and Scout would have given for such an opportunity. Small wonder the kidnappers had been ready to take Frisco and Sutter. The first strike in a new area could be the making of any man smart enough to take advantage of it.

He glanced up to find Callie watching him. She must have seen something in his eyes, for she shook her head.

Levi reached out and took her hand. "Don't worry, Callie. I'm in no danger of succumbing to gold fever again."

She cocked her head. "You sure?"

"Positive," Levi said, without so much as a twinge of regret. He reached out his other hand and caressed her cheek. "You are more precious to me than gold. I'm not going anywhere."

Her face cleared, her lower lip trembled, and he leaned in to kiss her. He barely noticed Mica crowing in delight or Beth tiptoeing past to see to her.

In the end, it was a sound of the door opening that made him raise his head. Callie's cheeks were rosy, her eyes shining and he was fairly sure he was smiling in just such a daze.

Almost as dazed as Beth as Frisco and Sutter ran into the room.

Callie pulled out of Levi's embrace to meet them halfway, hugging them close. "Are you all right? Where have you been?"

Levi snatched up the rifle and strode to the door, but a glance out into the night showed nothing but the moon glinting on the snow. Turning, he found the twins wiggling in Callie's arms, while Beth clapped and Mica squealed.

"We're fine," Sutter said, breaking free.

"We escaped," Frisco bragged, right behind him.

Levi shut the door before they could dash out, feeling as if the room was starting to spin. "What happened? Did Zachariah and Willard actually kidnap you, or was this all a game?"

Frisco and Sutter shook their heads, turning solemn.

"We found them in the house when we came back from church," Frisco explained.

"Looking under and inside everything," Sutter added.

Frisco rubbed his hand along his pants. "They said

they needed to find something. And they said you were a bad man, Uncle Levi, trying to take what was theirs."

Sutter hung his head. "We were still kind of mad at you, on account of what you done to poor old Scout. So we said we'd keep their secret."

Beth perked up. "Scout?"

He would have to share the whole story with his sister. "Go on," he told the boys.

"They said if we came with them, they'd take us panning," Frisco obliged. "They said Adam found gold, lots of it. His pockets were full of nuggets."

Callie met Levi's gaze. It seemed she and Beth had been right about the treasure map.

"We said we'd go," Frisco continued. "Only they didn't go anywhere. They stuck us in that little room at the back of the hall, said we had to wait until you told them where to go."

"So, when they got sleepy, we left," Sutter said.

"The hall." Levi met Callie's gaze.

"Of course!" she said. "There'd have been enough warmth from the dance, not to mention the food left over."

"They've been under our noses this whole time!" Beth cried.

"They were taking some chance," Callie said with a shake of her head. "What if we'd come in to clean?"

Beth's face darkened. "Oh, wait until I get my hands on them!"

Levi set the rifle down long enough to pull on and lace his boots. "We'll take care of this."

Callie touched his hand and nodded. "Yes, we will."

Levi returned her nod. They were partners, more so now than ever. "Stay here with Mica and the boys,

Beth," he ordered. "Callie and I are going to find the kidnappers."

No one argued with him as he and Callie headed out.

The light from the open door spilled across the snow, setting it to sparkling. The path was wide enough that Callie could walk at his side. She didn't speak, and neither did he. Instead they moved as one to the door of the hall.

Levi lifted the rifle, then nodded to the door. Callie swung it open so they could peer inside.

Anyone else glancing in would have thought the place empty. Perhaps that was what Zachariah and Willard had been counting on. The fire in the hearth had gone out. Snow had pushed in through one of the windows, leaving a melting puddle on the floor. The Christmas tree was listing in the corner, and it seemed to be missing some of the apples Beth and the logging crew had used as decorations. The tables along the far wall had been emptied of their food and stripped of their cloths, as if the dance had never been. The door to the pantry was closed, but a light glowed under it. He and Callie headed in that direction.

She paused as she reached the door as if afraid of what she might find. Keeping the rifle at the ready, he nodded encouragement. She took the latch and pushed the door open.

The tablecloths were piled up in the middle of the floor with bits of cheese, bread and apples scattered among them. Zachariah and Willard were curled up against the far wall, as if they had tried to escape from the twins. Levi nudged Zachariah with the rifle.

The prospector started, then opened his eyes, eyes

that widened as he took in Levi and Callie. He elbowed Willard, who woke with a snort.

Zachariah's smile was sickly as he sat up. "Guess you found us."

Willard glanced around them. "Guess we lost the twins. Thank the good Lord."

Levi kept the rifle trained on them. "I doubt God thought much of your plans for holding them for ransom."

Zachariah ducked his head. "We didn't think much of our plans once we had them in the room. It's not easy taking care of them." He rubbed his arm. "I've got bruises from where they hopped on me."

"Me, too," Willard complained. "And the noise! I thought sure they'd give us away."

"You got what you deserved, as far as I can see," Callie said, raising her chin. "What were you thinking to kidnap two innocent boys?"

"Innocent!" Willard sputtered. "They're wilier than snakes!"

"They may be," Levi put in, "but you're the ones who committed a crime."

"What was we to do?" Zachariah pleaded, getting his feet under him. "You wouldn't tell us where Adam found gold."

"We asked," Willard reminded them.

"You danced around the question," Levi told them, motioning with the rifle for them to stay seated. "We didn't know about Adam's strike until you left that note."

"You were so greedy to be the ones to find gold you couldn't even ask us the question straight out," Callie said with another shake of her head.

Zachariah and Willard frowned.

"How was we to know?" Willard demanded. He tipped his chin toward Levi. "He's a liar and a cheat. We didn't want to give him ideas if you hadn't let him in on the secret."

Once he would have felt guilt at their words. Now he knew that their choices, not his, had caused their predicament. Callie had shown him that.

"I don't care what you think of me," he said. "You vandalized the Murphy cabin searching for the map, tore apart the church, nearly damaged my family's Christmas and threatened to harm Frisco and Sutter."

"It was all a bluff," Zachariah insisted. "We wouldn't have hurt the little fellows."

"Much," Willard muttered.

"You can tell that to the sheriff," Levi said. "I doubt he'll be as happy to make your acquaintance as the boys were."

Zachariah struggled to his feet. "Now, see here. No call to bring in the law."

"We're prospectors, same as you," Willard agreed, joining him. "You know how it is. You fell prey to gold fever, too."

He had, and he'd done as much or more than they had. Yet he'd been truly sorry, had tried to find a way to make up for his mistakes. They didn't even seem to understand they'd done something wrong.

He must have looked conciliatory, for Zachariah's eyes lit.

"Tell you what," he said with a smile, "you share the location of Adam's strike, and we'll take you with us when we head north. What do you say, preacher? You can finally have all the gold you wanted."

Callie was watching him, and he thought she might be holding her breath.

Levi shook his head. "No deal, gents. I have everything I need right here. And there's a deputy sheriff who's been looking for you. I'd hate to disappoint him."

Chapter Twenty-Three

Harry, Tom and Dickie took turns watching the prospectors at the main house through the night. Beth had gone to fetch them and alert the rest of the family that Frisco and Sutter had been found unharmed. Harry was planning to ride for Seattle in the morning to locate Deputy McCormick.

While Callie was glad her brothers had bested the men, she couldn't like their attitude about the gold. Accordingly, when Beth left, she seated the twins at the table.

"Why do you want to pan?" she demanded. "And don't look at each other. Look at me."

Both her brothers squirmed. Levi, who was standing beside her, put his hand on her shoulder in support. She knew she could count on him. That was by far the best thing to come out of the night. Finally, someone who wanted to be with her more than gold.

"Adam said he was the man of the family," Frisco answered. "With him gone, I'm the man now."

"So am I," Sutter protested.

"Only the oldest is the man," Frisco told him, "and I'm two minutes older than you. Callie said so."

Sutter pouted.

"Go on," Callie told Frisco.

"As head of the family," he said, chin coming up, "it's my job to take care of the rest of you. I can't stake a claim to farm until I'm one-and-twenty. Mrs. Wallin said I can't work for pay until I'm ten. What else can I do but pan?"

Callie sagged. "Oh, Frisco. You don't have to take care of us. That was my job until Levi came for us."

Levi nodded, giving her shoulder a squeeze. "I promised to take care of you all, and I will."

"Even though you let Scout down?" Sutter asked.

The uncertainty in her brother's voice hurt. How much more would it hurt Levi? He looked from one frown to the other.

"Did you ever do something and later realize it was the wrong thing?" he asked them.

"No," Frisco said.

Sutter nudged him. "Yes."

Frisco sighed. "Oh, all right. Yes."

"Then you say you're sorry," Sutter told Levi. "Try to make amends."

Callie wanted to hug them close. She knew where they'd learned that lesson.

So did Levi, for he stood taller, as if a burden had been lifted. "That's right. That's the rule of this house. Are you willing to live by it?"

Her brothers exchanged glances. This time Sutter spoke first. "Yes, sir. But Pa and Adam promised Callie a big house and pretty dresses."

"You going to keep those promises, too, Uncle Levi?" Frisco challenged.

Callie spread her hands. "He already did. This house is plenty big enough for us. And I have two pretty dresses now. Nora and Beth and the others made them for me for Christmas." She gave in to her feelings and put an arm about each brother. "I have almost everything I could ever want, right here."

Her brothers wiggled under her hold.

"Almost everything," Levi murmured as she straightened. "What's missing, Callie? What do you want?"

From the beginning, he'd asked her that question. She never could think of an answer that satisfied, until now. She glanced at him, heart starting to pound. She knew ladies weren't supposed to ask this question, but Nora had done it. Why not her?

"If I tell you, do you promise to get it for me?" she asked him.

He nodded, taking a step closer. "Anything, Callie. I love you."

Her heart overflowed. With Frisco, Sutter and even Mica watching, she drew herself up. "In that case, Levi Wallin, I want you to marry me."

Levi stared at her, joy nearly lifting him off his feet. "I will. As soon as you want."

She stuck out her hand. "Partners, then, for the rest of our lives."

"Partners," Levi promised, taking her hand. "In everything." He drew her close and kissed her. For the first time in a long time, the world felt right, his dreams possible.

Thank You, Father.

From a distance, he heard Mica clapping and Sutter and Frisco making gagging noises.

"Does this mean you'll be our pa?" Sutter asked as Levi raised his head, keeping Callie in his embrace.

"No, silly, he's our brother," Frisco said.

"Brother-in-law," Callie corrected him. "He'll be my husband."

She looked so pleased by the fact that Levi wanted to tip back his head and crow.

"Too confusing," Sutter said, slipping off the bench. "I'm going to keep calling you uncle."

"Good idea," Frisco said, following him.

Levi was content to let them go, Callie warm in his arms, but she called after her brothers.

"Not so fast, you two. We still have to decide your punishment."

"How you're going to make things right," Levi amended.

Callie nodded, hair tickling his chin.

"Spending a day with those two prospectors was punishment enough," Frisco said.

"Talk, talk, talk," Sutter agreed, putting his hands over his ears. "Nearly gave me a headache."

Levi kept his face stern. "Still, you made quite a mess of the pantry. You'll clean the hall from top to bottom, until it passes Beth's inspection." He thought he saw them swallow.

"And there will be no sledding for a week," Callie added.

Their faces melted. "But, Callie," they chorused.

"But, Callie," Levi wheedled, giving her a hug. "The snow might not last that long."

Frisco and Sutter scurried back to their sides. "What if we cleaned the loft, too?" Frisco asked.

"Cleared a path to the woodpile," Sutter suggested.

"That's enough," Frisco said out of the side of his mouth. "Don't give them ideas."

Callie glanced over her shoulder at Levi. "I told you—you can't coddle them."

"We didn't," Levi said with a smile. "Besides, you could have been a lot harder on me, and you forgave instead."

She turned to eye her brothers. "Clean the hall for Miss Beth and the loft to my satisfaction, no grumbling, no complaining. You can start with the loft. Now."

Her brothers ran for the stairs.

Callie rested her head back on Levi's chest. "You're taking on a lot, you know."

"I know," he murmured against the silk of her hair. "I can't wait."

As it turned out, he had to wait a good six weeks. Beth needed that amount of time to arrange for the dress, minister, food and music. Callie could have told her none of that really mattered. Levi had met and fallen in love with her when she'd had nothing more than a buckskin coat and her mother's dress. He didn't need to see her gowned in silk any more than she did.

As it was, she had to argue Beth and Nora out of a white wedding dress. What use would she have for a white dress? Mica or the boys would only spill on it. She convinced them to make her an inset for the bodice of the ball gown instead. With a higher neck, she could wear the dress for church later when she played the piano.

In the meantime, Deputy McCormick came out to

take charge of Zachariah and Willard, who would be spending time in the Seattle jail while they awaited trial for their crimes. Levi and Callie debated what to do with Adam's map. In the end, they filed it away with the rest of his things to be given to Mica when she was older.

"Someone else will likely find the spot before then," Levi pointed out as Callie folded the paper.

"And I wish him the best," Callie replied. "But my family is done with hunting for gold."

Saturday, February thirteenth, the day before Valentine's Day, Callie stood up with her sweetheart in the Wallin Landing chapel, before all their friends and family and the Reverend Daniel Bagley from the Brown Church in town. Beth was Callie's attendant, Sutter was Levi's and Frisco in long navy pants that matched his brother's walked her down the aisle.

"You take good care of my sister, Uncle Levi," he murmured as he surrendered her hand.

"I will," Levi promised, gaze on Callie.

The older minister led them through the vows, but Callie knew the words by heart. Because Levi had taught her her letters, she'd read the marriage ceremony beforehand in the church manual. Still, nothing could prepare her for the emotions that surged through her when Levi vowed to love, honor and cherish her all the days of his life.

At last, they turned, hand in hand, husband and wife, to receive the applause of the congregation. From the front row, Mica waved from Beth's arms.

Callie felt Levi stiffen. "It can't be," he murmured.

She wasn't sure what concerned him, but his steps grew faster as they started down the aisle, until she had to lift her skirts to keep up.

He jerked to a halt beside the last pew, where a man about his age was standing, hat in hand. He wasn't as tall as Levi, and his frame was more slender. His dark hair was slicked back from a peaked face. His nose was just the slightest crooked, as if it had been broken long ago, and a scar ran down one cheek, the rakish line at odds with the soft look in his brown eyes.

"Congratulations, Levi," he said, then he turned a shy smile on Callie. "Ma'am."

"What are you doing here?" Levi asked, voice rough.

Callie glanced from one to the other. Tension strung like a wire between them, vibrating. Only one man she could think of might affect Levi this way. Could it be?

The other man spread his hands. "I came home."

Levi released Callie, face tight. "I'm so glad. I think of you every day. What I did was unconscionable. I should never have let you take the blame, even for a moment. I hope you can forgive me someday, Scout."

Callie sucked in a breath.

Levi's old friend held out his free hand. "No day like today. I've missed you."

Levi took his hand and pulled him in for a hug.

Callie bit her lip to keep from speaking, tears gathering in her eyes. Others were clustering around them, calling their welcome to Scout, their congratulations to her and Levi. Though Levi had confessed his past to his family in the last month, only she and Levi knew what this moment truly meant.

Levi's cheeks were wet when he pulled back. "Anything you need, tell me. I know your father lost your claim, but you can sleep in the loft at the parsonage. I'm sure Drew can find you work."

Levi's family chimed in their support.

Scout held up a hand. "Thank you, but there's no need. In some ways, Levi, you did me a favor by making me strike out on my own. I learned a lot about myself, what's important to me. And I found gold."

Frisco and Sutter pushed their way through the crowd.

"Where?" Frisco demanded. "Are you going back for more?"

"Can we come, too?" Sutter added.

"No," Callie said. "We've been through this. No more panning."

"No more panning," Scout agreed with a smile. "In fact, I sold my claim before heading south. I can pay my own way. You don't have to take care of me, Levi. I might even be able to help you for once."

"You already have," Levi assured him. He clapped Scout on the shoulder. "Come dance at my wedding."

Scout grinned. "First, you should probably introduce me to your bride."

"California Murphy," Callie said, sticking out her hand. When Beth coughed, she realized her mistake. "That is, Callie Wallin."

Scout shook her hand, his grip sure and firm. "Thomas Rankin, ma'am. My friends call me Scout. You have no call to remember, but I met you and your brothers once at Vital Creek. How'd you all come to be in Seattle?"

"I'll tell you all about it," Callie promised.

"But first," Levi put in, "I intend to dance with my wife." He took her hand and led her toward the hall.

It was a while before they could be alone. There were friends and family to greet, time to spend with Scout. Then they had to settle Frisco and Sutter with James and Rina for the next few weeks, to their chagrin.

"She's the teacher," Frisco complained. "She'll make us learn."

"I have work for you," James said with a grin to Callie and Levi. "The horses need exercising, and the candy bins at the store seem to be overflowing."

Frisco and Sutter exchanged glances. "I think we can help you there," Frisco said, while Sutter nodded, eyes shining.

Nora took Mica, the little girl going eagerly into her arms. Then it was time for Callie to throw her bouquet.

Beth held out her hand with a sigh. "You might as well give it to me. There aren't any other unmarried ladies present."

Little Mary, who was standing nearby, tugged on Beth's skirts. "I'm not married, Aunt Beth."

Victoria came up as well, nose in the air. "I have yet to be spoken for."

Callie grinned at Beth. "Looks like you have competition."

Beth rubbed her hands together, glancing at her nieces. "I welcome it. Come on, girls."

Beth stepped back with Mary and Victoria on either side. As the others separated to give them room, Callie turned her back and tossed the bouquet over her shoulder. Then she whirled to see who had caught it.

As Beth eyed the ceiling innocently, Mary clutched the flowers, gaze dreamy.

Catherine came to take her daughter's hand. "You'll need to wait a decade or two before you earn the right to carry one of those yourself."

"Yes, Mother," she said with a sigh.

Finally, Callie was sitting in the wagon with Levi. Lance and Percy stood in the traces, ready to take them to Seattle, where Callie and Levi would catch a ship to San Francisco for a honeymoon. It seemed fitting. That was where she'd started—in a gold rush camp outside San Francisco. Now she was returning as a bride with a much brighter future.

She linked her arm with Levi's as he called to the horses, and everyone cheered them on their way.

"I never dreamed when you walked onto our claim that I'd find myself a partner for life," she told him as they drove down the road, trees on either side.

"And I never dreamed I'd find myself a wife and a family," he told her.

She smiled. "Your Christmas family."

"Our family," Levi said. "From this day forward, for richer, for poorer, in sickness and in health. Forever, Callie."

"Forever." Callie snuggled closer under the woolen lap robe. "I like the sound of that."

* * * * *

Find more great reads at www.LoveInspired.com

Dear Reader,

Thank you for choosing Levi and Callie's story. The youngest Wallin brother has finally come into his own. I'm glad he found the right lady to stand by his side. If you missed the other stories about the Wallin brothers, look for *Would-Be Wilderness Wife* (Drew and Catherine), *Frontier Engagement* (James and Rina), *A Convenient Christmas Wedding* (Simon and Nora) and *Mail-Order Marriage Promise* (John and Dottie).

I smiled when I wrote about Callie throwing her bouquet. It is very like the scene at my own wedding. Most of my friends wanted to remain single at the time, so, when I tossed the bouquet, they punted it into the arms of my flower girl! She is happily married now with two boys of her own, but she did have to wait a decade and more.

I love to connect with readers. Please visit me at my website at www.reginascott.com, where you can also sign up to be alerted when the next book is out.

Blessings!
Regina Scott

Get 2 Free Books,

Love Inspired HISTORICAL

Plus 2 Free Gifts—

just for trying the Reader Service!

SPECIAL EXCERPT FROM

*Hoping to make his dream of owning a farm come true,
Jeremiah Stoltzfus clashes with single mother
Mercy Bamberger, who believes the land belongs to her.
Mercy yearns to make the farm a haven for unwanted
children. Can she and Jeremiah possibly find a future
together?*

Read on for a sneak preview of
AN AMISH ARRANGEMENT
by **Jo Ann Brown**,
available January 2018 from Love Inspired!

Jeremiah looked up to see a ladder wobbling. A dark-haired woman stood at the very top, her arms windmilling.

He leaped into the small room as she fell. After years of being tossed shocks of corn and hay bales, he caught her easily. He jumped out of the way, holding her to him as the ladder crashed to the linoleum floor.

"Are you okay?" he asked. His heart had slammed against his chest when he saw her teetering.

"I'm fine."

"Who are you?" he asked at the same time she did.

"I'm Jeremiah Stoltzfus," he answered. "You are…?"

"Mercy Bamberger."

"Bamberger? Like Rudy Bamberger?"

"Yes. Do you know my grandfather?"

Well, that explained who she was and why she was in the house.

"He invited me to come and look around."

LIEXP1217

She shook her head. "I don't understand why."

"Didn't he tell you he's selling me his farm?"

"No!"

"I'm sorry to take you by surprise," he said gently, "but I'll be closing the day after tomorrow."

"Impossible! The farm's not for sale."

"Why don't you get your *grossdawdi*, and we'll settle this?"

"I can't."

"Why not?"

She blinked back sudden tears. "Because he's dead."

"Rudy is dead?"

"Yes. It was a massive heart attack. He was buried the day before yesterday."

"I'm sorry," Jeremiah said with sincerity.

"Grandpa Rudy told me the farm would be mine after he passed away."

"Then why would he sign a purchase agreement with me?"

"But my grandfather died," she whispered. "Doesn't that change things?"

"I don't know. I'm not sure what we should do," he said.

"Me, either. However, you need to know I'm not going to relinquish my family's farm to you or anyone else."

"But—"

"We moved in a couple of days ago. We're not giving it up." She crossed her arms over her chest. "It's our home."

Don't miss
AN AMISH ARRANGEMENT
by Jo Ann Brown, available January 2018 wherever
Love Inspired® books and ebooks are sold.

www.LoveInspired.com

Inspirational Romance to Warm Your Heart and Soul

Join our social communities to connect with other readers who share your love!

Sign up for the Love Inspired newsletter at **www.LoveInspired.com** to be the first to find out about upcoming titles, special promotions and exclusive content.

CONNECT WITH US AT:

Harlequin.com/Community

 Facebook.com/LoveInspiredBooks

 Twitter.com/LoveInspiredBks

LISOCIAL2017

*Special Agent Tanner Wilson has only one clue to figure
out who left a baby at the Houston FBI office—his
ex-girlfriend's name written on a scrap of paper.
But Macy Mills doesn't recognize the little girl that
someone's determined to abduct at any cost.*

Read on for a sneak preview of
THE BABY ASSIGNMENT *by* **Christy Barritt**,
available January 2018 from Love Inspired Suspense!

Suddenly, Macy stood. "Do you smell that, Tanner?"

Smoke. There was a fire somewhere. Close.

"Go get Addie," he barked. "Now!"

Macy flew up the steps, urgency nipping at her heels.

Where there was smoke, there was fire. Wasn't that
the saying?

Somehow, she instinctively knew that those words
were the truth. Whoever had set this fire had done it on
purpose. They wanted to push Tanner, Macy and Addie
outside. Into harm. Into a trap.

As she climbed higher, she spotted the flames. They
licked the edges of the house, already beginning to
consume it.

Despite the heat around her, ice formed in her gut.

She scooped up Addie, hating to wake the infant when
she was sleeping so peacefully.

Macy had to move fast.

She rushed downstairs, where Tanner waited for her. He grabbed her arm and ushered her toward the door.

Flames licked the walls now, slowly devouring the house. Tanner pulled out his gun and turned toward Macy.

She could hardly breathe. Just then, Addie awoke with a cry.

The poor baby. She had no idea what was going on. She didn't deserve this.

Tanner kept his arm around her and Addie.

"Let's do this," he said. His voice held no room for argument.

He opened the door. Flames licked their way inside.

Macy gasped as the edges of the fire felt dangerously close. She pulled Addie tightly to her chest, determined to protect the baby at all costs.

She held her breath as they slipped outside and rushed to the car. There was no car seat. There hadn't been time.

Instead, Macy continued to hold Addie close to her chest, trying to shield her from any incoming danger or threats. She lifted a quick prayer.

Please help us.

As Tanner started the car, a bullet shattered the window.

Don't miss
THE BABY ASSIGNMENT by Christy Barritt,
available January 2018 wherever
Love Inspired® Suspense books and ebooks are sold.

www.LoveInspired.com